Baron of the North

Book 4 in the Anarchy Series

By

Griff Hosker

Contents

Baron of the North i
Part 1 The Blood feud 2
Prologue 2
Chapter 1 7
Chapter 2 17
Chapter 3 29
Chapter 4 38
Chapter 5 52
Chapter 6 64
Part 2 Treason and treachery 72
Chapter 7 72
Chapter 8 81
Chapter 9 92
Chapter 10 100
Chapter 11 110
Part 3 Miklagård 120
Chapter 12 120
Chapter 13 131
Chapter 14 143
Part 4 Odyssey 155
Chapter 15 155
Chapter 16 168
Chapter 17 177
Chapter 18 187
Epilogue 196
Glossary 197
Historical note 199
Other books by Griff Hosker 200

Baron of the North

Published by Sword Books Ltd 2015
Copyright © Griff Hosker First Edition

The author has asserted their moral right under the Copyright, Designs and Patents Act, 1988, to be identified as the author of this work.

All Rights Reserved. No part of this publication may be reproduced, copied, stored in a retrieval system, or transmitted, in any form or by any means, without the prior written consent of the copyright holder, nor be otherwise circulated in any form of binding or cover other than that in which it is published and without a similar condition being imposed on the subsequent purchaser.
A CIP catalogue record for this title is available from the British Library.
Cover by Design for Writers

Baron of the North

Part 1 The Blood feud
Prologue

The English Channel

I stood with Sir Edward at the prow of the King's ship, *'Hand of God'*. It was the largest ship in which I had sailed but I did not like the motion of the precocious English Channel. I had found that the only way I could endure it was to stand at the bow and watch the horizon. It calmed my queasy insides. On this particular voyage, I also needed to speak alone with Sir Edward. We had been tasked with escorting Empress Matilda to Normandy to allow her to prepare for the arranged marriage to Geoffrey of Anjou. Neither the Empress nor I were happy about the arrangement. Geoffrey was just fourteen and he was half of the Empress' age. It did not strike me as the basis for a successful marriage. For myself, I still harboured feelings for her. I loved my wife but within me burned a flame and that flame was Matilda. I was no fool and I knew that my love could never be consummated but I was still consumed with both frustration and anger. Sir Edward knew me as well as any, save Wulfstan, my mentor, and he stood by me at the bow looking out to sea.

"At least we will not have to stay long, Baron. Once we have safely delivered her to the castle at Caen then we can return to your castle in Stockton." I said nothing. That was a double-edged sword. I would be home with my family, whom I loved, but I would be parted, forever, from the other woman I loved. It was cold comfort. "And the King has rewarded you for your efforts too. You are now, since the illness of the Bishop of Durham, the only lord between the Tees and the Tyne who can stop the incursions of raiders. You are the Baron of the North."

Since Bishop Flambard had fallen ill, some said his end was close, there was no incumbent for Durham and I had been commanded to watch over the Palatinate. It was a poisoned chalice. I laughed, "And what does that get me? Nothing but more responsibility and the punishment should I fail. It brings me neither more land nor taxes. The taxes from the Palatinate still go to the church and to the King. I do the work and they reap the benefits."

Edward laughed, "You are too honest and that is your trouble. Any other knight being given this opportunity would find a way to increase his prosperity."

I had to smile for he was correct. "I am sorry if my honesty offends you Edward but it was the way I was brought up."

"I know and I am only trying to make you see the cup half full rather than half empty. The King shows you favour and this will lead to more, believe me."

I had no opportunity for a reply as the lookout on the masthead shouted, "Sail Ho! Sail to the East!"

A sail from the east was a threat. The Captain needed no orders from me to beat out to sea. I turned to Edward, "Get the men on deck. This may be a friend but, in these waters, it is more likely to be an enemy."

He headed down the centre of the ship. My three squires all appeared as though by magic. They presented themselves by my side. Two of them, Leofric and John were of low birth and were young. They might never become knights but they served me well. The third, Hugh of Gainford, was the son of one of my knights who had been killed by raiders the previous year. He was now my ward until he became old enough to hold Gainford for the King and for me.

"My lord?" As the eldest squire, Hugh took command.

"Bring me my helm, sword and shield. There may be danger."

They raced below decks and I heard the second shout from the masthead. "She is of Flanders! She has a consort!"

There were two ships now and the fact that they were from Flanders, an avowed enemy of Henry King of England meant that we were in danger.

Empress Matilda came on deck with Judith and Margaret her two ladies in waiting. "Baron?"

"Two Flemish ships seek us. You had best go below decks."

"Perhaps they have peaceful intentions."

I nodded, "And perhaps tonight the sun will set in the east. Go below decks please and let us defend you."

My squires brought my arms. We did not have armour. That was too dangerous at sea. If these two Flemish warships wished to attack us then we would show them that we were prepared. Dick led my archers up from the hold where they were berthed first. There were twenty of them and they were the finest archers in the whole land. Many of them had been outlaws in Sherwood but now they served me. Wulfric brought up the eight men at arms we had brought. The rest remained in Stockton protecting my family. Finally Edward and his squire, Hugh's cousin, Gille appeared armed and ready for war.

"Dick, have half of your men in the rigging and split the rest between the forecastle and the aft castle. Wulfric, divide the men. I know not which side they will attack. Sir Edward and I will deal with any who break through your ranks."

"Aye Baron."

We both sounded calm for this was not the first time we had been outnumbered and with no apparent means of escape. I peered to the east and saw that the two ships were slightly smaller than us but I knew that they would have larger crews.

"The King's nephew seeks his cousin eh, Baron?"

William Clito had attained the Flemish crown when Charles of Flanders had died. Louis of France played complicated games and the son of our King's brother was anxious to gain the Kingdom of England as well as the Dukedom of Normandy. These two ships had been sent to stop us from reaching Caen. Once there the Empress would be beyond his clutches.

I strode aft to consult with the captain. "Can you outrun them?"

He shook his head. "We could if there were but one. No, Baron, they will catch us. The only question is when."

"Dick I want your archers to go for the crew around the rudder."

"Aye Baron."

I turned to my squires and Edward, "Whoever they are I am certain that the six of us will have more skills than they do. We use those skills and we fight as one. This ship becomes our horse. Edward and I will be at the fore and you four protect our backs."

I saw that the two Flemish ships had more canvas than we did and they began to gain, inexorably. We were sailing through the channel, past the ports of Calais and Boulogne. They would be of no help; they were ports of Flanders. We had to defeat the two ships and continue our journey. There were six archers attached to the crew and they would augment my own. There lay our one advantage.

I called to the captain. "Take in some canvas captain. They are going to catch us and I would rather have a better platform for our archers."

"Aye, Baron! Two reefs!"

His crew scurried up the ratlines and within a short time we had slowed and our passage was smoother. We had taken the two Flemish ships by surprise and they hurtled towards us under full sail. I saw their crew as they hurried to slow their own ships down. They were just a couple of hundred feet astern of us. I saw Dick make a signal and his best archers released arrows to pluck the crew from the rigging. Their sails were taken in but it was slower than their captains had intended and they came abeam of us. It afforded me the opportunity to see what the opposition was like. I saw at least two knights on each ship but there were only four men at arms. The majority appeared to be just brigands and pirates. The danger lay in the crossbowmen. I did not need to issue orders. As soon as the crossbows were levelled arrows flew from our ship and either felled them or drove them to shelter. There is no enemy more despised by an archer than one who wields a crossbow.

The ship to landward was closer to us. "Captain, head for the ship to port!" We began to turn. It meant we would fight one ship for a short time before the other could come to his aid. "Let us deal with this nearer vessel first." Leaving Edgar with half of the men at arms we joined Wulfric.

The ship, I saw her name was *'Sainte Marie'*, was close to us and they obliged us by sending grappling hooks over. Those throwing them had no protection and my archers killed them. I saw the knight who led them had a yellow and black shield quartered by three lions. This was a knight of the household of William Clito. We had spears at the ready. When they came they would have to either use ropes to swing aboard or clamber over the side. Either way, they could not hold a shield and our spears would force them back. There were twenty men about to leap across the chasm. Although they outnumbered us as long as the other ship did not strike us soon then we had a chance.

They leapt. As I thrust forward with my spear and felt it tear into the unprotected chest of an axe-wielding Flem I noticed that the knights held back. Many of those who jumped fell to their deaths but the sheer weight of numbers meant that half of their number reached our deck. Edward and I moved forward. His left shoulder touched my right and I had some protection from his shield. Our spears were gone. Mine had broken and Edward's was at the bottom of the sea along with the man he had killed. Wulfric and his men parted as we approached. The two Flemish knights took the opportunity to swing on board and came at Edward and me. That suited me. It was not right for a squire to face a knight.

I found myself facing the one with the three lions on his shield. His helmet meant I could not tell his age but he was shorter and wider than me. He had a better balance than me on the pitching ship. I waited for I had fast hands and I would use them. He swung his sword at me. Leofric's spear darted out and the knight instinctively brought up his shield. I deflected the sword which did not have as much force behind it as the knight had intended. Rather than swinging down with my blade, I let it dart forward with all of my weight behind it. I did so confidently knowing that Edward protected my right. I felt my sword strike something soft. I pushed harder and then withdrew. I caught the sight of blood on my blade.

I heard Edgar shout, "Baron, t'other ship is close."
"Wulfric!"

"Aye Baron." I knew that Wulfric would take half of the men from this side and support Edgar. Our archers were whittling those down on this port side.

I punched with my shield. John son of Tan threw his spear at the warrior who hurled himself at my left side. He was thrown back against the side of the ship. The knight I fought was wounded and, when he slipped on blood he was forced back. I tried the same manoeuvre a second time. This time he managed to bring his shield down and my sword went into his leg. Edward slew the second knight and the Flemish sailors were forced back.

The Flemish knight shouted, "Back!"

Barely six men made it back to their ship and they threw the grappling lines into the sea. We had no time to gloat. We turned and ran to support Edgar and Wulfric. The departing Flemish ship and our bloody weapons were enough to send the crew of the second Flemish ship to reconsider their position. Had both ships managed to attack us at the same time then things might have gone awry. As it was our manoeuvre had taken them by surprise and we managed to defeat one. We had had a certain amount of luck but the backbones of my men had helped.

As we surveyed our naval victory my men all cheered. Out of the corner of my eye I caught sight of Empress Matilda and her ladies. They had defied my orders and now stood applauding with the rest. I saluted Empress Matilda who gave me a little curtsy and then blew me a kiss. My life was complicated and it looked as though it would become even more confused in the future.

Chapter 1

Stockton

I felt my usual sense of relief when I saw my castle in the distance. The light-coloured stone stood out against the river and the green behind rose towards the distant hills. After the plots, plans and power struggles of London and Normandy, it was a relief to return to a world over which I had some control. Both courts were full of fawning faces which hid the real intentions and thoughts of those who inhabited those rabbit warrens of deceit. It had been a wrench to leave Empress Matilda. Once we reached Normandy we had had to behave with more formality. We were in Caen. It was a castle riddled with prying eyes and potential spies. The journey she took to Rouen was under the eyes of a full conroi of knights. I watched her depart with sadness for she was not a happy woman and she was going to a marriage she did not desire. On the journey back to King Henry's court I had been distracted and kept to myself. My men knew me well enough to keep their distance.

When we reached London I reported to the White Tower where I had a private audience with the King. That was rare for he trusted few and showed that he valued me. He might use me liberally but he appeared to trust me.

"Now that the Bishop of Durham is very ill and close to death another Bishop will need to be appointed. The Pope will need a list of names from which to choose the successor. Neither the Archbishop of Canterbury nor myself have any candidates in mind and so, as I told you before, you must command the land around the Palatinate. You have done so before and I know that there is no better choice. You will keep the border safe. I have much to do in Normandy. The wedding of my daughter is a momentous event. It will secure our southern borders and bring a little respite to my Dukedom. Your news of the attack by the Flemish ships is, however, worrying and I shall have to return to Rouen sooner than I would have hoped. I will have to return for the marriage of my daughter in any case. With my son busy on the Welsh Marches you have a great responsibility on your shoulders. You will be my rock in the north."

"And the Scots, my liege, how do I deal with them?"

"A good question. King David might be related to me but I know that he covets the land north of the Tyne. He is, however, not foolish enough to risk war with England, not yet anyway. It is more likely that men will raid from the lands of the Scot and that is what you need to prevent. You should deal forcefully and decisively with any incursion which threatens our people of Durham and the north." He smiled but I knew King Henry, he was cold and calculating, "Do this for me and you shall be rewarded. Baron of the North is but one step. You shall be advanced."

That had been what I was afraid of. Advancement meant leaving the world I had built and being sent somewhere else. I did not want to leave my castle and my river. As we had headed north, with newly acquired horses and men at arms, I had discussed with Edward and my squires my new orders. We knew that protecting the Palatinate was achievable but the land north of the Tyne was less easy to patrol.

"You have good knights on the Tees, Baron. They are a barrier of iron!"

"I know Edward but they are on the Tees. The Tyne is almost forty miles further north."

Hugh of Gainford had gradually regained his confidence following the loss of his father and his family, "Baron, you could use that iron to make safe our valley and have a small force of horsemen who could patrol the Tyne."

Edward had agreed, "He is right, Baron. We have good mounted archers and men at arms. Use the revenue due to you from the Palatinate to pay others to guard Stockton."

By the time I stood on Ethelred's ferry across my river we had formulated my plans. We had but a short time until winter and I knew I would have to impose my presence upon the Palatinate and the land of the Tyne. There were many treacherous men who would seek to fill the vacuum left by the Bishop. I knew whom I could trust on the Tees. However, the further north I went the less I would know of the loyalty of the men there. Some would have allegiances and land north of the border.

I smiled as we neared my castle. Adela, my wife stood there with my young son, William, holding her hand and my daughter Hilda in her other arm. This was my rock. Behind her stood my steward, John, son of Leofric. He was a clever young man and his mind gave me the freedom to be a knight. He managed the manor and the revenue. I was able to be a knight because of his efforts.

Our slow and steady approach also afforded me the opportunity of examining my castle. The keep was not the biggest I had seen but it was well made and the curtain wall had been cleverly designed by my mason. And yet there was still something lacking. The idea was driven from my mind as we bumped against the jetty and William hurled himself at me as I stepped ashore. "Father, you are home!"

"I am indeed and what a fine fellow you are becoming!"

"Yes, father, and I am almost big enough to ride my pony!" He looked around, "Where is Uncle Edward?"

"He and his men returned to their castle. Fear not he will visit with us soon." Adela handed Matilda to one of her servants and I hugged her. "I missed you. Is everyone well?"

She knew what I meant; one of my father's retainers, Athelstan had died just before I had left to escort the Empress home. There were just two of them left now. "Osric and Wulfstan are in good health. Fear not for their health, my husband. And you carried out the task the King required of you?"

I took her arm and led her back into my castle, "I did and he has honoured me with more responsibility." As we walked up the ramp towards the solid door I told her of my new title and the task the King had set for me.

She was undaunted and actually excited, "It speaks well, my husband, that the King rewards you so. Why I expect you to be an Earl before too long."

I shook my head and laughed, "Let me get used to this title first before you make my head so big that I will require a new helmet."

The next day I rode, with my three squires, to visit with my knights at Elton, Hartburn and with Osric at Norton. They were the three manors that were the closest to mine and, while Edward guarded the south they had the crucial task of guarding the north. It had been many months since I had seen Wulfstan. He and his family were happy just a mile or so north of my castle. He had built a homely manor. He had no castle and his home was like a rambling rabbit warren filled with his lively and happy children. I sometimes resented the fact that he rarely visited. However, when I saw him playing with his sons I knew why he kept to his manor. He had been a soldier until late in life. Having found a good woman and become a father he was making up for lost time.

"Alfraed, it is good to see you!"

Wulfstan had been the warrior who had trained me and it was always good to see him. He might be a little greyer and his belly a little larger but there was no man I would rather have at my back in battle and that included Edward.

"And you." I waved a hand at his home. It was only built of wood but it was sturdy and could be easily defended. He had no men at arms now but his men were all fine archers and he had many good yeomen he had trained. If he were to be attacked then it would need a doughty enemy to best him. "I see you have made your home bigger."

Faren came to join him. As she wrapped her arm around his waist I saw that she was with child again, "My family is growing, Baron. And how goes it with you?"

I told him of my encounter with the Flemish ships and my new task. He nodded and gestured for me to sit on the bench which faced south and looked over the becks which edged his land. "Your father would be proud. You have taken the start he gave you and increased it. It will be Earl next."

I laughed, "You are as bad as Adela. One small step at a time eh?"

"You did not come here to watch the deer drinking at the stream, what is on your mind?"

"I cannot fool my mentor, can I? Edward suggested a way to protect the King's land while ensuring that the valley is not left vulnerable."

"Take mounted archers and men at arms and use the castles on the border."

I laughed, "You are a mind reader."

"No, it is obvious. It worked the last time but it is also clear that you cannot keep a large force-fed that far from home. You would need to make it small and you would wish me to watch your home while you were away."

I nodded, "I know that she does not complain but I hate to leave Adela alone."

Faren brought us some ale, "You have a good wife, Baron, as I hope I am a good wife too. Loneliness is a burden we bear and a price we pay for having a good man." She kissed Wulfstan. "Not that my husband needs to wander far these days."

"And who would you suggest I take with me as my knights?"

"Edward and Harold are your first choice?" I nodded, "Then Tristan of Yarm would be my third."

"That means we take two young knights and only Edward with experience."

"You were their age not so long ago. It will do them good and it leaves the experienced knights to protect the valley."

"We could find ourselves outnumbered if the Scots raid in numbers."

"From what the King said and from what I know King David will be reluctant to allow large numbers to raid. He would not want retribution from the King or Robert of Gloucester. They are a rapacious people. They want to take what our people earn with hard work. If they do send a larger conroi then you retreat to one of the castles and wait them out."

I nodded. It made sense. Hugh of Hexham had a good castle and there was another at Alnwick and Morpeth. "I will visit with Harold now. I will need many arrows. Ask Old and Young Tom for as many as they can manage."

"Old Tom is not in good health at the moment but Young Tom now has a son he has taken as his apprentice. You will have your arrows."

As we rode the few miles to Elton I reflected that Old Tom's illness was a sign of the times. He had been one of my father's first archers and now he was ailing. Age caught up with us all. Perhaps Wulfstan had the right idea and was enjoying the fruits of his labours.

Harold had been my squire and his manor showed his youth. It was half the size of Wulfstan's and he had barely six farms and only ten warriors but he was keen. The land would become more populated but Harold would need to do as Wulfstan had done and make it attractive to farm.

He was pleased to see me. He had only been elevated to the rank of knight recently and I think he was a little overawed by the responsibility. He had come from humble beginnings. The idea of having others obey his orders was foreign to him. "I will be pleased to follow you, Baron. A campaign with you is always profitable and I can turn my ten men into twenty and build a tower of stone."

"You need not a tower of stone. Your people are more than welcome in Stockton if there is danger and you know that."

He nodded, "And when do we leave?"

"The end of next week. This will be a short campaign before winter sets in. I use it to let those in the Palatinate know who their new lord is."

Although a temporary appointment I was wise enough to know that some might seek to use my relative youth as a weakness and try to take advantage of me. I had grown up in the east and I knew strategy. My last stop was Norton. As we rode there John, my squire, asked, "And what of our mail and our weapons Baron?" He pointed to Hugh who had a hauberk which was the equal of mine.

"When we have finished this upcoming campaign we shall see Alf and have yours made but Hugh here has ceased to grow. You and Leofric are still youths. I would not waste coin on armour which you will outgrow by the spring."

Hugh said, "Use the battlefield, John, to earn gold for yourself and increase your wealth. I bought this armour myself. It was not a gift from my father."

I saw John taking that in. He was the least experienced of my squires and he would, when he finished growing, be the biggest! He would need a mighty warhorse to carry him. He would be bigger than even Wulfric my sergeant at arms.

My visit to Norton was largely sentimental. There was no knight there for me to consult but the small church held the grave of my father and his dead oathsworn. The only one of them who remained now was Osric. It would be good to see him. As we approached I turned to my squires. "While I speak with the Steward take yourselves around the manor. Picture yourself as a raider. How would you attack it?"

Hugh was a bright youth, "You wish us to find its weaknesses."

"If someone comes south to raid the valley then it is here and Hartburn that will be attacked first."

They took Scout from me and I went into the church. I always went to my father's grave and spent a few moments there first. As I rose Father Peter approached, "I had heard that you had returned, Baron. Will you be at home for long this time?"

"No Father. I ride north to the borders but I will not be away for long. I go to secure our lands north of the Palatinate."

The priest had been one of those who had survived the early Scottish raids and he nodded. "The people miss you but they appreciate what you do for them, my lord."

Osric, too, had aged but he was happier than the last time I had seen him. It was summer that did that. Longer nights and sunsets had a way of making everyone happier. "We have had a good year, Baron. The crops are the best we have ever had and the Lord has been kind; our animals are healthy and multiply."

Since we had begun to slaughter less for the winter and to bring many inside our walls we had prospered. It was the wolves who now went hungry and not us. It was, however, a double-edged sword. It made us more attractive to raiders. "Good but remain vigilant. Do not let the ditches be filled with rubbish and keep up the practice with the fyrd."

He laughed, "Aye my lord and I daresay you will be teaching me to suck eggs sometime soon!"

I laughed, "You are right Osric. Perhaps I think I am speaking to my younger knights such as Harold."

"Fear not, my lord, they are good fellows and they will learn. They have a good teacher; you."

As we rode back the sun was setting in the west, lighting our way back home. "Well, what did you learn?"

"That it would be hard to take Norton using horses for the swampy ground protects one side and the other has deep ditches."

"Aye Baron but the gatehouse is weak."

Hugh had a good eye for such things. "Well done Hugh. We will improve it in the spring."

As we rode through the town I noticed, for it was now in my mind, that the gatehouse into the town was also a weak point. I shook my head. I was becoming foolish. It did not matter about the gate to the town for my castle was there as a sanctuary. It was when I approached my gate that I saw the weakness in my own argument. The river gave good protection but the gate could be taken by determined knights. The gatehouse was only as tall as two men and the towers were small. It needed to be much higher. I stopped and dismounted. I had asked my squires to picture themselves as attackers and now I did the same. Here, if I was a knight I could stand on my horse's back and scale both the walls and the tower. This would not do.

"Leofric take Scout to the stables. I will not need you again until the morrow."

Aiden, who scouted for me and acted as a gamekeeper approached me. "Baron, will you be hawking? Caesar and Sheba are in fine form."

I was about to say no and then I relented. I had little enough time to myself as it was. "We will go the day after tomorrow."

For some reason that seemed to please my former slave. "Excellent my lord. They will be ready."

John, my Steward, was also waiting close by. "My lord we need to hold a Session soon. There are many cases which must be heard."

"In seven days I travel north on the King's business. If it cannot be three days from now then the cases will have to wait until Advent."

"Three days from now will suffice, Baron."

"Good. Tomorrow I wish to speak with William the Mason and Sir Edward. Arrange it if you please."

"Aye my lord."

"And I need you at both meetings."

I had aroused his curiosity but he knew me well enough not to pursue the matter. I felt guilty when I entered my Great Hall. Adela and my children rushed towards me. I knew that I should spend more time with them but I always had so much to do. My childhood had been the same. My father had been away so much fighting the enemies of the Empire that I barely recognised him when he came home. I eased my conscience by persuading myself that William would have more of my time when he became older and could accompany me to war.

I smiled at him and swung him around. While I was at home I would make it up to him. After the servants had taken them both to bed and Adela and I sat before the roaring fire she put her hand on mine. "Thank you, my husband, that made all the difference to our son."

"I know I do not do enough but…"

"But you are a warrior and you are lord. Both of those are important. I understand. Do not fret."

"I have to leave again soon."

"I know. You will need to stop any raids for the animals and the crops before winter sets in and the harvest is stored. At least I know you will not be away for winter. I am content."

"I am lucky and I do not deserve you."

"Without you, my lord, I would have been as someone dead. You saved me and all that I am I owe to you."

My mason lived close to the castle and he arrived first for the meeting. I walked around the walls with him and with John. "How is the work going, William?"

"Thanks to you, Baron, I am kept employed as are my sons. The church will take time but your generosity means that it will be the finest south of Durham and north of York. I am proud to be working on it."

"Good." I pointed to the gate of my castle. It sat in the middle of the low curtain wall. "I would make my gate stronger."

"You have ideas, Baron? I fear that I have more knowledge of churches and cathedrals than castles. If you know what you have in your mind then I can build it but…" He spread his arms and he shrugged.

"I know exactly what I want. I would like the gatehouse to be as tall again as I am." William nodded. "And I want it connecting to my tower."

That shook them both. William said, "That will require a large amount of stone!"

John said, "And expensive!"

I smiled at John, "As it is my coin I will be using then it is for me to determine what is expensive and as for the amount of stone… can we get enough, William?"

"Aye, my lord. There is still plenty at Piercebridge but if the river freezes then we will not be able to get it."

"Then John, I want you to arrange with Ethelred to bring as much stone as he can fetch before the river freezes."

"Ethelred?"

"He is enterprising and he has a ferry. I am sure it is not beyond his wit to transport stone down the river. There will be profit in it for him. Just make sure there is not too much."

Edward arrived as we were finalising the details. He listened as I explained what I wanted. "That is an excellent idea, Baron. It will give you two baileys; both would be protected. An enemy would find it almost impossible to take the two"

"There, William, you have your plan. Take your measurements and give the estimate of stone to John. You have plenty of time."

He bowed and scurried off with his eldest son taking out his wax tablet. The three of us would have a great deal of time to talk. "John, Sir Edward and I will need to take some of our men north for three or four weeks. You have four days to gather supplies for us. I have the arrows already being made but we will need food and spears. You will need to see Alf."

"My lord, with the new gatehouse this will burden your treasury considerably."

"Do not worry about that, John. The King has made me Baron of the North. While the Bishop of Durham is indisposed I will be administering the Palatinate Treasury. The cost of our men in the north will be borne by Durham."

He brightened, "Then, in that case, Baron, I can have it all ready in four days' time. Will you use wagons or horses?"

"Horses are easier. I will take ten archers and ten men at arms. Sir Edward, you will need just five archers and five men at arms. We leave the rest to guard our lands." He nodded, "So, John, you need supplies for forty-five men. I will also require men to care for the horses so make it fifty and find me the men to look after the horses."

"Will you be taking your warhorses?"

"As it is the Scots we may be fighting then no. I would not risk Star with those savages."

He bobbed his head, "Then if that is all?" I waved him away.

The two of us walked my walls and looked to the south across the river. "Are you in better humour, Baron now that you have seen your family?"

"A little," I said nothing but stared across the river to Sir Edward's manor.

"She is the Empress no longer but she is beyond your grasp Baron. Firstly you are married. That is reason enough. And then there is the fact that none of us may like that she is marrying a child but it is the King's decision and we obey him. We still serve her but we cannot do that properly if you harbour these secret desires."

"You know?"

"I am not blind and I have seen the way that she looks at you but it cannot be. We both know that. You have a fine wife and family. Most men would be content with that."

"I know." I sighed, "And thank you. I needed someone to tell me what I knew in my heart. I will throw myself into this new task. Who knows there may be not only glory but rewards too?"

"There will be little glory, Baron; we go to fight the Scots!"

Chapter 2

The weather had become unsettled when we left for the north. It was a wet and windy day as we headed north from my manor on the Durham Road. The five men we had to care for our animals included the freed slave, Oswald. He was eager to help and to earn the coin John was paying. He had told me that his life began again the moment we rescued him and he would make the most of it. I had also brought Aiden for he had told me when we were hawking, that he missed the company of my archers and men at arms. He liked scouting. He would have made a fine warrior save that he was invaluable as a scout. Harold and Tristan had trained together as squires and they rode easily side by side. Hugh and Gille, Edward's squire, were cousins and they travelled as a pair. It was a small conroi of knights but we were close. In the dark days to come, that would prove vital.

We reached Durham and the Castellan, Hubert of Lincoln, appeared pleased to see me. "We were told of your impending arrival by a messenger from the King. I, for one, am more than happy that it is to be you who will defend the border."

"I must warn you, Castellan, that I do not intend to base myself here. My men and I will make a show of force along the border and then winter back in the valley. We will return in the spring. I am not here as a guard but as a deterrent."

"I understand and you are close enough for us to send to should the Scots make another surprise attack."

"Your words suggested that there are some who are less than happy at my appointment?"

"Many lords have left their lands in England and gone to their estates in Scotland. More left when the rumour of your arrival spread."

I smiled, "I cannot help that. Is Sir Hugh Manningham still on the wall? The lord of the Manor at Hexham has not departed has he?"

"He is, Baron, and he is like a rock. I am grateful for his presence."

"Good. Now we will need supplies when we come in the spring. I wish to move quickly and I do not want to have to bring a month's supplies with me."

"I will see the reeves and the stewards and it shall be arranged." He waved his arm towards the keep. "You will stay tonight, Baron?"

"I will."

The castle at Durham made my own seem like a Saxon hut. The Great Hall was large enough for a huge conroi, far larger than mine. There were just the ten knights and squires who ate with the Castellan and the Dean. The rest of our men ate in the warrior hall. It suited us better;

Wulfric was adept at garnering information. When Hubert had had a few goblets of wine he opened up a little. "There is a new baron who has been threatening the border castles."

"Is he from England or is he a Scot?"

"Neither. He has come from Anjou."

"Who is he?"

"Sir Guy Fitzwaller. He has six household knights and many men at arms and crossbowmen with him."

The name made me freeze. It was like an icicle in my heart. I knew the name. Edward asked, "What is it, Baron? You look like you have seen a ghost."

"Not a ghost but an unpleasant memory. When we travelled from the east we saved the King from this Fitzwaller's father whom I slew. The King took a heavy ransom from him and his family. He was supposed to swear allegiance to King Henry. If he is troubling the border then he is forsworn."

"He may have renounced his allegiance. He is in Scotland, Baron."

"You are right, Sir Hubert. This complicates matters. He hates me and swore to kill me." I swallowed the last of my wine. "Tell me when did he arrive in Scotland?"

"I am not certain. Perhaps a year ago, maybe less."

"About the time the king began to plan to marry the Empress and was seeking suitors. It begins to make sense now. He must have had wind that Geoffrey of Anjou was available. I must warn you, Sir Hubert, this is a cunning knight. He and his father were willing to kill a king. That tells you much. He is someone who is used to playing for high stakes."

"It does indeed."

"And where is his castle?"

"Skaithmuir, close to Berwick."

"Then it is some way north of here."

"It is but he has raided as far south as Rothbury. He took many slaves and cattle last year."

"And why did you not seek help then?"

"The Bishop had other matters on his mind. It was just before he went back to London and now..." He crossed himself, "God will watch over him I am sure."

It may sound callous but the Bishop's soul was not my concern. I had ridden north feeling confident. We had trounced every band of raiders sent against us but this was different. This was an Angevin raider. This was someone who had fought King Henry for many years and survived. He would not be as easy to defeat and he had twice as many knights as I possessed. I would need to be on my guard.

As we rode the thirty odd miles to Hexham I told the others of my earlier encounter with this Angevin knight. I gave more detail than I had to Sir Hubert. "Believe me he is both cunning and cruel. He almost had King Henry in his grasp and in those days he was much younger. I doubt not that he will now be both clever and even more devious. I am glad that we have brought Aiden for we will need his skills."

"Do you know that part of the country, Baron, the land close to the coast?"

"No Harold. I have never been there. I know that it is a wild land and desolate. It is one reason they raid so far south. They even struggle to grow barley and oats in that region. If there is one consolation it is that the men of Anjou will not find it to their liking."

Sir Hugh had heard of the raids, "The bastards come nowhere near me but I have received many refugees who fled their privations. Do you want my men to accompany you?"

"Not this trip but I would appreciate a couple of local men who know the area. We will return in the spring and then we might need some help. All I intend to do with this visit is let Fitzwaller and the other knights know that I am here to stop their raids."

The two men he gave to us were Cedric and Garth. Both were foresters who had lived further north until the frequent raids had driven them south. They hated the Scots more than most. They and Aiden would be our eyes and ears. We left just after dawn. The showery, windy weather had given way to a grey overcast sky and scudding winds that drove into our faces. It was not pleasant riding. We headed for Otterburn first and then Elsdon. There was a tower at Otterburn and a motte and bailey castle at Elsdon. It remained to be seen if they were still occupied by the English. The castle and manor at Morpeth appeared to be although they had not been large enough to stop the raids. I knew that they had raided Rothbury. It seemed prudent to begin there.

I turned to Cedric. "Will we reach Rothbury this night?"

"No Baron. We will reach Otterburn but even Elsdon is too far."

"And is there a lord at Otterburn and men at arms?"

"No Baron. The lord of the manor took the cross these ten years. He has a steward who runs the estate for him. The people fear that their lord has forsaken them and has found a better manor in the Holy Land. Outremer attracts many knights who wish for a better life than here in the harsh cold north."

"Fear not, Cedric, when King Henry hears of this he will appoint another lord. Who is the lord?"

"Richard D'Umfraville. His grandfather was given much of the land around the Coquet. I fear the grandson did not feel it was good enough for him. His younger brother stayed. It is he who lives in Elsdon."

The lassitude of the King was causing more problems than he knew. I now realised that he saw the Palatinate and Northumberland as barriers to prevent the Scots from raiding the richer lands to the south. Our valley was the real border. These lands were too poor to be profitable. It was why his father had laid waste to so much of it. I saw forests and I saw moorland. It might make good land for hunting but I would not like to farm here.

"Aiden, go with Cedric and scout out Otterburn and the land around it. I will take no chances with this Fitzwaller."

Hugh nudged his steed next to mine as the two scouts rode off. "Baron, this land is not worth defending. Why not go back to Hexham? Does it matter if the Scots have this moor and forest?"

"You may be right Hugh but what of the people who live here? They are English are they not? Do they not deserve our protection?"

"Are we not Norman?"

"The moment King William landed at Pevensey then every knight who took land on this isle ceased to be Norman. They became English. The trouble is many knights do not realise that."

Edward growled, "And the three knights who lead this conroi, young Hugh of Gainford, are all English! Your land is in England and that makes you English!"

I heard the anger in Edward's voice and Hugh mumbled, "I am sorry I have offended you, Sir Edward."

"He is a squire, Sir Edward and he has much to learn. Give him time."

I saw Edward nod but knew that he was still seething inside. Edward was English through and through. He spoke Norman when he had to but his heart was in England and not Normandy.

Otterburn had a simple tower amidst the huts that made up the large village by the river. We reached it in the late afternoon. It had been sited well and had a good view across the land. The villagers must have seen our approach for the door of the tower was shut.

"I am Baron Alfraed and I am here on the King's business." A head appeared from the top of the tower. "Are you the Steward?"

"I am, my lord."

"Then open the door so that we may take refuge here for the night." I saw him hesitate. I took off my helmet. "If we were enemies then we could take this tower with ease."

I did not need to glance behind me to know that Dick had the archers stringing their bows. The head disappeared. I dismounted and handed my reins to Leofric. "Wulfric, set up camp behind the tower. It looks to be sheltered and there is water below."

"Aye, Baron."

The door opened and a nervous-looking man opened it. "I am Gilbert of Otterburn and I am the reeve and steward here. I am sorry we barred the gate, Baron but we have had many raids from across the border and it is safer to be in here."

I waved a hand. "Have you been raided of late?"

"A month since, riders came from the east. We had a warning for we saw smoke in the distance and we hid within the tower. They took the sheep and cattle from the fields but left us alone."

"You will find it hard to survive in the winter."

"Aye, my lord. We only grow oats and barley here and they will not last the winter."

"Then as your lord is absent I give you permission to hunt this winter for rabbits and deer."

"Thank you, Baron. Would you care to sleep this night within the tower?"

I shook my head, "I did not give you hunting rights for my own gain. I will camp with my men. The King wishes his people to be safe. When I next speak with him I will tell him of your plight." He nodded his gratitude. "Tell me Gilbert what of Elsdon and Rothbury? If you were raided then what of them?"

His face darkened. He gestured for me to follow him inside. The tower was crowded with people, "You are safe my friends. Return to your homes. Tonight we are under the protection of the Baron."

They knuckled their foreheads as they left the tower. There were no steps leading to the top; it was a series of ladders. It was not easy in my armour but I deemed that he thought it necessary. I saw that Edward followed me. We reached the top. The sky was darkening towards the east. He pointed to the northeast and there was a faint glow against the skyline. "That, Baron, is Elsdon. The smoke began this morning and the fires burn still."

"Then you did right to be wary of us. Tell me, Gilbert, when you were raided for your animals was Elsdon not raided too?"

"I think not for Ralph of Elsdon came with his three men at arms the day after the raid and offered us help."

"Then there is a knight in the castle?"

"No, Baron, Ralph is the son of the knight, William D'Umfraville. He is but a squire. His father was killed six months since when he went to the aid of Rothbury."

"But the castle was not attacked?"

"I think not. There are many roads from Rothbury to Hexham, lord. Elsdon blocks one as we block this one but there are ways around it and the Scots are cunning. He only has ten men to defend the castle and it is made of wood." He pointed again, "I fear the worst."

It was too late to risk a night march. I descended. It was almost as difficult as climbing to the top. "Dick put two men on the top of the tower. I fear the Scots are in Elsdon."

I gathered my knights and squires around me. "We need a good guard keeping this night and we leave before dawn. The Scots are causing mischief to the north of us. This may well be the new frontier!"

That evening as we ate a frugal meal Tristan and Harold questioned me about the D'Umfraville family. "If the king charged Baron Richard with defending this land and gave him castles why would he leave?"

"Taking the cross and going on Holy Crusade is seen as a noble and holy pilgrimage. We know that it is the way to riches and a more comfortable life but the church and the king encourage knights to do this." I waved my hand around the huddle of poor and crude huts. "The people here are the ones who suffer. You would both do well to remember that. Tristan, you have no manor as yet but your father is a fine example of a good lord of the manor. Copy him."

We had brought lances but this was not the land for their use. There were steep-sided, wooded valleys and crags and hills. We left them at Elsdon with our spare horses under the charge of Oswald. He had proved himself a good man. He took charge when he had to and his experiences as a slave had hardened him. We rode faster without the supply horses.

"Aiden and Cedric, scout out Elsdon. I would know if there is danger before we reach it."

We rode with half of the archers before us and the rest as a rearguard. Edward and I were behind the vanguard with Harold and Tristan behind. It was a tried and tested formation. Cedric came galloping back when we were just a mile from the castle. His face was grim. "They are all dead, Baron."

Had this been Aiden I would have had a better report. I could not blame Cedric; he did not know my ways. "Who is dead, Cedric? Men? Men and women? Who?"

"Just the men, Baron. We found no sign of women and children."

"Take Garth and rejoin Aiden. I want the three of you to discover where they have gone and we will remain at the castle."

As the two of them rode off Edward shook his head. "It is like Norton when you arrived, Baron. An empty manor filled with the dead."

"It is and that makes me angry." I waved a hand at my conroi. "This is enough to frighten a few brigands but the King should come north and teach these Scots a lesson that they will not forget. He should be as William the Bastard was, ruthless."

We were approaching the smoking ruins of the castle. Edward said, sadly, "The King is ruthless but Normandy appears more important than England at the moment. After the marriage that may change."

I had not needed that brought up but Edward was right. I liked his forthright honesty. "Dick, secure the castle."

The archers galloped around the far side of the castle. I could see that it was an old-fashioned although well-constructed motte and bailey castle. There was a keep on a high hill, the remains of a bridge which connected it to a lower ward and a palisade around the side. With enough men, it could be easily defended. Poor Ralph had been a squire with a handful of men.

The heads of what I assumed was Ralph and five of the defenders greeted us as we dismounted. Their heads were atop spears as a message. "Get the heads down and find the bodies. We will bury them."

I saw that the six squires were all shaken by the head of the brave Ralph. He looked to be of an age with them. Edward pointed, "Ten men could not hold each side of that castle. It would have been a massacre."

"And yet what could he do? If he had run then he would have been deserting his people."

"The result is the same, Baron."

Edward had been a man at arms, a sword for hire and sometimes that showed in his practical attitude. I had been brought up as a noble and that gave me more responsibilities than rights. I left Scout with Leofric and made my way up the slope. In places, it was slick with the blood of the defenders. The blackened walls had burned to the ground in places. The hall, however, had had a turf roof and that had saved a little of it. We found two bodies there. I could see why their heads had not been spiked on spears; they had been badly hacked. The white hair on one of them showed that he was an old retainer.

"Here are two died defending their lord."

"There is no point in surrendering to a Scot, Baron, the result is the same."

There was little left in the hall. It was a simple affair but there was enough left to show the mark of a woman. Where were the women? We headed for the lower bailey. Tristan and Harold were there already. "It looks like there was a stable." Harold knelt and examined the ground. "The horses were taken."

Baron of the North

We descended to the bottom of the hill. "Edgar, there are two more bodies in the Great Hall." My men were digging graves. It was not just the heads that had been disfigured. The bodies of the dead showed that cruel and unnecessary wounds had been inflicted on them after death. The grim faces of my men told me what they would do to these Scots if they found them.

Cedric galloped in. He had returned sooner than I had expected. "They did not go towards Otterburn, Baron. I went along the track over the hills and there was no sign but, to make sure, I rode to where I could see the tower and it was safe yet."

"You have done well."

We had buried the last of the dead when Garth rode in from the south and east. "I have found them, Baron. They are heading for Morpeth."

"How many? And do they have captives?"

"No captives. They have at least twenty horses and there looked to be forty men."

There was little point in berating the forester for his faulty information. He might not know the difference between a knight and a man at arms. At least we knew the captives were not there. "And the road, is it a good one?"

He shook his head, "It is little more than a track Baron."

"How long will it take them to reach Morpeth?"

"They will be there this evening, my lord."

"Then we cannot catch them for they have a head start and they will move as swiftly as our column does. One man might make it though. Garth, could you get ahead of them? Could you warn Morpeth?"

He nodded, "I could try. I can take the forest road. It is quicker for a single horseman."

"Then go and may God be with you."

"You will not pursue them, Baron?"

"Not until Aiden has reported back. I doubt that they will attack this night but the captives are more important right now."

Aiden appeared from the northeast. He dismounted and approached, "I have found the captives and the animals, Baron. They are at Rothbury. The Scots have taken the town."

"Is it fortified?"

"They are using the stone church as a castle. It is surrounded by carts on three sides and the river on the fourth."

"How many men?"

"I only saw one knight, Baron, and he appeared to have a wound. His head was wrapped in a bandage. There were four men at arms but the rest look to be brigands from Ireland, mercenaries. I counted fifty of them, at least."

"Then we know what we have to do. We ride to Rothbury and rescue the captives."

"And the raiders?"

"If we follow the raiders then the captives may be moved further north." I turned to Cedric, "Ride to Otterburn and tell them that the Scots have moved towards Morpeth. Then ride to your master and ask him to move towards Otterburn and Morpeth in case this is a Scottish trick."

"Aye, Baron."

I waved over Dick and Wulfric. "I doubt that they know we are here. We will use that to our advantage. I want the archers to get around Rothbury and stop them from leaving. I intend to attack as soon as we get there." John will sound the hunting horn when you are to attack, Dick."

"Do you not wish us to soften them up first, my lord?"

"No, I want them demoralised. They will see our small numbers and assume they can win. When the horn sounds and your arrows rain death upon them they will not believe that such a large number of arrows comes from a handful of archers."

He nodded and they rode off. I could rely on Dick for he had a great tactical sense. He would use the land to maximum effect.

"We will attack on foot. Aiden, John and Leofric will dispose of any sentries and then we will move silently into their camp and begin the slaughter. Leofric will sound the horn on my command when we are deep inside their camp. Tristan and Harold, you will secure the captives."

They nodded. It was a hurriedly concocted plan and I would not have tried this had we had a larger number or more men that I did not know. These were my oathsworn and they had been blooded already. They would not fail me.

We crossed the col above the Coquet and headed down into that fertile, narrow valley. Ominously there was no sign of any animals on the hillsides. The Scottish scavengers had picked them clean. I had not been here before but Aiden told me that the road was hidden from view by trees. We could reach Rothbury unseen. We took our time. I wanted to reach there by dark. There was no need to rush and tire ourselves out. Darkness would disguise our numbers and they would be more likely to be off their guard.

Aiden stopped us just half a mile from the town. Any closer and our horses might have alerted them. We did not have the luxury of any spare men to guard them and so we hobbled our animals. There were not many of us and I hoped that the twenty-six of us would be able to frighten over forty wild Irish warriors. Edgar led Edward's men at arms and half of mine on the left. Wulfric had the others on our right. Wulfric hefted his war axe. I pitied anyone who faced him in the dark. He was a terrifying warrior. Our three killers slipped off through the dark. All of them were extremely effective at moving through the undergrowth and remaining unseen. They were all in their own natural element; the woods and forests. I had confidence in my assassins. The rest of us kept moving forward in a long line. We were no more than a pace and a half apart. I drew my sword before I left the safety of the woods which lined the road leading to the town. The Coquet Valley was verdant and it afforded good cover.

Up ahead I heard the noise of the camp. It was a mixture of laughter, shouts, squeals and screams. The warriors were enjoying themselves but the captives were not. There was also a background noise of the penned animals. There was a large fire burning. It gave a hint of what was going on ahead of us. I had seen that when I had left the road. From the smell they were roasting meat; obviously, one of the animals they had captured. We were not concerned with sentries on the river nor on the northern side of the settlement. I could not see them having more than a couple of sentries there in any case and their attention was more likely to be on the camp rather than outside. They had reached here unmolested. They had no idea that we were close.

Aiden materialised out of the dark and held up two fingers. The sentries had died. I nodded and signalled for him to return to the horses. The carts were interlocked but were intended as a defence behind which to fight. Undefended they were no barrier to us, even wearing hauberks. We crept in a perilously short line and stood behind the carts. Now we could see within the camp. Many of the children and the women were huddled together in terrified groups. Some of the older girls and younger women were the subjects of the attention of the mercenaries. The wounded knight and the four men at arms were seated away from the deprivations and appeared deep in conversation. My men all looked to me. I climbed over the cart and nodded to Leofric. We moved forward into the camp even as the strident notes summoning my archers were sounded by my squire.

There was immediate confusion. The horn's sound seemed to swirl in the air. Those within were disorientated. I slashed at the neck of an Irish warrior who was straddling a young woman. He was straining his head to hear the horn when I decapitated him. I made for the knight and the men at arms. They were the danger. The mercenaries would be wild fighters but the danger lay in the five professionals. The knight reached for his sword as two of his men at arms advanced with swords and shields. They had grabbed them far quicker than I could have anticipated. Even so, we had momentum with us and I punched with my shield as I swept my sword around to strike at the nearest warrior's middle. Although he managed to get his shield to block my blow my punch made him reel and he began to lose his balance. I pulled back my sword and brought it over my head. He had to readjust his feet to try to block my next blow. He fell backwards and my sword split his helmet and head in one blow. His headgear had been poorly made.

A sword darted out at me. Had I not had quick hands then the wounded knight would have done for me as he stabbed towards my side. I swept the blade away and brought the side of my shield around. I hit him in the neck with the edge. My left arm is almost as strong as my right and the shield tore into his throat. He died spraying blood over the last two men at arms.

Tristan and Harold quickly finished the two remaining men at arms. I saw huddles of bodies looking like hedgehogs with arrows sticking from them. Dick and his archers had done their job as well as ever. The last of the mercenaries were being backed towards the wall of the church and Wulfric and his men were relentlessly driving into them. Wulfric favoured a one handed war axe and I saw it rip through a shield and across the collar bone and chest of a terrified-looking warrior who died against the church wall.

One of them shouted, "Quarter!"

I glanced to my left and a mother comforting a girl of no more than fifteen summers. "No quarter!" They were butchered where they stood. They had no armour to stop our blows and they were drunk. It was a job of work. Dick and his men rode in with swords drawn. I looked up at my captain of archers. "Did any escape?"

"None, Baron!"

"Good. Have these carts filled with the captives. We start back now. See if there are any boys who can drive the animals. If not then we shall have to do it."

Tristan said, "We go back immediately?"

I looked at the young knight who had acquitted himself well. He deserved an explanation. "We have a warband to find and I want these in Otterburn by dawn. They will be safer there than here."

We used oxen and horses to pull the carts and the boys, supervised by Aiden, drove the animals. We had little time to search for treasure but there was little to be had anyway. It was just the knight and the men at arms who had been worth searching. The mercenaries must have been promised animals and slaves. I rode next to a cart where the woman who had been comforting her daughter rode. She was facing defiantly forward. Her daughter, at least I assumed it was a daughter but I supposed it could have been her sister, sobbed still.

I spoke gently to her for I could see the anger in her face. "Were you from the village of Elsdon?"

She shook her head, "No, my lord, a village far to the east. They killed my husband and my son and took us. We had little enough but they took it anyway."

The girl looked up, "They killed my dog. Why did they do that?" Her mother put her arm around her and pulled her in tightly.

"You will be safe now. We will take you to Otterburn Tower."

The woman shook her head, "And then what? What can two women do there? The Scots will come again. Better we had died with our men than live as slaves or worse. We will not stay at Otterburn!"

I had no answer for her but she set me to thinking. I nudged Scout forward. I was weary but I had to keep alert. The woman was correct in one respect; the worst thing I could do would be to abandon these people in Otterburn. She had not been scathing about my fatuous comment but she would have been justified had she done so. What was I thinking? Abandon these people and impose them on others who were as poor as they were and in just as much danger? I could not do that. The King had appointed me protector of this land. I would have to use my mind to come up with a solution.

Chapter 3

It was after dawn when we reached Otterburn; we were all exhausted and weary. Oswald and my men had been preparing for our arrival and they had a fire going and food which they had hunted. I waved him over, "Oswald you were a captive for many years; these women need care. You will understand their needs better than I. Look after them for me."

He dropped to a knee, "It will be an honour, my lord!"

I took off my helmet. "John, get this armour off me. I will bathe in this river."

The captives look on in amusement as I stripped down to my undergarments and stepped into the icy river. The cold was soon replaced by refreshment. It awoke me and made me less weary. Harold and Edward joined me leaving a bemused Tristan to shake his head. He would learn. "We need to leave before noon."

"The men are tired and some have wounds, Baron."

"I know, Harold, but we must end this sooner. If word gets out that we are in this valley then they will be prepared. It is why I sent for Baron Hexham. His men will be fresh and might give us the edge we need. We will leave any wounded here to protect the captives and we will only take the fittest of palfreys."

Edward rose from the water and headed for the bank. "And what do we do with the captives?"

"Is my mind that easy to read?"

"I know you, Baron. You worry o'er much about people."

"We will let any who wish to either stay here or return to Elsdon. The rest can return with us to Stockton." Edward nodded. "It is the Christian thing to do and, in all conscience, I cannot abandon them."

Leofric helped to dress me while John put an edge on my sword and my dagger. We were six men at arms and two archers weaker following our attack. It could have been worse but it meant we relied upon Sir Hugh Manningham bringing his forces to aid us. Gilbert told me that the fastest route would take us back through Elsdon. It could not be helped. "Have the men at arms take a lance each. They may be useful if we are to catch them on the road." We had just over twenty miles to cover and we were well-mounted. It was fortunate that we had brought so many arrows for we would need them.

Aiden went ahead to scout for us while one of Dick's archers went the longer route south to find the men of Hexham. Enough of the men at Otterburn had been to Morpeth to give me an idea of its defences. It relied on a small hill and the river to protect itself. The bridge, if they were warned of our approach, could be held. I counted on Garth being able to reach the castle and alert the defenders.

Aiden returned when we were just five miles from Morpeth. He had a grim face. "Baron the castle is barred to them but they have burned many of the farms and manors which stood around the castle and they have captives." He pointed to the north, "They are riding back to Berwick."

"Which road do they take?"

"They are heading up the coast road."

That worried me. Was Alnwick held? "Can we save time by cutting across country?"

"I believe we can take the road to Ugham. I saw a Roman road marker back there, Baron."

I had to detach another archer to fetch Sir Hugh and his men to join us. My only hope was that those heading north would be slowed down by the captives and if we could attract their attention then Sir Hugh might actually reach us. We only had to travel a mile or so off the road and we were soon making good progress. The land here had been cleared and some of the fields were ploughed while others were for pasture. We found the first body just five miles up the road. It was an older woman. Perhaps she could not keep up but whatever the reason she had her life ended by a spear thrust into her side. It pained us but we could not afford to bury her. We had the living to consider.

We were close to the bridge over the Coquet when Aiden spotted them. He had spurned the road in favour of the higher ground to the west. "They have stopped at the bridge, Baron."

"How many are there?"

I hoped that they had lost some during their march south. "There are six knights, four squires and ten men at arms. They have ten crossbows and the rest are foot soldiers although some of them ride."

Edward nodded, "The captured horses."

"How many captives?"

"There look to be thirty or so. This time they have some young men with them. It looks like they have them driving the cattle and the sheep."

"Dick, take the archers and find some high ground. I want the men with crossbows taken out." He nodded and led his small band north. "We will try to use our one advantage."

"What is that Baron?"

"Lances, Tristan. We have just five fewer mailed men than they do. If we can surprise them then we might cause enough damage to slow them down and Sir Hugh can join us."

It sounded flimsy even to me but they nodded as though it was sound advice. John and Leofric had barely begun to train with lances. John was powerful and I hoped that his strength would outweigh his lack of skill. The road on which we travelled was the old Roman Road which went north. It was unerringly straight but, more importantly, it had a good surface and would be wide enough, between the ditches, for us to have four knights and three squires in the first rank, then the men at arms and John and Leofric would bring up the rear. John was carrying my banner. This time they would know whom they faced.

We reached the top of the rise leading down to the bridge. They were a little slow to react to us and we had cantered fifty feet before we saw the panic begin. I spied the blue standard with two yellow stars and fleur de lys. It was Fitzwaller. He was there. The men at arms all wore his livery while the others looked to be Scottish knights. I stored that information. Fitzwaller was organising his knights and men at arms to face us. He waved and his crossbowmen and foot soldiers spread out on either side. We trotted easily down the gentle slope and we were soon just two hundred paces from them. Fitzwaller put his horses in a line and had a single line of spearmen before him. He had been fooled. He had thought we had no archers.

At one hundred and twenty paces we lowered our lances and Dick's archers targeted the crossbows. The Flemish mercenaries were waiting until the range was close enough to puncture our mail and they paid for the delay with their lives. Dick and his archers could release a large number of arrows very quickly and they had a big target at which to aim. At fifty paces I spurred Scout on. Dick and his archers concentrated upon the left flank of Fitzwaller's line. That way he would not risk hitting us and he would weaken one flank.

Horses will not charge a solid line of men and this was a solid line. Those who rode with me knew that. At five paces we pulled back on our reins so that our horses slowed and then, we jerked their heads up to make them rear as we lunged forward as one with our lances. Our weapons were longer than those held by the foot soldiers. Those who were not speared tried to flee but were prevented by the horsemen behind. The thin line of spearmen died quickly.

"Change!" We had practised this manoeuvre many times. The knights and squires peeled off to ride back along the ditch while the men at arms charged the horsemen. With no spears to protect them the second attack of lances all struck targets. Four men at arms fell mortally wounded while another three reeled back from the onslaught.

"Fall back!"

There was little point in risking casualties for we now held the advantage. As we moved back up the road and some of the more foolish Scots tried to pursue us they were cut down by Dick's arrows. Fitzwaller led the retreat across the bridge.

"Regroup!"

"Baron, Gille and Hugh have been wounded!"

"Leofric see to them. John, join us in the front rank. Who has an unbroken lance?"

Roger of Lincoln rode up, "Here Baron, I found flesh and not mail."

With an unbroken lance, I led my horse down the road. The bridge was a maelstrom of chaos and confusion. The horses had crossed but those on foot were crowded as they tried to escape from my archers' deadly missiles. Dick's arrows continued to rain death. We struck the stragglers piecemeal. Some threw themselves into the Coquet to escape the snapping jaws of our horses and our deadly spears. We did not wait to finish them off. I wanted to destroy this war band's will to fight.

I heard a horn behind and, glancing over my shoulder, saw the conroi of Sir Hugh Manningham as they thundered down the road to our aid. It was as well for our horses were spent. I finally broke my spear on a Scot who tried to use his shield to defend himself. The spear spun the shield around and broke as it entered his chest and caught on his baldric. He was the last man I killed that day. I reined in Scout. He was sweating heavily. I waited for Sir Hugh and his men to join me.

"A timely arrival, Sir Hugh." I pointed ahead of me, "My horses are spent."

"Do not fear, Baron, we will chase them back beyond the border."

"Do not risk your men. This Fitzwaller is no fool and I fear Alnwick has fallen too."

He nodded, "Aye Baron. Your commands will be obeyed." He and his horsemen galloped off. The fresher legs of his horses showed as they began to gain on the fleeing Scots.

"Wulfric, finish off the wounded and collect the coins from the dead." He waved, dismounted and took off his helmet.

I took off my helmet and allowed the coif to drop too. Edward joined me. He dismounted and began to tend the cut on his horse's neck, "Damned barbarians!"

"We were lucky there, Edward."

"I know." He glanced to the top of the hill, "I wonder how Gille is?"

He had lost one squire before and it had upset him deeply. "Edgar will tend to him and he is a good healer." Once again I regretted not bringing a priest with me.

Dick and his archers rode up. "Dick get the captives and animals; head back to Morpeth. We will clear up here and follow you."

"Aye, Baron."

"And Dick, once again your archers made the difference. We must try to get a few more."

He shook his head, "I fear it takes too many years to make a good archer and those from Sherwood are now but a distant memory."

"This winter travel the manor and seek any yeomen who have the potential. Your archers are the difference up here in this border country."

"I will do so, Baron."

I watched the captives nod and mumble their gratitude as they headed south. They would know how close they had come to a life as a slave. They were more fortunate than the people of Elsdon. Here Fitzwaller had kept some of the men alive to care for the animals. The rescued captives had disappeared over the hill when I saw the first flames flicker around the pyre of the dead raiders. With winter coming it would not do to tempt the wolves down from the hills for easy pickings. We mounted and made our way back up the hill. I saw that Gille and Hugh were alive and both were heavily bandaged.

Edgar was washing the blood from his hands. "They are both lucky but they will need Father Matthew's hands and some rest. They will not fight again this campaign, Baron."

Hugh tried to rise but his heavily bandaged leg would not support his weight, "I protest, Baron! I will do my duty!"

"And your duty is to obey me! Put them both on a cart. They return to Stockton and Father Matthew." My voice had been forceful and I smiled to soften the blow. "Do not worry Hugh and Gille, I have a task for the two of you."

We stayed at Morpeth where we were greeted and treated as heroes. I did not relax until I saw the banners of Sir Hugh and his conroi return from the north. I breathed a sigh of relief when I saw that they only led one horse. Sir Hugh shook his head as he dismounted, "You were right Baron. He is a sneaky bastard. Alnwick has fallen and we might have ridden into an ambush close to the Aln but for your warning. I lost my scout only. Do we try to take Alnwick back?"

"We have neither the men nor the time. This and your castle are now the border. Next spring I will bring a battle and we will try to retake Alnwick. When the cold comes and I return south you and your men will need to ensure that Morpeth and the road to the New Castle are safe."

He nodded. "And where will you and your men stay while you are here?"

I shook my head ruefully, "We will wear out saddles riding twixt Otterburn and here. I have no doubt that they will send spies to see if we have left. I will make my handful of men an army."

It was a day later when we returned, weary, to Otterburn. I saw the relief on the faces of the former captives and the residents of the tower. We arrived in the late afternoon for I had not wanted to push the weary animals too much. We had also been hampered by having our wounded squires in carts.

I used one of the carts as a platform and I addressed the host before me. "We have driven the Scottish raiders hence and I cannot see them returning this year."

There was a cheer at that. The woman whose daughter had been assaulted said, "That is all well and good, my lord but what about next year? Will they return again?"

I nodded, "Probably. The Romans tried to build a wall and even that is south of here. There are good knights such as Sir Hugh Manningham who will try to deter them but…"

One of the men of Otterburn said, "We could improve our own defences here. The tower is strong."

"That is a good idea and, while we remain here, my men and I will help you."

The woman was persistent, "Walls and ditches did not help at Elsdon. It is warriors that we need."

"I cannot conjure warriors." I saw faces filled with despair. "If any of you wish then you can make new homes further south. I know that the Palatinate will be defended and I watch over the Tees."

For some reason that brought cheer to their faces. The relentless woman said, "I for one would take you up on your offer, Baron."

There was a chorus of, "Aye."

I saw Edward shake his head. He would have left them to their own devices. "Then on the morrow, all those who wish to travel south will be escorted by my squire, Hugh of Gainford and my wounded warriors. They will protect you but you must watch your own animals on the way south."

The news filled them not only with hope but activity too. They all departed save the relentless woman whose daughter clung to her skirts still. "I am sorry that I appeared obstinate, my lord, but we had been driven to Elsdon from our home in the east. I lost my men I would not lose my daughter."

"What is your name, mother?"

"Judith wife of John, this is my daughter Susan."

"I do not blame you Judith wife of John. I would do the same for my family if I were in danger but I do not promise an easy life in Stockton."

"Just so long as you promise me protection then we will fend for ourselves."

After she had gone I summoned Oswald, Hugh and Gille. "You will need to be patient on the way south. I know that we could travel the distance in one day. These people cannot."

Oswald nodded, "I will watch over them, Baron. I have spoken with them for the last few days and they are good people."

"And I am honoured that you put them under my protection too, Baron. We will treat them as though they are our own." Hugh was taking his responsibilities seriously. That was a good sign. He would soon be ready for knighthood.

With the wounded men and those, like Oswald, who had been caring for us left, we were a small number. We spent the next two days improving Otterburn's defences. The ditches were deepened and my men gave the villagers lessons in using weapons. It was not enough but it was all that we could do. On the third day, I took my conroi on a leisurely ride through Elsdon, Rothbury and back to Morpeth. There was no sign of the Scots save the devastation they had left. We saw flocks of carrion in the skies over farms where the living had been replaced by corpses. My warriors too were depressed. We had driven the Scots hence but this still felt like failure.

Edward asked me, as we rode south from Rothbury, "This Guy Fitzwaller why do you think he is here?"

"He is an opportunist. We have had them before, have we not? And, more importantly, if the Empress is to marry Geoffrey of Anjou then there will be little opportunity for him to ferment rebellion in his homeland. What surprised me is that he has not gone to Italy. The rewards are greater there than on this border."

Tristan had been listening and suddenly said, "Baron, perhaps you should look closer to home for the reason."

"What do you mean?"

"If you and your father were responsible for his family losing their estates and their money then it may not be the King alone who is the object of his hatred. Is it a simpler answer that he comes for you? It is no secret that you defend Durham and the borders. He can find allies aplenty in Scotland. As we have seen it is not an easy place to defend. He can become rich, gain power and build up an army. He can seek greater power. Who knows he may think he can gain a throne up here."

Edward laughed, "You have a fertile mind, Tristan." The young knight coloured, "No, I do not disagree with you. I think your assessment is a good one it is just that I am a simple soldier and I would not have made all those connections."

I nodded. "And I, too, think you are right. We will spend the winter planning how we deal with this threat. I would rather campaign here than have to defend my land."

"And do not forget the Irish mercenaries. You bloodied the noses of the Vikings and the Irish last year but both places are filled with swords who seek a lord." Edward shrugged, "I was one such was I not? They can find many such warriors. They are easy to kill but they can still cause us hurt."

We rode in silence as I sifted through all of the information I had just received. Even though we had hurt them over the last few years there would still be individual knights who would join Fitzwaller. He now had the winter to improve his defences and build up his army. We had given him a setback but if Alnwick was in his hands then he would attract warriors.

We stayed for three more weeks. We saw no Scots but we were aware of their scouts and their spies. Aiden found camps and hiding places close to our patrol route. They had learned to evade Aiden's scrutiny. However, we knew that they had not departed completely. It was the weather that made us return south. The first of the hard frosts came followed a day later by a flurry of snow. Although it soon melted in the morning light we knew that it meant winter was coming. We left Otterburn. The tower and the village were stronger than when we had arrived but the villagers were unhappy at our departure.

We spent one night with Sir Hugh. We could have hurried home and reached it in one hard day but I needed to inform the Baron of the situation as I saw it. "I intend to seek permission from the King to take a battle north and recapture Alnwick next year. To do that I will need the help and support of all the knights who have manors north of Durham."

"What you really mean is loyal knights." I nodded, "Then I will send spies to find out their affiliations. This is a good manor and I would not lose it."

"And Alnwick, what kind of castle is it?"

"Potentially the most powerful castle in the north for the site is a natural fortress but it is still a wooden structure. I think that was why your enemy captured it with such relative ease."

We left the next day, calling only briefly at Durham to inform Hubert of our news. "I will return in the spring but I will need soldiers from

Durham if we are to retake Alnwick and, more importantly, drive these usurpers back to Scotland."

"Then I will spend the winter building up our forces, Baron."

I left him and the Dean preparing for winter in what was now the most important castle in the north. If a large enough army came then they would sweep through Morpeth and Hexham. Only Durham would slow up an invader.

Chapter 4

By the time we finally reached Stockton the winter had begun in earnest. In days of old, this would have meant that many animals would have either been killed by the cold or butchered to be preserved. We had perfected the technique of sharing homes with our animals so that far more survived than when I had first arrived. It explained our prosperity. Many of those displaced from Elsdon had settled across the river. Thornaby and Preston, as well as Elton, were growing quickly. New huts were already in evidence. I understood the reasons behind the choice. There was the barrier of my castle and then the river. A raider from the north would be hard-pushed to break through those barriers.

Oswald and Judith had set up home close to the Oxbridge. Since the attack by wolves, we had cleared much of the land and Oswald had built a large hut. Hugh told me how the two had been inseparable on the way south. Judith was not a poor woman; she had three cows and four sheep. She had had more but they had been lost in the attack. Her daughter, Susan, was also less fearful of gentle Oswald than my warriors. She had been damaged in the attack. For them both it was a new start and I was pleased for them. They were like Wulfstan and Faren. They had found each other when they were older.

I was just pleased to be in the bosom of my family once more. The last nights in the north had been fearfully cold. I was too used to my warm castle. The first thing I did, however, after greeting my family and playing with my children was to summon John, son of Leofric, my steward and clerk and dictate a letter to the King. I sent a copy each to the Archbishop of York and Robert of Gloucester. I would have sent one to London and the Bishop of Durham but the bishop, it was rumoured, was even closer to death now. He seemed to be hanging on to life as though it was a prize. The Emperor of the Holy Roman Empire had done the same. I would have thought a man of God would have welcomed the chance to go to heaven.

I left nothing out of my report. John's eyes widened once or twice but he remained silent. I wanted the King to draw his own conclusions but I knew what I wished for. I wished for knights who could be trusted to come to the borderlands. Finally, the missive was finished and John made two more copies. Getting the message to York was relatively easy but I was lucky that Olaf had one more visit to our port before winter set in. He would deliver the two other messages to London. I had no idea where the King was but I hoped that the message would reach him.

Then we prepared for winter. I took John and Leofric hunting before the snow began to lie. Wulfric had our men cutting down as much firewood as possible while Dick and his archers made bows and fletched their arrows. The little money we had made went directly to Alf who made the arrowheads and the new spearheads. War was expensive. However, as Edward pointed out, peace came at a very high price- much higher than war.

Winter proper arrived a week before Yule. Although the river did not freeze there were thin patches of ice upon it. Edward, Richard of Yarm and Harold joined me in sending men out to hunt the wolves. This was the time to seek them for the cold made their sense of smell weaken and they had yet to create their cubs. The meat, whilst a little tough would augment our supplies. The late winter was always a time of tightening belts; even for lords of the manor.

It was close to Candlemas when I received a reply to my letter from the King. I had not expected a reply to my other letters. I sat with Hugh, John and Leofric when I read it. I did not read aloud but I commented to them as I read.

Stockton,
I was most disturbed to hear that the Fitzwallers still harboured treacherous thoughts. Your prompt action is gratifying. I am also more than a little angry that many of my lords have decided to abandon their people.

I have summoned D'Umfraville back from his crusade. He owes me his fealty! I am concerned that there are so few in that part of my kingdom.

I will visit the north when next I visit England. You have my authority, in the meanwhile, to take whatever action you feel necessary to regain Alnwick and to make the borderlands safe. New lords will be appointed. Until that time you will continue to protect the lands north of the Tees.
Henry Beauclerk
By the Grace of God
King of England, Count of Maine and Duke of Normandy

The seal which was attached to the letter was all the authority I would now need. It was a terse letter and to the point but it matched the King. He wasted nothing!

"Well, what do you make of that?"

"You have more power than any other lord save the Bishop of Durham, Baron."

"But you miss the point, Hugh. It is now my responsibility. If I do not recapture Alnwick nor keep the border safe then it is I who will suffer and my family. You assume I can do both successfully."

"You can my lord."

"Thank you for your confidence, John, but I have never taken a castle by assault. The border is many leagues from here and we have fewer knights than the Scots."

Hugh nodded and then leaned forward eagerly, "But it is not the Scots is it, Baron? It is a rebel knight and the sweepings of the gutter."

"Others will join him. The rebels I fought two years ago will fight alongside him. They have nothing to lose. If I defeat them then Fitzwaller will take the blame. If I am defeated then they will all benefit from the victory. Many will fight behind false liveries; I have seen it before in Flanders. We have this winter to make the three of you into fine warriors. With luck, Hugh, you shall be knighted next year."

"I fear I have much to learn and… to be truthful, Baron I am a little fearful of going back to Gainford."

"I can understand that. You should be looking around now for those men at arms you might like to follow your banner when you have one. It would not do any harm to visit Gainford now and again. Remember what Dick said about archers. If I were in your position then I would train up a large number of archers."

"But will we be campaigning in the coming year?"

"Aye. As soon as the first sign of spring comes then I will send for my barons and we will move north. We will have to leave before the lambing season and before the animals are returned to their pastures."

Often times we make plans and when we attempt to put them into operation they fail. At other times you make plans and they are jeopardised from the start. My most reliable knight, archers and men at arms belonged to Edward. He came to see me a week after I had received the letter from the King. His face told its own story as he approached me in my inner ward. "Baron, I have been summoned to Anjou to attend the wedding of Empress Matilda and Geoffrey of Anjou."

Now I saw the reason for the short letter from the King. The King knew what he was doing. "It is not your fault, Edward."

"I know but you are going to campaign in the north and I will not be there."

"But you go to guard the Empress, possibly for the last time. I am happy that you, Rolf and the Swabians will be there to watch her once more. It is right that you go."

"I do not need to take my whole garrison."

"No, but you will need to leave some men to guard your manor. I shall be away and Wulfstan will be hard-pressed enough as it is."

"Baron, I leave you with a heavy heart." His face showed his earnestness. "Beware this Fitzwaller. Your young knights think that they have easily bested him but from what you have told me he is a cunning warrior. Be wary. Expect tricks and expect treachery. I have served such knights when I was younger. I know what they are like. I will return as soon as I am able."

"Thank you, Edward; I too will miss your mighty right hand. When you see the Empress…" I trailed off lamely.

"I know Baron. I will find the words."

"The words are easy, old friend; they are goodbye."

Without Edward, I had more planning to do myself. In this, I was aided by both Hugh and John my steward. John and Leofric were both willing squires but they were unused to such enterprises. We spent the next few days poring over lists and musters and determining which knights we should take and how many of their men. It was not as large a list as I had hoped. We only took archers who could be mounted. That limited my choice for some knights did not have horses for all of their men. We had to leave men at arms and archers to guard the castles and manors we left behind; I was mindful of the words of Edward and, as we would be away during the busy season on the land we could take no servants with us. It meant we had but eight knights, ten squires who would be required to see to all of our needs, forty-four men at arms, forty archers and five crossbows. I know that Dick would be angry at the crossbows but, if we were to assault a castle, then I needed all the missiles I could muster.

I spent a week, with my squires, riding around the manors and telling them of my orders. They were all gratifyingly happy. Tristan was convinced that he would gain a manor in the north from this. I did not like such overconfidence. The others had not campaigned with me in the autumn and were eager for action. We left at the end of March. Even that was later than I would have hoped but it took time to gather such a force together. This time we took our warhorses as well as palfreys and sumpters; Fitzwaller had knights.

Hubert had not found as many men for me as I would have hoped. I was disappointed in his efforts. In fact, I was not even certain he had bothered to gather a muster. He had Ralph Espec who brought with him four men at arms and four archers. He had had more but they were not mounted and I wanted a swift force. I also refused the fifty men of the fyrd who had been raised. They were unreliable and more trouble than they were worth. They either charged off, as they had at Hastings or fled the field when things went badly. He did, however, give me a priest, Father John, and the standard of St. Cuthbert as well as a holy relic. Two other priests accompanied Father John. I knew how valuable such a Pyx could be. Finally, we were ready and we rode north under fine banners and standards. As we headed along the Roman Road towards Hexham, Richard of Yarm and Raymond de Brus flanked me.

"My son tells me that you sent back a larger force at the Coquet. Perhaps that bodes well for us."

"No, Richard, we dispersed Irish mercenaries. Not a knight was taken and they have had the winter to gather allies. I have no doubt that they have been doing as we and building up their forces."

Raymond had little experience this far north. "And can we expect much help from the local lords?"

"Sir Hugh is the most important. Guiscard of Morpeth too can be depended upon but the main lords, Gospatric and the like have fled to their Scottish lands. They will not show themselves in open rebellion but they side with the Scots. The D'Umfraville family was given the land but, until they are summoned back from the Holy land there is an empty land where there should be bristling spears."

Hexham brought hope to my heart. Sir Hugh had not been idle. He had improved his defences and spent his money wisely. He would be supplying twenty men at arms, ten archers and he had six foresters as scouts. We camped close to the castle next to the river on the wide flood plain. I held a council of war. I had more knights this time and I wanted them all to know what was in my mind.

"We will travel to Morpeth and move up the coastal road. Our first aim is to recapture Alnwick. Once that has been achieved then we will drive any other Scots back to Berwick and the border."

Ralph Espec was new to me. I felt happy about the qualities of the rest of my knights but he was an unknown quantity. "Have we the men to attack a castle? Where are the fyrd who will make the assault?"

I smiled, "I have only attacked one or two castles but even I know that sending the fyrd to make the assault would guarantee failure. We weaken the castle first and then we use knights and men at arms to capture it."

Ralph shook his head, "That too would be doomed to failure."

Before I could speak Harold said, "It is how the Baron took Hexham from the rebels and now Sir Hugh has improved it."

Ralph looked at Harold who still looked little older than a youth. "You fought here then? Were you a child?"

That could have caused offence but Harold merely laughed, "I have been fighting since I was but ten summers old. Do not let my lack of a full beard deceive you."

They all laughed and I said, "If age and beards were qualifications to fight then I would have brought my old men with me. Fear not Ralph of Fishburn; I will not waste lives and we will capture the castle." I spoke with a confidence I did not feel. I had a plan but I wanted to see the castle first.

We picked up Guiscard and another fourteen men from Morpeth. It would not do to leave that most important of river crossings unguarded. It gave us ten knights and, more importantly over seventy men at arms. Wulfric was my Sergeant At Arms. He knew how to command. Dick was my Captain of archers. Some of those we had brought were not of the quality of Dick's finest but they would do. They were all mounted and would be able to move swiftly around the field of battle. Their arrows would whittle down the enemy but it would be Dick and my best archers who would win the day.

We reached the mouth of the Aln. Although a wide estuary, it was shallow enough at low tide not to present an obstacle. The scouts we had brought told us that the castle was on the southern side of the river which was narrow and easily fordable. We crossed the estuary and made camp on the northern bank. I had no doubt that we were seen. We were too large a band to be missed. Although most of those in the area might be loyal to King Henry, it had changed hands too many times over the years for that to be certain. I wanted us to be seen. I needed our enemies to come for us.

Once we had guards set I gathered my knights. "Tomorrow we advance upon Berwick!"

I waited as the knights erupted. "Berwick! I thought we came to recapture Alnwick!"

"That is our intention and believe me, Sir Raymond, we will."

"Baron, we have few enough men to attack Alnwick why would you risk going further north and taking us closer to enemies?"

I stood and drew my sword. I marked some lines in the sand. "Here is Alnwick and here we are at the Aln. As you can see the castle cannot be supplied from the sea. The land to the west is poor and has little growing there at the moment. To the south is the land we now hold and control. If we besiege Alnwick from where will we get our food?"

"Why the land around of course."

"Exactly Sir Hugh and that land belonged to our people. They will either have fled or have been captured. The result is the same, there will be no farms there and no food. Alnwick has to get its food from the north. We will move into that land. We are now in Scotland. From now on every mouthful we take is taken from a Scotsman."

Harold suddenly laughed, "You do not mean to take Berwick."

"Of course not. Do I look a fool? I ride north so that we cut off the supply of food to Alnwick and threaten the north. We will take food from the Scots north of here. Fitzwaller will have to come forth from his castle to eliminate us. He will already have sent a message to his allies further north that we threaten him. When he realises we are heading to Berwick he will send more riders for help and we will stop them. I intended to use some of the archers and scouts to cut the north road. They will ambush any riders. Before dawn tomorrow they will go here." I jabbed my sword into the sand. "Warenford. It is far enough from Alnwick for the riders to think they are safe." I smiled," We will also gain some horses. We isolate Alnwick and take the battle to the enemy rather than wasting men assaulting a castle."

"And how far north do we go?"

"Before I left Durham I spoke with the Dean there and looked at some old maps. There used to be a castle at Bamburgh but it was reduced by the Vikings. King William also laid waste to it. As far as I know, it has no castle there now but it is a good site and easy to defend. We draw them there."

"And if they do not come?"

"Then after laying waste to the area and gathering supplies, we head south for by that time the garrison will have eaten any supplies they laid in for a siege. If they remain behind their walls because they fear an attack then that fear will grow each day we do not attack. We move slowly and care for our horses. We eat everything we find north of here and we keep together. "

Dick chose just four archers for the ambush. Those and the four foresters would be all that we would need. They were not there to stop an army just single or pairs of riders. Ralph of Wales led them. Dick and I made sure that they understood their task and we told them where we would be. As well as stopping news from leaving they would gather news for us and keep us informed.

The land north of the Aln was made up of small farms and farmsteads. Although the people fled they were not able to take their animals. We captured and slaughtered as we went. I knew that some would flee to Alnwick while others would head north. It suited us for it spread panic. Fitzwaller would know it was me and be wondering what were my intentions. When the animals were butchered the archers spread hunks of meat on either side of their horses' rumps. We would eat well. The going, however, was slower than I had hoped. The roads were small roads and we only made the small fishing village of Craster by nightfall. Many of the fishermen and their families fled by sea when we approached; others just headed north.

We found food in the homes and the fish they were drying. We demolished a hut to make the fires to cook the meat. The men were in excellent spirits as we dined like kings on beef, mutton and smoked herrings. Far from being hungry, we had food to spare. An army that was well fed fought better than one with empty bellies. We moved along the coast towards the small village of Seahouses. Unless I missed my guess many of those who had fled Craster would have taken refuge there. As we approached the cliffs which guarded the southern side I sent my archers north of the town to make sure that the people who fled took as little as possible with them. The high ground afforded a view into the small bay. We had been seen and I saw a veritable fleet of small ships heading north to Berwick and safety. We found more supplies for, like Craster, the people here smoked and dried fish. More importantly, they left food in their homes too.

"We will camp here for the day."

Sir Geoffrey approached me, "We could move far quicker if we need to, Baron."

"But there is no need. What is travelling far faster than we are, is the news of our advance and the panic is setting in. Fitzwaller may not be concerned that we are here, as yet, but the Lord of Berwick will and he will mobilise men soon enough."

"You want to fight the Scots?"

"I want to fight them on ground of my choosing. If we besieged Alnwick then we might be trapped between two forces. This way we eliminate the threat whilst keeping Fitzwaller nervous. The King has charged me with recapturing Alnwick and this is the only way I can see to do it with the forces I have at my disposal."

A messenger came from Ralph of Wales. He had with him two horses. "They sent a pair of messengers yesterday, Baron. We took this document from them."

I opened the hastily scrawled piece of parchment. I saw a seal at the bottom. I did not recognise it but I took it to be that of Fitzwaller.

To the Earl Gospatric,
I am trapped inside Alnwick. The Baron of the Tees has come north and is ravaging the country with a large battle. He has many knights with him. We need help. Our supplies are running out.
Fitzwaller

I smiled. He had overestimated my forces and now I knew of Gospatric's continued treachery. I would show this to the King.

"Have you stopped any messengers from the north?"

"We have seen none. The road is quiet, Baron."

"Then we will continue to annoy the Scots and weaken their resolve." The fact that there were no supplies moving south told me that the villages we had emptied must have been the ones supplying the castle.

We moved towards Bamburgh. It was on a small promontory surrounded on two sides by the sea and on the other two by dunes. The wooden remains of the old castle could still be seen but the Vikings had done a good job of demolition. It would need work to make it habitable once more. We set up camp on the high ground across the bay while I went with Sir Richard and Hugh to inspect what remained.

There was a ramp and we walked up it. To our right, the rock rose naturally and I saw, at the top what had been the wooden stakes driven into the earth. The gatehouse, or at least its remains, showed signs of burning. Once inside the ground rose steadily to the stone and wood keep. Little remained. The stones had fallen in when the tower was fired. The seas protected two of the sides while there was a ditch running around the other two. The sand dunes would stop a rapid advance. I wondered how the Vikings had managed to take such a formidable castle.

Hugh scratched his head, "I can see how the Vikings took it. The ditches would have caused little trouble to them."

I laughed, "If you had examined the gate you would have seen that was the way they came. Unless I miss my guess at high tide this ditch fills with water. It has not been cleared for some time but you can see weed at the bottom and there the sand is damp. That is why the gatehouse is burned. They must have set fire to it and then rushed in but they would have taken many casualties."

"You have a plan, Baron?"

"I do, Sir Richard. We put the archers and crossbowmen in here. When the men of Gospatric come from Berwick the knights, squires and half of the men at arms will appear to flee for we shall be frightened. We will appear to be heading south and we shall ride along the side of what the Scots will think is a deserted castle. The archers and crossbows in the ruins will whittle them down and the rest of the men at arms will attack from the west while we turn and attack from the south. They will not know in which direction to turn." I turned to walk back to our horses. "Come we shall put the archers and crossbows in here now. Dick can improve the defences and make the attack more effective."

I sent our scouts north towards Berwick. It was just twenty odd miles away. I suspected that the fleeing ships and those who had been displaced would have reached the town in the last couple of days. They would have waited a short time for news from Fitzwaller and to gather more warriors. I estimated they would reach us by the next day but I wanted confirmation from the scouts.

I allowed the men to shed their armour, at least for half a day. Our war horses were taken to the remains of the castle where they would be ready should we need them. When we fled they would be waiting for us south of the castle. We would charge on fresh horses. I also had our supply of lances left there. The priest and the Pyx, along with the banner of Durham, would remain hidden until my archers' attack. It would have an effect on those men who had followed Gospatric. It would show them that we had God and St. Cuthbert on our side.

That evening as we ate the last of the meat we had collected and the smoked fish, Sir Raymond asked me about my plan and how I had devised it. "It is not my own, Sir Raymond. I stole it from the Parthians. The Romans invaded their land and the Parthians led them on for they were a nation of mounted men. When they had them where they wanted them they sent in a force of horse archers. The Roman cavalry pursued them. They turned and destroyed them with their arrows and were then able to surround the Romans and slaughter them. It was a huge defeat."

"But you have changed it."

"Of course. I looked at the terrain and I have used what was available. They will have foot and when they chase us the knights and men at arms who are mounted will outrun them. They will be the ones we destroy first and then we can fall upon the foot."

"It sounds easy."

"Every battle plan sounds easy. Ask me again tomorrow after the battle. There are a hundred and one things that can go wrong. If they do then I will have to adapt my plan."

The scouts returned the next morning. "Baron, there is much activity at Berwick. We waited until late at night to return as there was much going on at the castle. Many knights arrived with their conroi and they had mercenaries who came from the west."

"Exactly what sort of activity?"

"Riders coming from the south and from the north; people fleeing north too."

That worried me. If they had messengers from the south then it suggested that, perhaps, they had found a different route north. Gospatric would know who faced him. It could not be helped. I gathered my knights and my captains. "They may come today. Wulfric, take half of the men at arms and wait to the west of the town. There are hills and folds in the land which will hide you. Dick I know you will have put markers out for the distance I suggest you put traps on the western side of your lines to deter them. It will keep the archers occupied. Leofric, go with Dick. I want the warhorses on the southern side of the castle ready for us to change."

The three of them left. "I want us to appear surprised. Squires, as soon as you are given the command I want you to gallop south as though the devil himself was after you. Ride to Leofric and help him with the horses. You will make as much noise as you can as you run. The rest of us will appear indecisive. The fact that our banners are fleeing south should encourage them to keep up the chase. They will be eager for revenge and see a small number of knights fleeing them. I have made a nuisance of myself before now. I will give the command for the squires to run, then the men at arms and finally for the knights. It must appear as though we have been taken by surprise and we are frightened. I want their horsemen to be encouraged and to pursue us closely. Do not worry; our horses will be fresher and we will be riding down the slope towards the castle. We will easily outrun them."

I had the scouts to the north of us. I sent them in pairs so that one could rest and one could watch. What I could not possibly know was the makeup of the army or the conroi which was heading south. I would have to judge that myself.

The thunder of hooves told me that the scouts had returned. "Baron, they are right behind us. They spotted us. I was asleep."

"Do not worry, now gallop south." I heard the host but could not see it as it was hidden by a fold in the land. "Squires, prepare!" I saw the banners begin to appear. "Squires flee!" I lifted the reins and made Scout rear. It added to the illusion of panic. "Men at arms! Go!"

The enemy knights and warriors were just four hundred paces away when they appeared over the crest. This all depended now upon timing. I was already pulling Scout's head around when I shouted, "Retreat! We are doomed!"

Harold laughed but he obeyed my command. The ten of us spurred our horses. I glanced over my shoulder and saw the men who pursued us were just a hundred paces from us. The knights at the front of the Scottish line were leaning forward eagerly. I noticed that they had neither spears nor lances. It was hard to estimate numbers for the vanguard hid those who followed. Our fresher horses began to extend our lead. I saw that the knights were riding their destrier. Our palfreys were faster. Ahead I saw the men at arms as they disappeared into the sand dunes. It would appear as though they had panicked. We headed that way too. Our lead was now almost two hundred and fifty paces. We galloped through the dunes and I saw the squires waiting. I leapt from Scout and mounted Star. He snorted and stamped his foot. He was eager for war. John handed me a lance. The scouts would follow us but not until we were all armed and ready.

I whipped Star's head around to the northwest and spurred him. "John! The standard!" John leapt on his horse and held the standard high. The standard from Durham was held by another squire and we turned to ride north.

We were not in a solid line as we emerged from the dunes but we did not need to be. The enemy knights were just level with the castle and the arrows and bolts flew into them. It was as though the Scots had ridden into a stone wall. Horses and men pitched into the ground. John nudged his horse next to me. Harold and Tristan flanked the two of us. I saw the line spreading like a long V. One or two of the knights had been a little tardy in mounting their warhorses but it did not affect us over much. I steadied Star so that we could make a continuous line. The enemy knights and men at arms were confused. They turned to face the wrecked castle walls from whence they were assailed by arrows and then they saw us. Some of those who had not been struck tried to bring their horses around to face us.

I tried to identify the banners as we closed with them but I recognised none. They were following neither Gospatric nor King David. That did not mean that this was unsanctioned. I pulled my lance back. I was at the head of the arrow of knights and a brave knight tried to charge me. His horse was spent and Star was not. My horse was eager to get to grips with the enemy and it took all of my strength to hold him back. The knight had no lance and mine took him in the throat. He had no gorget and the spear penetrated all the way through. He tumbled from the back of his horse and I lowered the lance to allow him to slip off without breaking my lance. I saw that the enemy was trying to rally. Wulfric's men at arms would not strike until the men on foot came to the aid of their horsemen.

I saw a shield before me as a knight tried to rally his men. I punched hard and my lance struck his shield so hard that it shattered and threw him from his saddle. I threw the broken lance away and drew my sword. I stood in my stirrups as I saw a knight turning to face me. I brought my blade down over my shoulder and it tore into his body between his helmet and his shield. I felt the edge grind against bone and then he just fell to one side, dead.

I saw the foot soldiers as they raced towards us. There was no order. They were a rabble. To the west, I saw the line of men at arms as they

Baron of the North

charged into the flank of the enemy. I spurred Star on. I drew my sword back and began to swing it as I approached the men armed with spears and swords, shields and helmets only. They had not one piece of mail between them and when I swung my sword it struck flesh and came away bloody! Star must have terrified them. His mighty head and jaws snapped to both the left and right. He trampled on one poor fellow. The foot did not stand against such an attack for they had no line and no cohesion and they turned to flee. That suited us and we charged through them laying to our left and right at unprotected backs. By the time we had reached our camp from the previous night, all opposition had ceased. We had not slain them all but we had destroyed them as a fighting force. They would not stop running until they reached the safety of Berwick castle.

I reined Star in at the top of the hill and turned around so that I could spy the field. It was littered with the enemy dead. An exultant John was there and I noticed that the tip of the banner and the banner itself were bloodied. He had used it as a weapon.

Sir Richard reined in next to me. "A victory, Baron, and they outnumbered us by over two to one!"

"It worked, Sir Richard, but it could have gone awry. We will thank God this night."

As we rode back through the corpses I had my men at arms search the bodies for anything we might use. I took off my helmet as I rode and handed it to Leofric who had appeared, as if by magic on my left. I saw that his sword, too, was bloodied.

As he took it he said, "That was easy, my lord. They just ran!"

"They were brave men but they were surprised and badly led."

I saw four of the five enemy knights were being guarded by my men at arms; some had surrendered. Roger de Bertram rushed over to me as I dismounted, "What a victory, my lord! These men surrendered."

My face must have been black as thunder for Raymond de Brus said," We will take ransom, Baron will we not? You did not say no quarter."

"We will take ransom. Share it between the knights and the squires but I will take none."

Sir Richard said, "But you should take the largest share! You led, Baron, and it was your plan."

"I was just doing what my King commanded. Collect all the spare horses and use them to carry the armour, weapons and the treasure."

"And the dead? "

"Bury ours and leave theirs. We head for the Great North Road. Tomorrow we retake Alnwick!"

Baron of the North

We turned as we heard hooves to the south. Four riders had escaped the net and were galloping south. Our horses were spent and I let them go. We would catch them soon enough. The only place they could go was to Alnwick and that would now soon fall to us. Hubris is a dangerous thing; I would soon discover just how dangerous and I would regret not stopping those four men to my dying day.

Chapter 5

We had done well out of the skirmish. We had four destriers as well as another fifteen horses. There was also a good quantity of mail and some swords. Although inferior to those of my men I knew that they would prove invaluable for the fyrd. We had enough to give each leader of the fyrd in each manor a sword. Although a small gesture, it would enhance the position of each elder. Every one of the men at arms and archers had profited from the coin we had taken and they would all fight harder next time. All in all, it had gone far better than I could either have expected or hoped.

We met our archers at the ambush site. There were another two horses. "We caught these two today, Baron."

"And there were no other riders either north or south?"

"None."

"Good, you have done well, rejoin Dick."

Sir Hugh rode next to me. "Send your men to scout out Alnwick. Fitzwaller has had plenty of time to prepare tricks. With no danger from the north now we can take our time with the siege."

He sent forward his scouts. "That was a good site for a castle, Baron. We could have fortified it."

"We could but we have few enough men as it is. I will write to the King. Perhaps he has a lord he wishes to reward."

"Would you not wish it?"

I laughed, "It is like saying would you like to own a wasps' nest? I will stay with the beehive which is Stockton. There are dangers but the rewards outweigh them. Besides I like the people who are there."

"You are lucky. It is lonely at Hexham."

"Aye, but you have sons and they can have manors. You can put your children close by and that will give you security."

"If we had women that would be true but there seem to be more knights than ladies to bear them children."

"That will change. Wulfstan, the Lord of Hartburn, has a daughter who is ten summers old. In four summers she can be a bride."

My squire, Hugh, who was behind us said, sadly, "My two sisters would have been of an age to marry had the raiders not slain them."

We rode in silence for a while. Such memories were not to be dismissed. It showed the dead no respect. Then Sir Tristan said, "And I have sisters too, Sir Hugh. Perhaps you need to visit the Valley and see what hardy flowers bloom there."

He laughed, "Quite the poet eh Sir Tristan! Honey-tongued, you shall soon have a bride."

"Like Harold here I will have a bride when I have a fine home which can be defended. I am still young and riding beneath the Baron's banner brings me regular coin. I will serve for a while."

The scouts came hurrying back and, ominously, there was a black cloud of smoke rising to the south. "My lord, Alnwick has been razed to the ground and the people were slain!"

There was little point in speculating until we had seen it with our own eyes. The foresters were good scouts but they could not read the land as Aiden could. Not for the first time, I regretted leaving him at home. "Dick, take the archers and secure the castle."

We rode faster now. My heart was heavy. Had someone else attacked the castle? I could not see who. The fact that the people had been slain pointed to Fitzwaller but what had made him leave? The closer we came to the burned-out ruin that was Alnwick the clearer the picture became. When the riders, who had escaped, had reached the castle, Fitzwaller must have known that he would get no help. But where had he gone? He had not headed north; we would have seen him.

A sad sight greeted us. Everyone had been slaughtered; men, women, and children, all lay dead and many were dismembered. He was not burdening himself with prisoners. That was ominous. He would move swiftly. Even as I dismounted to inspect the ruins I ran the different routes he could have taken through my mind. He had not gone north we would have seen him. He could have gone northwest. There were some Roman roads that headed over the high moors to Scotland. That would have been my choice but if he had gone in that direction he could have taken some slaves. He could have gone west and travelled to the west coast north of the wall. There he would reach safety and allies. The last two routes were either towards Hexham or Durham. If he was foolish enough to take that route then we would have him for that was not border country and there were castles that would bar his progress.

We spent the rest of the day burying the dead and examining the castle. "Sir Hugh, we need to ensure that Fitzwaller has not gone to Hexham and headed north-west into Scotland. If he has not then I wish you to return here and rebuild Alnwick. You will hold it for the King until we can send a new garrison."

He nodded, "Until the people return it will be a poor manor."

I pointed to the south, already I could see movement. Our banners had shown the people that the Scots had gone. They were hardy folk in these parts. They would return. "It will be poor for a while. Tax those merchants who venture south with their goods. That shall pay your men and the building of the castle. Let the Scottish merchants pay the price for this treachery."

"You are right, Baron, first we see if he has gone to Hexham!"

We reached Sir Hugh's home the next morning. The clearing of those slain and the burial rites had taken time. The dead deserved dignity in death. We had seen no sign of the rampaging conroi as we had headed towards the Tyne. I sent a rider to the New Castle. He returned while we were still at Hexham. They had not seen the raiders.

Sir Hugh seemed satisfied, "They have headed west and travelled north of the wall."

"I am not certain. If they have gone west then they have escaped me for they have a head start. I will leave the knights to be ransomed here with you. I will take the rest of the conroi south and we will make sure they have not travelled to Durham to cause mischief. "

He laughed, "Then they would be foolish! I know not how many men he has but he would never be able to take that mighty fortress."

"He does not need to. They have few men in the fortress and he could rampage through the countryside causing mayhem."

Thankfully we saw no sign of them as we approached the mighty citadel. Hubert was relieved that we had achieved our aim with so few losses. "I would not tell that to the people of Alnwick, Castellan. They have lost everything."

"You are right. And the banner, did it help?"

I nodded, "We have never lost as few a number of men before." I looked at the walls which appeared undamaged. "The raiders did not pass by here?"

"We had no sign of them although we heard reports of the thunder of hooves in the night. Some of the outlying villages such as Trimdon and Sedgefield hid in their homes and feared the worst but they were untouched."

"Then we must continue our quest. I will not be satisfied until this Angevin knight is in my hands!"

As we left to head south this was when I realised that I missed Edward the most. He always had sage advice. I could have asked Wulfric but it would have been seen as a slight to my knights. I chose to take the road to Sedgefield and Trimdon. Perhaps the villagers might have more information for us. It was late afternoon when we approached the village of Thorpe. It was just a huddle of five huts. As we neared them my hand went to my sword. "There is danger! Archers!"

Dick and his men galloped around the outside of the huts. There was no sign of life. As we moved into what had been a quiet community I saw that even the dogs had been slain. The bodies had been dismembered and scattered as though by wild animals. Dick and his archers rode towards us. "There is no sign of life beyond the village and no tracks save our own. Whoever did this came by the road and left the same way."

I felt my heart sink. Stockton lay less than five miles away and we had left perilously few guards there. "We ride to Stockton with all haste. Dick take the archers and see how the land lies."

We rode quickly and Tristan and Harold flanked me. Their manors were close to mine. If mine fell then all would fall. I cursed Fitzwaller as I rode. It was now obvious to me that he had been intent upon revenge. My knights had been right. I was the reason he had come to England. His object was to destroy what I had. I put my spurs to Scout. My family and my people were now in danger. We passed many small farms and rude huts. One or two showed signs of life but two others were eerily empty as we headed to Stockton.

It was with some relief that I saw my banner still fluttered from my tower but I saw smoke rising. There had been some damage. Approaching the river I saw that the ferry had been destroyed. It was now just a burnt pile of timbers. The gate was open and I saw Dick at the gatehouse. I galloped the last four hundred paces and threw myself from the saddle as soon as I was through the gate. John was there, and, thankfully, Adela. She wrapped her arms around me. "I knew you would come! We were so afraid!" She began to cry and the sobs wracked her body.

I looked beyond her to John who bore a bandage upon his arm. "Tell me all."

"They came yester evening. The guard saw them and, at first, took the banner for yours and then Will the Wanderer spotted the fleur de lys and the alarm was sounded. Only a handful of the townsfolk made the castle but the ones in the town successfully barred their gate and held off the enemy. Alf and the people of Stockton rained missiles and arrows upon them as did we. Your lady had water and oil boiled but it was not needed. When they had lost four men at arms they fell back and set fire to the ferry." He shrugged, "I think it was a petty gesture for they had lost."

I nodded. I saw Will the Wanderer and Thomas of Ulverston, they were speaking with Wulfric. I would soon have a different perspective on the events. John was a good Steward but he was no warrior. "Where did they go?"

"Go, Baron? I know not. It was dark by the time they left." He waved vaguely to the west. "That way I think."

My knights and men at arms were dismounting too. "Mount up. This is not over yet."

Raymond de Brus said, "But they have gone!"

As I mounted Scout I said, harshly, "Where to? We have manors and farms to the west. You saw what they did to Thorpe."

"But Hartburn is well-defended."

"We ride!" I was in no mood for a debate and I led my weary warriors west. The sun was already dipping in the sky and I saw the ominous black cloud spiralling ahead of us. I feared the worst. I heard the keening of women as we approached the manor. Flames still flickered amongst the huts. Fitzwaller had vented his spleen upon Hartburn and Wulfstan.

"Douse the flames. Dick, ride to Elton, take Sir Harold with you." Harold and his squire joined my archers as they raced to the next manor just two miles away. I dismounted and approached the home of my mentor. The walls were charred and still hot to the touch. Inside I saw Wulfstan my first knight and the finest warrior I had ever known. Around him lay the bodies of five men. He had died well. Behind him, I saw the charred remains of what I took to be Faren and her children. Wulfstan's son would never be a knight like his father. Before the grief consumed me I gave orders, "See who lives. Find the dead and we shall bury them."

Wulfric, John and Leofric were all as touched as I had been. Wulfstan had been as much a part of their lives as mine and he was now gone. I put my hands beneath what had been Wulfstan's arms, his body was still warm from the flames which had singed and I dragged him from the building and the dead raiders. I saw that it had been the fire that had killed him. He still held his sword. Without a word being spoken Wulfric and my men at arms carried the corpses of Faren and her children. I saw that Wulfstan's son still held his seax in his hand. He had died a warrior. I had no doubt that his father would be proud. I was not proud, I was angry and full of vengeance.

Richard of Yarm brought forth four women of the village and a youth I vaguely recognised. They were young and they were tearful. "These are the only survivors, lord. They are the family of Old and Young Tom the fletchers. We found the two Toms. They took many with them."

"Tell me what happened?"

The boy stepped forward to speak, "We heard the sound of battle, Baron. My father sent me to look after the women, my mother and my sisters. He told me to shelter by the beck. We hid deep in the undergrowth." He bit his lip. "I wanted to help but my father had told me to watch for my family and I obeyed my father."

I ruffled his head, "You did the right thing. What is your name?"

"Tom, son of Tom the Fletcher."

"And can you fletch?"

"I was learning, Baron."

Then you can bring your family to the castle and you can fletch for me there." I nodded to Tom's wife. "You will be safe within my walls."

She said, gratefully, "We are indebted to you, Baron."

"But Baron, the willow grows here by this beck! I will need these to make my arrows!"

I laughed, "Young Tom, the new fletcher of Stockton, it is but a mile or two from my castle to this stand of willows. You have young legs and you will manage. Now," I became serious, once more, "How many men did you see?" I had a sudden idea. "Can you tell the difference between men at arms and knights?"

"I think so, Baron." He pointed to Wulfric, "He is a man at arms."

I nodded, "How do you know?"

"His weapons Baron, his mail and his hair." He looked at the horse Wulfric was holding, "And you have a better horse."

That made even the dour Wulfric laugh. "Then how many knights and how many men at arms?"

"There were five knights and I think, four squires. Twenty men at arms and then there were others."

"Others?"

"Aye, Baron. They had no mail and they rode small horses which were little bigger than ponies. They had markings on their faces and some had spiked hair. There were a large number of them." He shook his head, "I would be guessing but I think forty, maybe more."

"You have done well. Roger of Lincoln, escort this family back to the castle."

Tom's wife said, "Baron, we would like to bury my husband and his father if you please. They loved this land and I know the very spot."

"Of course. Roger, take a couple of men and help them."

"Aye Baron."

It set my mind to thinking of Wulfstan and his family and their grave. Before I could attend to the matter I heard the sound of hooves in the twilight and Harold and Dick rode in followed by Tristan. Harold's face was as black as thunder. I knew what he would say before he even opened his mouth. "They have been there, lord. They killed all of the men, burned my hall and took the women and children as well as the animals. I would go after them!"

"And we shall but not until the morning." He opened his mouth to argue, "I command here!" My voice softened, "Aiden can pick up their trail when it is daylight and we will have fresh horses. We have not eaten and our mounts can go no further this day." He did not look convinced. "Where can he go?"

Richard of Yarm said, "My family!"

"I think they will be safe but take Tristan and your men and go to your home. If it is secure then send Tristan back in the morning with your archers. They can join my pursuit."

Geoffrey of Piercebridge said, "And my home?"

"I fear he will be heading there. He can cross the river. But it is no use travelling there this late. We will head there in the morning. Now let us bury a great man and a noble warrior."

We dug a grave facing west. I took a shovel and helped. I had to be part of this funeral. The land was on the slope above the beck. We carefully laid the shrouded bodies in a line and I placed Wulfstan's sword across his body. We piled earth on the top and then laid stones we gathered from the stream. Finally, we placed a cross. Father Matthew could come and say the words which were necessary but I would not leave my friend and his family above ground for the rats and foxes to feast upon. We made a sad procession back to my castle. I was weary but I knew I would not sleep over much that night. I was too angry for that.

My wife was wonderful. When she had heard of the horror she had known what to do. She had put on a feast, not only for my knights but for the men at arms and archers. It was not a celebration but a feast of thankfulness. More might have died. I knew it was appreciated although neither Harold nor myself ate much. We were both filled with regrets. For myself, I regretted not spending more time with Wulfstan as he aged. I know I still had much to learn. I regretted not forcing him to live in the castle whilst I was away. He would still be alive. Most of all I regretted my delay. Had I started south earlier I could have saved his life and that would live with me forever.

We left Stockton with a pared-down conroi. I left more men at arms to protect my family. I left Star in my stables and took another palfrey. This would be a chase. I also took Aiden. He was like a hound and he would sniff them out. He left before dawn and rode west to find these killers.

We approached Piercebridge with caution. Aiden had not returned and that had worried me. Sir Geoffrey led his men ahead of us and galloped off to see if his home had been damaged. We arrived and I saw the walls still standing. They had been attacked; the bolts in the walls told me that but they had not crossed the river. The barrier of logs showed that the defenders had fought hard to keep this wolf from the door. I now knew why Aiden had not returned. He had seen that the castle still stood and the passage over the Tees had been barred. He was on their trail. I did not stop and we carried on. Sir Geoffrey would catch us up.

Aiden did return to us shortly after we had left Piercebridge. He galloped up to me and whipping his horse's head around he pointed to the northwest. "Baron, they have left the road and they are heading to the north and west."

This needed words with my knights. "They are not heading south and if they head to the north and west they must come up against Barnard Castle. That cannot be taken. Its lord is noble and would not side with the rebels. Which way would they go?" I was stumped. I had been outwitted again.

"They must be heading back to Scotland. Do you think they know we pursue them?"

I was about to answer when Wulfric said, "My lord they have left no one alive and taken only prisoners to pleasure them. They think they have vanished. It is an old trick." He smiled, "When I was younger and wilder... well, let us say I know how this works. He goes back to Scotland and he goes by secret paths and hidden ways."

"Then he will try to get back to Scotland using the lesser-known paths. He will avoid Durham and Hexham and we know he heads north and west."

"Carlisle bars his way there."

"But the border is close. He will cross between Hexham and Carlisle. I do not think he can cover that in less than two days. It is almost ninety miles. He has to cross the wall and that means using one of the passages and gates in the wall." I turned and summoned Dick. "I want four good archers to accompany Aiden and keep on the trail of this conroi. We will travel to Barnard and thence to Brampton. If this knight looks to deviate from the course I have predicted find us. We will ride a parallel course and will be just a few miles from your men." Aiden had been listening and he nodded. The two rode away.

The hooves of Sir Geoffrey's men made us all turn. "They came to my castle, Baron. It was a half-hearted attack. They stood off and used bows and crossbows. When my men resisted they turned away."

"Your people did well."

He nodded, "We had the lesson of Gainford and we have made our castle stronger."

We halted at Barnard. Guy de Balliol had been given the castle by King Henry's father. Although old he was still a force to be reckoned with. He offered some of his men to accompany us but I saw that many were as ancient as Sir Guy and they had not been in combat for some time. I deemed it safer for them to deny the passage of the Tees to any raider. We left early knowing that we had to have had a more comfortable night than Fitzwaller and his men. They would be ahead of us but we were rested and our horses had had grain. We also had something else driving us; vengeance. We pushed hard.

With Aiden away to the east of us we used Dick and Roger of Lincoln to scout. When they did not return we knew that the road was clear and we rode into Brampton as the afternoon became evening. There was no castle. Carlisle was but nine miles away. We warned the villagers of the potential danger and we set sentries as we awaited our scouts.

Griff of Gwent rode in soon after dawn. "Aiden sent me. They have headed north to cross the Irving close to Lanercost."

I had almost been outwitted. Instead of being able to bar their return I now had to follow. He had found somewhere to cross the wall. The advantage I had was we had fresher horses. As my men armed and mounted I asked my scout, "Did you watch the camps?"

"Aye, Baron, we were hidden and were able to get a close look at them."

"Have they lost many through desertions?"

"There have been some fights in the camps and we saw four of five bodies on one morning as we passed through. They are not a happy band of warriors. They still have more warriors than we do."

I nodded. I turned to my knights. "We have nearly been outfoxed but the nearest crossing of the river is closer to us. We ride north and we will meet them at Walton." There was another crossing of the Irving not far from Brampton and we would, once again, get ahead of them and this time we would end this chase.

We reached a peaceful and sleepy Walton less than an hour after we set off and as we halted on the eastern side of the huddle of homes we saw that we had arrived in the nick of time. We spied the banners and the sun glinting off the armour as Guy Fitzwaller brought his raiders to us. "Lances! Archers to the flanks."

My conroi was practised now and they moved swiftly and efficiently. I had John behind me with my banner. Harold rode to my right and Sir Richard to my left. I saw that they outnumbered us but their superiority was in the wild Irishmen who rode the small ponies. They would not fight on the ponies. They would fight on foot. Fitzwaller had his men at arms before his knights. They would bear the brunt of our attack and blunt our blades. He was a cunning adversary.

I turned to my men. "We ride to avenge Wulfstan and those who fell at Elton. No mercy and no quarter! Forward!" Our horses moved down the slope, which was gentle. I spurred Scout to make him move a little faster. We would not gallop but we would have more speed than the weary-looking Scots. We rode together but not quite knee to knee. Dick and his archers had galloped forward and were ahead of us. They dismounted and, using horse holders, began to shower the enemy with arrows. They aimed at those on foot and it was their archers and crossbows who fell first. As I had expected the wild Irish did not take kindly to the rain of death and they hurled themselves up the slope after my archers. We had not discussed it prior to the encounter but Dick would take advantage of it. Dick ordered his archers back on their horses and they fled up the slope with the foot in hot pursuit. It left the men at arms at our mercy.

    I spurred Scout again as we approached to within twenty paces. I pulled back my lance and then stood to punch at the man at arms before me. His horse flinched and Scout headed for the gap as my spear struck him on the shield. The weight of my blow, my armour and Scout made his shield ineffective and the spear plunged into his chest. The head sheared off my weapon as he fell to his death. I threw the broken haft like a spear high in the air and drew my sword. I headed for Fitzwaller. I tightened my grip on my shield and urged Scout on.

    Fitzwaller swung his sword at my horse's head but I was ready for such tricks and I wheeled away and smashed down on his sword with my own. There was a loud clang of metal on metal and sparks flew. We both had well-made swords. Rather than turn Scout to the right I continued to wheel him around and the manoeuvre fooled Fitzwaller. I appeared on his sword side. Neither of us could use our shields for protection. I stood in the stirrups to bring my sword down on his head. He had quick hands too and he brought his blade up to counter the blow. The force of my strike was so powerful that it bent his blade. He threw it at me and took the war axe from his pommel.

    "Your Saxon dog died badly, Greek! And his family joined him screaming and weeping! I have begun to pay you back!"

    "And how would you know? You were not there. You sent your animals to fight him and he slew them all. It was the fire which took his life and you shall burn in hell for your crimes!"

    I saw the anger on his face and he swung backhanded at me. The axe head barely missed Scout's head and it cracked into my shield. It could not take many blows such as this. I stabbed forward as our horses jostled together. Surprisingly he did not manage to get his shield down in time. My blade slid along the cantle of his saddle and across his hauberk. As I drew it back I heard it tear the links.

    We were oblivious to the battle raging around us save that I was aware of John and Leofric guarding my back and my banner fluttering above my head. Fitzwaller brought his axe over his head to strike at my upper body. I brought my sword up and the edge bit into the haft and stuck. We pulled back and forth. I stood in my saddle and leapt at him. I struck his body sideways on and we both tumbled to the ground. I heard the air pushed from him as we crashed to the ground. I found myself rolling to the side but the sword had freed itself from the axe. I was the first to my feet. As I did so I saw Leofric take the head from Fitzwaller's squire who held the banner. The flag fluttered to the ground.

Fitzwaller swung his axe at my legs as he rose. I managed to leap backwards and we circled each other warily. I saw that his hauberk was hanging down at one side. My sword and the tumble had weakened it. It would drag him to the right. I could use that. An axe was a wicked weapon but it had a tendency to make the user overbalance. Whilst in the saddle he had been protected by the cantle which held him in place Now he was on foot. He would also find it hard to counter my blows. I swung my sword at head height and he brought up his shield. When he swung his axe at my head I stepped back with my left leg while still holding my shield. He struck the shield but began to overbalance. I accentuated it by stepping forward with my right and bringing my sword hard round towards the top of his shield. He brought his shield up but my blow made him step back and he had to take extra steps to regain his balance. I continued my attack and swung backhand. I saw a huge chunk of wood fly from the haft of the already damaged axe.

Fear filled his face as I swung my sword at his shield once more. I was tiring but I knew that he was tiring more. An axe is a heavier weapon and more of his mail links had severed. The end of his hauberk was trailing along the ground. He tried to rally and force me on the defensive. He swung at my shield again. This time he anticipated my move and put more force into the blow. I did not step back and I put my shoulder behind my shield. The blow numbed it but I heard an ominous crack from the axe.

Our faces were close together. I hissed my words at him. "This time there will be no ransom. The Fitzwallers die here in this empty space between Scotland and England. Your bones will whiten the ground and no one will remember you or your evil. It will be as though you never existed!"

He punched with his shield and we broke apart.

"There is no Wulfstan and his seed is ended that is proof that I existed, Greek bastard and son of a peasant and my mark will fill your heart until you die."

I smiled for he was deliberately antagonising me. It would not work for I was as cool as ice. I swung my sword and he did not dare counter with his axe, instead, he used his shield. I could see that it was badly cut already. It smashed into it hard. I pivoted and swung backhand. He tried to move his feet to bring his shield around and they became entangled in the hem of his hauberk. He only kept his feet by stepping rapidly back. My sword tore across his upper arm and this time it was not just the sleeves of the hauberk which was torn, my sword came away bloody. I could barely raise my sword for I was exhausted but I forced myself. I pulled it all the way behind me and then swung it high over my head. I aimed it for his right shoulder. He held up the axe and the shield but my sword shattered the axe shaft in two and continued down to bite deeply through the mail and into his shoulder and neck. It continued down until it jammed between his bones. He screamed; it sounded like a vixen protecting her cubs. I tore the blade from the wound and I felt it grate along his bones. He crumpled dead at my feet as his blood flowed freely.

I stood panting and then I heard a cheer and my voice being chanted. I turned and saw my warriors behind me. The field was filled with the dead who had followed Fitzwaller. He had gambled and failed. My superior numbers and better-trained knights, squires and men at arms had proved too much for an already exhausted force. We had won.

Chapter 6

As we counted the cost I realised that we had been lucky. There were few of my men who did not have a wound. Roger de Bertram's squire had died and others had lost men at arms. It was just the archers who had avoided heavy losses; when Dick returned they had lost but three archers. "And the Irish?"

"Most were slain but some may have escaped. We did not pursue for very long for I worried about how you might fare." He shook his head, "I should have known you had the beating of him."

I spread my arm around me. "We bury our dead. Build a pyre and we will burn the dead when we have taken all that we can from them. There is no ransom but they will have pouches filled with their ill-gotten gains." I pointed to the small village on the hillside. "We will camp there this night and head east tomorrow."

Wulfric nodded and pointed to the dead horses, "At least we eat well tonight and we go home rich men!" As ever Wulfric was the practical soldier. He had survived and that was what was important. There would come a day when he would not but Wulfric would not begrudge those who lived the spoils of war. Most of my men at arms felt the same way. I knew that I thought about things too deeply; I could not help it.

Everyone seemed in good spirits. Everyone that is, save me. I would have traded all of our success for my old mentor to be alive. He had made me the knight I was. When I had come from the east I had been an arrogant and spoiled young man. I was not fit to lead brigands let alone fine warriors such as I now had. Wulfstan had changed all of that. Now just Osric was left. I had travelled far with fine companions and now they had left me. My world would never be the same.

I led Scout towards the circle of huts and farms. My squire, Hugh, followed me. He now bore a wicked-looking scar across his cheek and had come within an ell of losing his eye. "He must have hated you, Baron."

"How so?"

"He travelled all the way from Alnwick just to hurt you. He could have travelled west if he had wanted safety. He could have abandoned his men and sneaked back across the border to Scotland but he came to revenge himself on you and yours. This was hatred."

"True and he could have stayed at Alnwick if he had wanted to kill just me. This was an old-fashioned blood feud, Hugh. My father told me how the Vikings and some Saxons would lose all sense if they felt they were honour bound to avenge a family member. I killed his father and he wanted revenge on my family. He was arrogant enough to believe that he could hurt those that I loved and then kill me. Perhaps he thought I would be weaker if they were dead."

The villagers had had a fine view of the battle and they stood fearfully watching now. The headman bowed when he spied me approaching. "I am Baron Alfraed of Stockton and the King's appointed Baron of the North. We have defeated some rebellious Normans and Scots this day. We will spend the night here and you are more than welcome to share our food."

He nodded, relief etched across his mahogany-coloured face. "Thank you, Baron." Sometimes victors would not be sated by the blood of their enemies and would wish more.

"Have you an alewife?"

"Aye, Baron."

I took a silver coin from my leather pouch and threw it to him. "Then we shall buy all that she has!" He hurried off and I turned to Hugh, "Take my hauberk from me. I am weary and then get John to put an edge on my sword." I suddenly realised I had not seen my young squires since Fitzwaller's squire had been slain. "Where are they?"

"They were searching bodies with Harold, Baron. They did well today. They were fearless and slew many who tried to attack your blind side."

I smiled, "And I have no doubt that you did the same. I am fortunate to have such skilled and brave squires."

I felt much better without the hauberk and I walked to the end of the huts to watch the pyre of bodies as they were burned. I knew that the farmers of Lanercost would find a use for the dead. Their ashes would be spread and the fields fertilised. This was a cruel land and little was wasted. The better crops of the following years would be down to the men who had fought and died here. Gradually my men headed up the hill. Harold, John and Leofric were amongst the last ones to join me. Harold held a pouch in his hands.

"Treasure, Harold?"

"Of a kind, Baron. We found them in the saddlebags of Fitzwaller. They are letters and documents. He was a clever man, Baron. We wondered why he did what he did. It was not just for revenge. He was paid to do so." He held up three pieces of parchment each one bearing a seal, "The De Vries family, the Le Hongre family and the de Bouvilla family all had a hand in this venture." He handed them to me and then proffered the last one, "And this is the authority from Earl Gospatric to take the historic lands of Scotland."

I was both excited and saddened by the news. Excited for it meant we had evidence against these traitors but saddened for it meant I would have to take them to King Henry. He would need to see the documents before he acted. The phrase *'historic lands of Scotland'* was important. The Scots believed they had a right to all the land as far south as Hadrian's Wall. That was ominous. Gospatrick wished to be the earl of the old land of Northumberland. It was almost a kingdom. The old man was gambling for a throne. "You have done well. The light is too poor this night. I will read them in the morning before we leave." I noticed that John and Leofric were carrying suits of mail. "What have you there?"

John grinned sheepishly, "I found a man at arms who was the same size as me." He held up the hauberk, "And I slew him. I will now be better protected."

"And I have the hauberk of the squire I killed. It is not as long as John's but it is well made."

"Good and this day will serve you well in the future. The experience will make you better knights."

The horsemeat was good but I barely touched mine. Wulfstan's demise had robbed me of all appetite. Harold, too, picked at his food and Tristan spent the whole night trying to cheer up his friend. He had his mind on his dead people too.

I barely slept and I rose before dawn. My mind was on the four documents which Harold had discovered. I took them out and saw that they contained revelations that would have an impact beyond my little valley. Individually they told a tale of intrigue and plots but when taken together they were a threat to both England and Normandy. The impending marriage of Geoffrey and Matilda had not brought peace it had induced fear, for King Henry was seen as an Empire builder. Not for the first time I missed Edward. He always had sage advice and a sound mind. Wulfstan too had been someone in whom I could confide. I trusted my knights but the conspiracy I had uncovered was beyond their comprehension. My father had told of the plots at the court of the Emperor and this ranked alongside those. I replaced the documents in the leather pouch. I would have to keep a close watch on it until I could deliver it to the King or Robert of Gloucester.

We took three days to return to Stockton. We had much armour and weapons to transport and there was little point in making tired men and horses work harder than was needed. We went east to Hexham. I confided in Sir Hugh that Fitzwaller had been involved in a larger plot but not the detail. I warned him not to trust Earl Gospatric.

He had snorted, "Trust Gospatric? The man has more faces than a broken mirror! I know not why King Henry allows his knights to own land in Scotland and to swear fealty to King David for their Scottish lands! They have to break one oath. I know I would not do that for I would not be foresworn."

"You are right. I will need to travel to Normandy with the information I have. While I am away, keep a close watch on the borderlands. My knights will be ready to return should you need them. I will leave a large garrison at Stockton and they are soundly led by Wulfric."

"Aye, you are lucky there. He is the best Sergeant at Arms I have seen."

"Have the ransoms arrived yet?"

"Not yet but I will see that the knights and their men receive their share. It is time we made a profit from this land!" He was a bluff knight but he showed that he had a soft side. He put his arm around my shoulder, "I never met this Wulfstan but I know how much he meant to you. I am sorry for your loss."

I nodded my thanks but his sympathy would not bring back Wulfstan. His young sons would never grow up and there would be a black hole where they had once lived.

Our last call was at Durham. I told Hubert and the Dean of my fears. And, as with Sir Hugh, I warned them of the Earl and his treachery. When I said I intended to visit with the King in Normandy Hubert became concerned and agitated. "You would leave the land undefended?"

I sighed, "Not undefended. My knights will still be here and we have ended the threat for a while. You have knights who never stir from their manors, Castellan. They should bear some of the responsibility of defending Durham from the raiders."

"You are right but they are now accustomed to the Baron of the North taking on that mantle. I confess that I sleep easier knowing that you and your knights ride the northern fells."

"And they will still be here. I take just my squires. I should not be away for too long. Who knows the King may even be in London when I reach there."

"I doubt it. Empress Matilda marries next month."

"Nonetheless I shall be away for the shortest time that I can."

The reminder of Matilda's impending marriage put me in a black humour all the way back to Stockton. My other knights all left me as we headed south so that, when we reached Norton, I just had Harold and my conroi left. Harold would stay at Stockton for a while. It would be too cruel to return him to the charnel house that was Elton.

I left my men outside Norton when I went in to speak with Osric. He had heard the news already. My wife must have sent him word. He looked ashen and to have aged ten years. "Wulfstan was younger than I was! I had thought he would stand at my grave and say words over me." He took my hand and I noticed how thin and bony his old hands were. They were crisscrossed with purple lines. "I pray, Alfraed, that you take care of yourself. I cannot outlive you. We swore an oath to your father to protect you and I am the last."

"And I now have my own oathsworn. End your days in peace, Osric. You have done all that an oathsworn should do. I am honoured to have known you. I want you to be there to be a grandfather to my son. I want you to tell him tales of the Varangian Guard and Miklagård. Your work is not yet done!"

He smiled, "I can still tell a tale."

Even as I rode through my half-finished gatehouse I knew I would have to leave again within the week. The plot I had uncovered would not stop and I had a duty to the king. The letters had to be delivered personally.

William the Mason was working on the gatehouse as I rode past him. "Baron I have hired more men to build this gatehouse. I hope you do not mind. Your Steward seemed unhappy about the cost."

"The recent attack showed the value of your fine stonework, William. Hire as many men as you wish. I will speak with John!"

I greeted Adela and my children with even more warmth than hitherto. The charred bodies of Faren and her children sprung to mind. That would not happen here. "Harold will stay here for a while, I do not want him alone."

She nodded, "He is more than welcome and you know that. What is the real reason, husband?"

"Can you read me so easily?"

"I am learning."

I waved the servants over to take the children away. When we were alone I told her of the letters, "There is a plot to undermine us here in the north and to attack the King in Anjou. I have to take the letters to him. He must read them for himself and see the seals."

"Then you must go. I will get your fine clothes ready."

I kissed her. "You are a good wife but I do not leave until the end of the week. I have matters which need my attention here before I go. I will just take my squires."

"Is that safe?"

"I am travelling through the heart of England. I will be safe. And now I must have words with John."

She smiled, "I see William has spoken with you."

I nodded, "The trouble with John is that he thinks it is his money!"

I went to the door and waved a servant over, "Tell my Steward to meet with me in the west tower." As much as I wanted to take off my hauberk and bathe I had to deal with John first. He hurried in, "I am sorry about Wulfstan, Baron, he was a good man."

"Thank you; he was. I will come directly to the point John, William the Mason can hire as many workers as he deems necessary to build the gatehouse. He is an honest man and he will not rob me. I trust his judgement."

"But my lord the cost!"

"Ride to Hartburn and see the cost!" He was silent. "John, am I running out of coin? Do we lack gold?"

"No, Baron, but we must be thrifty and use the gold wisely."

"I agree and a wise use is to ensure it pays for a solid castle and men to defend it. That is my priority. Is that clear?"

"Yes, Baron."

"And we have made coin from this latest conroi. Do not cross me on this matter." He nodded, "Now, on to more urgent matters. If there are new settlers then they should be encouraged to go to Elton and Hartburn. I will appoint a new lord of the manor when I have spoken with the King."

"The King comes here?"

"No, John, I go to him. Use your skills to encourage farmers and merchants to come here and to prosper under our protection so that we may tax them fairly and increase our gold."

He brightened at that, "I have some new ideas, Baron. If…"

I held up my hand. "When your ideas are crystallised then tell me, for now, I need to change from this bloody armour and bathe."

He backed out, "Yes, Baron, and, my lord?"

"Yes, John?"

"I am sorry. You are right I know."

I was delayed by a week in order to make my manor and those nearby as safe as possible. It was urgent that I deliver the messages but I would not leave an undefended land. Edward was still away. It would soon be midsummer when every hand would be busy either in the fields or toiling in their workshop. Ethelred was still building his ferry. He was philosophical about the loss. "I can improve the design, Baron, and it will make all those who use it appreciate even more the fine service I provide!" He and John knew how to make money.

The main reason, however, was to spend as much time with my family as I could. My daughter was still so small that I was not even certain that she knew who I was but William did and spent every moment he could with me; he strode after me trying, vainly, to match my step. He had a wooden sword which he wore, as I did, at my waist. He was a delight. Within a few years, he would be able to begin his training as a knight and the wooden sword would be a smaller version of mine. The horror of the scene at Hartburn had shown me what I had. As the week raced by I forced myself to concentrate on my journey. This time I would need servants for we would be at court. I could not travel lightly. Matthew and Mark were older men who had sought service with me some time back. Neither were farmers and both had arrived with refugees from the coast two years since. The others had taken farms but Matthew and Mark had wished to serve in the castle. Adela told me that they had been so fearful of being raided that they wanted the security of my walls. I understood. Adela had told me that they would be the best servants to take for they were hard-working and quiet. She knew me well enough to know I appreciated those qualities.

We did not take spare weapons save a few knives and two swords but we had to take more clothes than we might normally. With food for the journey, we needed two sumpters. We now had horses aplenty. I did not take Scout this time, he had worked hard and he was no longer a foal. I took my second palfrey Night Thunder who was a jet black mount and looked to be a smaller version of Star. He was younger than both of my main horses and this would give me the opportunity to school him. We had almost two hundred and fifty miles to go. It would take up to six or seven days.

We were the first to use the new ferry. Harold would act as my deputy in the absence of Edward. I knew that Adela would bring him back from the dark place in which he had hidden. When I returned I had no doubt that he would be the happy knight whose laughter had once filled my halls. Wulfric and Dick were the rocks on which he would depend. I told both of them to hire any prospective men at arms and archers. The news I was taking to the king was ominous. Over the next few years, good warriors would be both scarce and, at the same time, vital. I was planning ahead. When trouble came I wanted to be able to respond quickly.

"Keep in touch with the other manors. I know the ransoms are nearly all paid and they will be enjoying the fruits of their labour but have them remain ever watchful, Harold."

"Will they listen to me?"

I pointed to the banner which fluttered from my topmost tower. "They will obey that. I will return as soon as I can. If the winds are right and fate is on my side then I may be back in less than two months. In all events, I will be back before harvest."

I left my home on another journey and, once again, I had a heavy heart.

Part 2 Treason and treachery
Chapter 7

We pushed hard the first day as I wished to spend the night at York. I needed to speak with the Archbishop and Baron Clare. We rode hard and I had to smile at the discomfort of Matthew and Mark. They bore the bouncing rumps of the palfreys stoically but I knew that they were in agony. They suffered in silence. We were travelling through lands that were prosperous and were safe. That was in no small measure down to me. Those who toiled in the fields recognised my banner and waved as we passed. We entered York through the old Roman gate. Here the Roman walls still stood, augmented and added to by William the Bastard. The minster was close to the northern gate and I rode directly there. We discovered that the Archbishop was with the King at his daughter's wedding. I reached the keep and discovered that Baron Clare had also departed for the wedding. His son, Ralph, who was younger even than Harold, commanded.

"It is good to see you, Baron. We have heard, through those who pass through our city, that you have defeated Scottish raiders and kept our city safe."

I had to hide my smile. His words sounded like those of an old man. I was used to plainer speaking. "We have been lucky but I urge you to be vigilant. With so many lords in Normandy and Anjou, the Scots may decide to take advantage of the situation."

We left the next morning for the next leg of our journey. I intended to stay as close to Doncaster as I could. Hugh was observant and he had watched Ralph during the meal. "He is young to command such a castle, Baron."

"He is of an age with you Hugh and I would leave you in command of Stockton if I had to."

"You would?" I heard the surprise in his voice.

"Wulfstan and my father trained me to take responsibility. I hope I have done the same with those that I train. I have seen you on the battlefield and I believe that I know what you are like." I saw him nodding. Soon I would elevate him to his own manor at Gainford. He was becoming ready.

The two young squires joined in the conversation about their hopes and dreams for lives as knights. We stopped, whenever we could, in the towns and villages through which we passed. Many did not have a manor and there were few castles. This was not the borderland. This was safe rich land protected by York and the people prospered.

It was in the late afternoon when Leofric's horse picked up a stone. He said, "I have a stone. There is a stream yonder. I will catch you up."

A short while later we heard the hooves of his horse as he galloped up behind us, "Baron, we are being followed."

Leofric and John had both been falconers and had been trained by Aiden. They both had an innate sense which came from hunting animals. Hugh made to turn and I said, "No Hugh, carry on looking ahead if you please. How do you know, Leofric?"

"I saw some men in York when we were there. They had the look of warriors and yet they wore neither livery nor armour. I would have thought that they were seeking work but they watched us too closely. As we rode south I sometimes turned to speak with John in the hope of catching sight of them but they were just a movement in the woods. I would have thought it was my imagination if I had not seen them again when we stopped in Selby. I was returning from the privy when I spied one. Then, when I was returning here I saw them again as I rejoined the road. They did not see me for I was hidden by the trees."

"How many were there?"

"I think eight."

"What think you, Baron?"

"I think, Hugh, that I delayed too long to bring these precious parchments to the King. I allowed our enemies to hire men. I believe they will try to stop us. Do not look around. I know where they will try to reach us."

"Where, Baron?"

"The forest of Sherwood is vast, Leofric and the Roman Road passes through the heart of it. There are few villages for many miles and if our butchered bodies are discovered then the blame will fall upon outlaws."

"If you had brought Sir Harold instead of me, then you might have had protection."

I laughed, "It is many years since Harold lived in the forest. Dick and the others are the last of those whom Harold knew. Besides, I fear not outlaws. Harold and Dick have told me how many nefarious and deceitful deeds were done by men in mail but blamed on men in green. It was ever thus. Keep looking ahead and we will enjoy a comfortable night in Doncaster."

The castle at the crossing of the Don was a formidable one and it was a busy town. The Castellan was more than happy to accommodate me. Thanks to my deeds in Wales and on the borders my livery was known and I was afforded the finest of hospitality. Before we left, the next morning, I gave a short sword and a dagger to both Matthew and Mark. "But Baron we are not warriors!"

"No Mark but you are men and men know how to defend themselves do they not? If we are attacked then we will be outnumbered. My squires will acquit themselves well but these assassins will go for you two as an easy kill. You will make it hard for them. Fight as one man. Stand back to back. When you use your blades go for the eyes and use the full force of your arms."

They did not look convinced but I was happier that they each had two weapons strapped to their sides. They would not be defenceless. They had teeth.

As we headed south I contemplated heading either east to take us through Lincoln or west to travel into Nottingham. Both would add to our journey and neither would be absolutely safe. We would head for Grantham and hope to reach there before dark. At least in daylight, we would have warning of an attack. We had not ridden with helmets before and I was loath to do so now even though it would afford us more protection. We needed our eyes and our ears. As we left through the gates I sent John to ride at the front whilst Leofric and Hugh brought up the rear. I wanted a longer line of riders. I had no idea what they would try but crossbows and arrows would have been my choice. If we were spread out then we spread the danger.

There had been a time when the forest grew thickly along the road but it had been thinned out over the years as the trees were used for buildings. It meant that we passed areas that had been cleared and then thicker areas of growth. When we stopped at the occasional houses and farms to water our horses we casually inquired if there were other travellers. There had been none that told me that they had left the road to set up an ambush. Leofric could not detect the sound of any hooves following us.

At noon, as we left the farm where we had watered our horses and I had bought ale for each of us, I warned the others to be even warier when we came to any undergrowth. We passed four or five dense areas. We knew that they were safe for us when birds took to the skies at our approach. John was a good woodsman and when he approached the next stand of oaks and elms he imperceptibly slowed down and I saw his hand go to his shield which was hanging from his cantle. It was a warning sign and I turned and nodded to the others.

As I turned back I leaned forward to speak to Night Thunder. It allowed me to loosen my sword. My shield was strapped around my back and I could pull it round in a moment. I began to think that John had been wrong when he suddenly brought up his shield and a bolt smacked into it. I drew my sword and then pulled my shield around as I dug spurs into Night Thunder. It was none too soon for two more bolts flashed through the space I had just occupied. I heard a cry from behind me but I ignored it. This was not the time for defence. I hurtled into the woods to my left. John joined me. I held my sword slightly down and behind me. I caught a flash of flesh and I swung the sword up. The man had been busy reloading his crossbow. My sword sliced up and, after smashing the crossbow in two hacked into the jaw and skull of the man.

Even as I wheeled Night Thunder to the right I took in that they had to have four crossbows. I saw John as he hacked down at a second crossbowman. The other two were busily trying to reload. A bow is better for it can be reloaded in a flash. Had these warriors been archers then John and I would be dead. We both crashed into them at the same time. I slashed across the neck of my target while John smashed his sword to split the assassin's head in two.

I heard cries from behind and I turned Night Thunder to ride back through the woods. I saw Matthew standing over Mark who looked to have been wounded. He was swashing his sword and dagger before him. Hugh and Leofric were engaged with two horsemen while a third lay dead. I did not hesitate; poor Matthew could not survive much longer. I thundered up behind the killer. He turned as he heard me and I impaled his chest on my sword. The blow was so hard that it tore the sword from my hand. I continued riding towards Leofric who was struggling against a powerful warrior. Leofric did not have the strength of arm that John possessed. I drew my dagger and stabbed the mighty warrior in the kidneys with my only weapon. As he tried to turn Leofric finished him off with a slash to the throat.

Even as we both reined around to aid Hugh, his opponent fell to the ground. John and Matthew were kneeling next to Mark. "Baron he has a bolt to the shoulder."

"Take it out and have bandages ready. Matthew, tear the tunics of the dead. You did well, Matthew!"

"I was terrified, lord."

"Which makes your courage all the more commendable."

The man who had just been felled by Hugh was still alive. Hugh had a dagger to his throat. "Who sent you? tell me and I will ease your passing." I saw that Hugh had managed to open the warrior's guts. It would be a slow death.

"I need no pity! I am a warrior and I will die in my own time." His accent was from the north of our river. These were not killers hired in Scotland as I had assumed. He was local; he was from the land around the Tees.

I turned to Leofric. "Go to the forest and there you will find four dead crossbowmen. Search them and bring anything which will identify them: coins, documents, tokens, anything and find their horses too."

The wounded man must have had another wound for he suddenly sighed and died. I began to search his body. In his pouch was a gold piece and some smaller coins. There was naught else to help me. I examined the coins. Hugh took the weapons from the man. "This is a good sword, Baron. This is a knight's sword."

"And where did he get it from?" I held out the coins. "What do you notice about these coins?"

"That he was well paid?"

I shook my head, "No, they are all from the Durham mint and this one," I held up the gold one, is brand new! This man was sent from Durham. It seems we have an enemy there too."

I returned to Mark. The bolt was out but he had lost blood. "John, you and Matthew make a litter to go between two of the horses. We have eight more beasts now. Make sure he drinks and, if possible eats something."

Hugh and I searched the other dead. They all had the same about them. The four we had slain were each paid a gold piece to kill us. Leofric returned with the horses. The crossbowmen had a silver piece instead of a gold piece but they were freshly minted and from Durham. We left the dead. The animals would feast on their flesh.

We would be lucky to reach Grantham now but we pushed on anyway. I spoke with Hugh as we rode south to clarify my thoughts. "There were just two in Durham who knew what we had found, the Dean and Hubert."

"They could have told others."

"True but that makes them equally guilty for I told them to keep my news secret. I remember the last Dean was treacherous and sold out the castle to Gospatric I wonder if the Bishop appointed another viper."

"Hubert seems an honest man. I cannot see him being a traitor."

"Honest men can adopt the mask of Janus when it suits but I agree with you and I will reserve judgement until we have more information. First, we must see to the care of Mark."

Before we reached Grantham we heard the tolling of a bell. There was a monastery or church nearby. We followed the sound and found a small monastery. There were armed guards outside and tents. Spears were pointed at us until I spoke my name. A young priest stepped forward. "This is fortuitous, Baron. We have Bishop Flambard within."

"The Bishop of Durham? I thought that he was close to death?"

"He is, Baron, but he wishes to die in Durham. We are taking him home."

"It is indeed fortuitous for we have a wounded man with us too. Could you have him tended to?"

"Aye, Baron." He turned to a monk, "Brother Oswald could you care for the man. Come, Baron, I know the Bishop will wish to speak with you."

We entered the monastery and we were taken to what must have been the abbot's quarters. Bishop Flambard was lying in the bed. He looked pale but he was conscious. He smiled in surprise when he saw me. "Baron, how did you know that I was here?"

"I did not. I believe God sent me here." I looked at the attendants, "May we speak alone, Bishop?"

He frowned and nodded, "You are not a knight given to alarm easily. Leave us I will be safe and have the Baron's people seen to."

When we were alone I said, "I was told that you were close to death. Some said you were dead."

He tried to laugh but failed, "I am dying but I fight against it. Many say that I should go peacefully to my God but my work is not finished. I heard of your exploits in the north. Why are you not there still enjoying the fruits of your victory?"

I told him all including the ambush. I held out the coins. He frowned. "Then it is as well that I travel home. I will get to the bottom of this. This is treason, Baron."

"I know."

"And you do right to tell the King." He took one of the rings from his hand. "Take this, it is the seal of the See of Lisieux. It will ease your passage to Normandy. I will not need it any longer for I go home to die." He handed me the ring. He sighed and closed his eyes as a wave of pain passed over him. When he opened them he said, "What will they say of me when I am dead, Baron?" I hesitated, "Do not flatter me for a dying man deserves the truth."

"I believe that they will say you were a man who helped to make England what it is today but there will be your enemies who will spread lies about you. That is in the nature of men and we live in treacherous times. Those who know you will speak well of you."

"I confess that, in my younger days, I did not always behave as well as a man of God should have done but I have tried to make amends in my old age and I have given much to the poor."

"Know that I will speak well of you, Bishop."

"I know and I thank God for the day that you met King Henry for without you who knows what the North would be like."

We left the next morning and Mark was taken with the Bishop. The spare horses we left with the Bishop enabled the Bishop's people to move much faster. I never saw the Bishop again for he was dead before I returned from Normandy but I always honoured him. Matthew had been badly shaken by the attack and the wound to his friend. "Matthew, you did all that I asked of you and more. You will be stronger as a result of the attack."

"But Mark could have died."

"We all die, Matthew, but it was not your friend's time. Be resolute and learn from this."

We made the journey in a further two days. I went to the Tower to see if the King was there. Apart from the constable of the Tower, there were no lords. It resulted in accommodation for us but I could not risk giving my information to the constable. I knew him not. If there was danger In Durham with men I thought I trusted then my news had to go to only two people: the King and his son. The next morning I journeyed to the river to try to gain a voyage to Normandy. Most of the ships were going elsewhere. The wedding had taken place even as we were journeying south and so many of the ships which normally plied that route were on their way back from Normandy having taken more guests for this most momentous of marriages. I discovered that there were ships due at the end of the week. We would have to bide our time until then.

It was as I was watching by the river that I remembered the house which the brothers Stephen and Theobald of Blois had used. It was across the river. I spied it. There was a banner flying from it. One of the brothers was in residence. Sometimes we do things and know not why. I did this act deliberately. I took my squires, crossed the bridge over the Thames and rode by the manor.

They had cleared the land around the hall and we headed to the forests beyond, ostensibly for a leisurely ride. We had no sooner entered the forest than riders erupted from the hall. Although they had no unsheathed weapons they glared at us belligerently. "What are you doing here?"

"This is England is it not? We ride for pleasure. Who says we should not?"

The men at arms parted and I saw Stephen of Blois. "Is it Baron Alfraed?"

I smiled, "It is. Have I committed an offence, Baron?"

I saw the look on his face; he was shocked. "Of course not it is just I had thought you to be on the Tees." That was a lie. He had thought I was dead; I could see it in his eyes.

"I am headed for Normandy." I was deliberately obtuse in my words.

"You must join me in my hall. I have some fine wine from Burgundy."

"I fear I must decline. I have business on the river. This was just a minor diversion twixt meals. I thought you might have been in Normandy for the wedding."

His eyes narrowed, "No, Baron, my brother Theobald attended, I had business here in England."

I could see that he had not expected to see me, not just here in London but at all. I did not like Stephen of Blois but was he a traitor too? I wondered what had made me cross the river. "Your business must have been important to miss the wedding of your cousin."

He nodded, "And you, Baron, I thought you were a Knight of the Empress?"

"I am but I had to quash a rising in the north."

"It seems to be a dangerous place to live."

"It is but living there makes us strong and able to withstand powerful forces which would upset the balance of nature."

"Balance of nature?"

"Yes, Baron, when evil tries to usurp good when foreign forces try to change a people. In the north, we have a fine balance. We may not grow wheat but there are good people there and no one can change that. Rebellion and treason might come naturally to some but those who live in my Valley are loyal to the King and will fight to the death to protect their way of life."

I saw his face as I spat each word out. It was as though he had been assaulted by me. I had shocked him. Now I knew why I had come here. I was throwing down a gauntlet. I had no evidence but I knew that Stephen of Blois had been involved in the Scottish raid and the attempt on my life. He was a confederate of either Fitzwaller or those in Durham; perhaps both.

"How long will you be here in London? Perhaps we could go hunting."

I knew what the prey would be, me! "A kind offer but I will have to decline. I have delivered my message to the Constable. I have a family and game aplenty. You must come and hunt with me."

"I will take you up on that but for now I have things I must do."

As we rode back I could feel the daggers in my back. John asked."What was that about Baron? " We had been speaking Norman and some of the words were unknown to my young squire.

Hugh explained, "I heard the same words John but the Baron was testing the Lord of Blois. He has told him that the documents are with the Constable."

"Indeed. You are right Hugh and when we leave we go without horses and without Matthew. I wish to disappear from London. This Stephen of Blois is a dangerous adversary. He may be the King's nephew but I trust him not. He would take the throne from the Empress. I want to be away from England before he knows. I am hoping I have set his eye to search the north road for us."

"Why would that be a bad thing, lord? Empress Matilda is married to an Angevin. What is the difference?"

I could not speak from my heart for I kept that part of me hidden. "The Empress has a heart which is English. Stephen of Blois would make England part of his own Empire. He would rival the Holy Roman Empire. My father returned here because he was English. I am English and I will fight for England!"

Chapter 8

The Constable was quite happy to house our horses and to watch over Matthew. For his own part, Matthew was happy to be spared the journey across the Channel. We found passage on the *'Jerusalem'*, a small cog which carried messages between London and Caen. The ring of the Bishop and the weight of the Archbishop of Canterbury ensured four berths. It was fast enough to avoid any pirates and it carried messages between the King and his ministers. The Archbishop of Canterbury entrusted some parchments to me for safe delivery to the King. I asked them to be discreet but I knew that someone would know we had gone to Normandy and our secret would be out but any delay was useful.

We slipped out on the first tide of the day. Dawn had not yet broken and we, I hoped, vanished from sight. The captain was a dour, silent man and that suited me. I had made faster time than I had hoped. I had only left home fourteen days since and within another two I would be in Caen. My meeting with Stephen had made me more fearful of my home than before. This was a man with his eye on the throne and I was an obstacle in his way. In many ways, I envied Harold and Edward. They had no family to lose and to be held a hostage to fortune. I did.

The winds were against us and it took more than a day to beat down to the Orne and Caen. Even worse, when we arrived I discovered that the King had gone from Anjou to Rouen. The four of us spent a frustrating night in Caen. I did not wish to risk moving at night. A few days more could not make a difference. Speaking with the Castellan I discovered that Robert of Gloucester was with his father. With an alliance secured in the south, it did not take much thought to realise that the King could now advance on Flanders. Unless the king of France was willing to risk war King Henry could teach his nephew a lesson.

We had to wait longer than I wanted to leave for horses were in short supply. In the end, I bought four. It was better than waiting. As it turned out the delay was propitious for Edward and his men rode in as we were about to leave. His face lit up, "Baron what are you doing here?" My reaction was less happy than he expected. "What has happened?"

We were in the full gaze of many men. "Accompany me to Rouen and I will tell you all."

It speaks well of my knight that he and his men, even though they had been anticipating a journey home, all of them acceded to my request without a murmur. When we were out of earshot of the castle and on a lonely stretch of road I told him all. It took some time. Behind us, I heard Hugh telling his cousin Gille the same information. By the time I had finished, I saw that Edward was becoming angry. His knuckles were white.

"I never met this Fitzwaller but I wish you and your father had slain him. Wulfstan was a good man and deserved a long life." He shook his head. "I wish I had not had to attend the wedding."

"It would have made no difference. Had you been with me you would not have been able to prevent Wulfstan's death."

"You are right but I feel I have wasted months being… well, I am not sure what I was." He shook his head, "The Empress is marrying a child! It is not right."

"You did not express such views before the King did you?"

He laughed, "Baron, you will be teaching me to suck eggs next! No, I kept a dispassionate face. But the Empress was angry, and she did not hide it. This marriage will not be a happy one. Of that I am certain."

Surprisingly that did not make me happy.

We rode in silence for a while as he took in all that I had said. "We knew about Blois of course but this new development concerning Durham worries me."

"It worries me and it worried the Bishop too. I pray that he has strength enough to do something about it before the end."

"He is as ill as that?"

"They have been reporting his death these six months and I can see why but he clings on to life. He wishes to make amends for the mistakes of his youth."

"If we all did that then we would live to be a hundred!"

Rouen now had the air of a capital. It was as busy as London. As we rode north I discovered that the King's nephew, the Count of Flanders, had died suddenly. Edward did not know if this was an act of God or something more sinister. Henry was at Rouen in strength to show King Louis that he had the power to take Flanders if he chose. "You have been with him more recently than I have Edward. Will he challenge Louis and take Flanders?"

"I doubt it, Baron. The land of Flanders has little to offer King Henry. So long as the new Count is amenable then I think the King will let that particular sleeping dog lie." Behind us, the two cousins were laughing. Edward smiled, "And Harold, how did he take the loss of his people?"

"Badly. He went into himself and I left him with my wife. If anyone can bring him out of his humour it is she."

It was a sign of my new position that the two of us, Leofric, myself and the precious leather satchel were admitted to the King immediately. As soon as I mentioned the word treason the room was cleared leaving just myself with the King and his son.

"Treason is a dangerous word to use, Baron. I hope you have proof."

In answer, I took out the four documents. The two men read them both and then asked, "This is proof but your words imply a greater conspiracy."

"When I was heading south we were attacked by men who sought the satchel. The only people who knew of that were Hubert of Durham and the Dean. None else, save Harold of Elton knew of it. The Bishop told me he would seek out the guilty party."

Robert of Gloucester shook his head, "The Bishop is a sick man. He should be making his peace with God."

"Amen to that. my lord. We also found freshly minted gold on the killers. They had come from Durham. Then, when I reached London I ran into Stephen of Blois." The lie almost stuck in my throat. "His shock made me think that he thought I was dead." I picked up one of the letters from Normandy. "In here it speaks of a new King. Stephen is a potential heir is he not?"

The King waved a hand, "I agree with all of the rest but you are wrong about Stephen. Matilda is now my heir and Stephen is happy about that. Why his brother Theobald came to the wedding and affirmed his support for my daughter."

I nodded, "And yet Stephen stayed in London."

I could see that the thought had not occurred to either of them. "Thank you for your concerns, Baron. You did right to bring this to our attention. Those lords of Anjou will be dealt with. It means, of course, that I will not be able to return to England to deal with the threat there. My son will have to be my right arm here as we ensure that all danger of rebellion here is quashed. The treason and treachery in the north will have to be contained by you."

"But…"

"But nothing. I have appointed you Baron of the North and you have shown you can do the task well. When you have defeated Gospatric then you will be Earl of Northumberland."

"He is clever, my liege, and hides beneath Scotland's skirts."

"And you were brought up by the Greeks. I am certain that you have the wit and the wherewithal to outwit an old man like that. Do all that is necessary to protect my borders."

I was not certain but I could tell that the interview was over. "Yes, my liege. What of the border. Can I pursue across the border if I need to?"

"Were my words not clear? Do all that is necessary. There is nothing more important than protecting our lands."

"Then with your permission, I will return to England and begin preparations."

The King stood and beamed, "There, that is better. I will have a war chest prepared for you. Stay this night and on the morrow, you can return to England."

I joined Edward and Leofric; we walked the crowded streets of Rouen. I told him all. He seemed happy about the idea. "You should not be so fearful of the responsibility, Baron. This way you answer to no one save yourself and if you have a war chest then we can hire more swords."

"I was lucky with you, Edward, but there are many out there with false hearts. Remember Richard?"

"I do but we have a core of brave knights. Leave the choice to me." He smiled, "This is a fine town with many merchants. Perhaps you could take presents back for your wife. I know women like pretty things."

I bought some delicate lace for Adela and gifts for my children. When we returned to the castle Robert awaited me. We had had a disagreement during the Welsh campaign and although the rift had been healed our relationship was still strained. I no longer trusted him. I suppose I could not blame him; he was illegitimate and had to watch out for himself.

"Here is the war chest my father promised. Use it wisely for there will be no more. If you want my advice," he laughed, "which I doubt, but you shall have it anyway then I would make the Scots pay for your war. Do not fight in your own land but in the borderlands." He proffered a document. "Here is your authority to appoint new lords to empty manors such as Elsdon and Alnwick. Use your own judgement." He smiled, "I trust it." My orders were quite clear. Pursue our enemies into Scotland.

It was a few days later that we approached the English coast. I now had a greater responsibility than I had had before. I was young to be appointing lords and yet Robert of Gloucester was not much older than I was. I hoped that the D'Umfraville heir would return from the Holy Land. I knew that one of the line had given his life to defend the castle and that kind of loyalty deserved a reward. We gathered my horses and headed north. This time I did not worry about the road. I was protected by Edward and his retinue.

Edward and I decided to change my livery to reflect my new status. I would retain the blue but the yellow stars would be replaced by red ones to reflect Wulfstan, Athelstan and the others who had died. Their blood had bought me success and they would be honoured with the three red stars which would adorn my surcoat. The war chest would pay for the changes. We also halted at Nottingham to hire more men at arms and archers. I had worried about making such selections in London. Stephen of Blois was cunning enough to have his own men pose as mercenaries. The King might trust his nephew but I did not. I had fought him when he had disguised himself as the Red Knight.

We left with six more men at arms and six archers. It was not enough but it was a start. Edward had been given gold by Empress Matilda and he gained four men at arms. Our retinue was growing.

Finally, we called at York where I closeted myself with the Archbishop. Archbishop Thurstan was a wise man. On his journey north, Bishop Flambard had told him of my fears and he had taken steps himself. "I sent four priests with the Bishop. They are all true men of the Church and can be relied upon. Are your churchmen reliable?"

"They are." I smiled, "It was I who appointed them."

"Good, you know your own mind. I will have the lords of the manor south of the Tees be more vigilant but I am afraid they will be loath to venture into the land of the Scots."

"I intend to improve the castles there, your grace. We will stop their privations and their raids that way."

Before I left he drew me to one side. "I see dark times ahead, Baron. I pray you let me know of any threat to the security of the north. York is the jewel of the north and if it were threatened then it would lay the rest of the country open. You are the last barrier from chaos and vigilance will be needed."

I knew he was right and I would do all that I could but we were spread thinly. I hoped that my knights had used the money from the ransoms to build up their forces rather than wasting it on fine clothes and furnishings.

My castle looked reassuringly solid as we approached. It was September and I had been away longer than I had wished. As we crossed on Ethelred's new and improved ferry I turned to Hugh. "You have served with me for over a year now. Are you ready yet?"

"Ready, Baron? For what?"

"To be knighted and become lord of Gainford. You know that I need every knight I can get. You should also know that I believe you are ready. The question is, do you?"

"It is a mighty step, my lord, from squire to knight."

"And that is why I ask you. If you are not ready then speak for I will be neither offended nor upset. However, I believe you are your father's son and that you will make Gainford a strong defence. The lord of Barnard is old. If you take over the fief then it will not be easy."

The ferry bumped into the jetty and he turned and smiled, "I will, Baron. I can still serve you and I now see hope here where I once saw despair."

"Good. I will give you a couple of my men at arms until you hire your own."

"There were many likely youths at the manor before ..., well before. Some were of a mind to be warriors."

"And your steward had husbanded your taxes well. John has cast his eye over the accounts and you have coin. Use it wisely."

"Could I use William? I would have some stonework in my new castle."

"When he has finished my gatehouse then he is yours."

My wife and children greeted me and I saw Harold in the background. To my relief, he was smiling.

William ran up to me. "Have you a present for me, father?"

"That depends, my little warrior, have you been good?"

"I have and Sir Harold has been teaching me to fight."

"Good, then I have." I waved my arms and John and Leofric handed the presents to my son, daughter and wife.

My daughter was now growing quickly and when she received her poppet she ran to me and hugged me. My children were growing and my daughter knew who I was!

Before we entered the castle I kissed my wife and whispered, "Harold looks happier."

"That was your William's doing, not mine. He pestered him to play and Harold became so involved in our son that he forgot his own troubles." She looked around, "Sir Edward has not returned?"

"He has but he went directly to his manor. I have been charged with more responsibilities and I fear the winter will bring more trouble with it."

She nodded, "Bishop Flambard called in when he headed north and he returned Mark to us. He was not a well man. I fear he has not long left on this earth."

"I know. I shall visit with him in the next few days. I have messages from the King and the Archbishop."

As it was on my mind I sent a rider to Durham to warn the Bishop that I would visit him in the next two days. I thought I was doing the right thing...

I could not have left any earlier for John insisted that I hold a court of sessions. There were many cases awaiting my judgement. He was right to chide me so. A Lord of the Manor had a duty to administer justice. I had two arduous days of listening to complaints, issuing judgements and imposing fines. It was almost as exhausting as combat.

I left Hugh at my castle. "You should talk with Harold for when I return I shall knight you. He was knighted recently. I will tell the Bishop of my decision."

"Thank you, Baron. I confess I am a little nervous."

"You will make a good lord of the manor." I took my two squires, Wulfric and four men at arms. I was not going to war.

I loved the start of autumn in my valley. The east, where I had grown up, had been a brown and desiccated place at this time of year. Here it was still green and lush. In the next few weeks, the leaves would begin to turn but in the middle of September, it was a green and pleasant land. It put me at peace; for a few miles at least. I knew that something was the matter when we saw the banners at the castle; they were at half-mast.

We entered the gate. "Is it the Bishop?"

"He died last night, Baron. He will be missed for he did much for the poor."

So much for the delay. Had I ridden immediately then I would have been able to speak with him. I wondered if he had discovered the treachery. The Dean and Hubert came to greet me. Both appeared as friendly as they had always been but one of them might be a traitor. "How did he die?"

"In his sleep, Baron. When I went to take him his medicine he lay at peace."

"Was he alone then, Dean?"

"He was."

For some reason that made me suspicious. He had known of the danger and I could not see him allowing himself to be placed in such danger. I knew that I would have to tread carefully. "When is he to be buried?"

"Tomorrow Baron. We have his tomb read at the chapter house."

"Then my men and I will spend the night." I turned to Wulfric. "Take the men to the warrior hall. We will stay in the castle." I nodded meaningfully. Wulfric knew of my suspicions. I had told him on the journey north.

"You can rely on me, Baron. Shall I take the squires with me or will they be staying with you?"

"I think they can stay with me." They left and turned back to the Dean and Hubert. "The Archbishop said he sent four priests with the Bishop. I would like to speak to them."

The two of them looked at each other guiltily. "When the Bishop became ill again we sent them away. They were not helping."

"They were sent by the Archbishop of York! When did you send them away?"

"Four days ago."

"I did not pass them on the road."

The Dean shrugged, "They seemed capable of looking after themselves. We sent a letter to the King asking him to appoint a new Bishop."

Something did not smell right to me but I needed to investigate more. "Where are the rooms for my squires and me?"

"We have spare rooms in the south tower. If you would follow me." Hubert led us to two small rooms just below the top of a guard tower. I could have been offended at the poor quality of the accommodation but I was distracted. I left the two squires to arrange the rooms and I descended to the Great Hall where Hubert and the Dean awaited me. "Where is the Bishop? I would like to pay my respects."

The Dean shook his head, "It is not seemly, Baron. I..."

"Seemly or not, Dean, I will see the body. Firstly I have a ring to return to him and secondly," I smiled as I took out the two documents from the Archbishop and the King giving me powers in Durham, "I have these."

Hubert looked at the Dean and gave the slightest of shakes of the head, "Very well, Baron, come with us. We have nothing to hide."

That did not ring true. There were two armed guards outside the Bishop's chamber. They looked at Hubert before moving. The Bishop was lying beneath a white shroud. I pulled it back. His face looked drawn and he did not have a peaceful expression on his face. I moved the shroud down so that I could put the ring back on the Bishop's finger. I noticed that there was skin beneath the nails of his right hand and, as I pulled the shroud up I saw marks on his neck. I covered the body and crossed myself.

"Farewell Bishop Flambard; your work will continue."

As I left the Dean asked, "His work?"

"Of course; he gave to the poor and he defended the north against the Scots and rebels. That will continue will it not?"

"Of course, Baron, of course."

"I will see you this evening when we dine. Until then I think I will explore this castle a little closer." I smiled, "My other visit came when the rebels captured it. I suspect this may be an easier visit."

Leofric and John awaited me in the Great Hall. "John, fetch Wulfric and the others. Have them meet me in the Cathedral."

We walked across the green. I wanted to delve into the depths of the castle but I wanted Hubert and the Dean less suspicious. A visit to the Cathedral would seem natural. "Baron is there aught troubling you?"

"Yes, Leofric. I like not what I have seen."

We entered the huge doors of the mighty cathedral and I went to the altar rail and dropped to my knees. I closed my eyes in silent prayer and waited until I heard footsteps behind me. I stood and saw Wulfric and the others. I was suddenly aware that we were being watched from the sides of the church by four or five priests. What struck me as strange was that they had not approached me when I had come in.

Once outside I walked across the Green where we could talk without being overheard. "The Bishop was murdered, Wulfric."

"How do you know, Baron?"

"He had marks on his neck and his fingernails had skin beneath them and one of his fingers was blackened as though it had been broken. When I saw him last his fingers were whole." Wulfric nodded, "And there is something else, there are four priests missing. The Archbishop sent them here with the Bishop and I am told they returned to York. They neither passed through Stockton nor sought me out. That, I find suspicious. I had thought that either Hubert or the Dean was a traitor. It may be that both of them are. We will explore the castle, ostensibly as guests but keep your eyes and ears open."

There was an air of disquiet in the castle. Servants looked nervous and the guards fingered their weapons. I felt a little isolated with just six of my men. Wulfric led us to the guard room. "This is where we sleep, Baron, should you need us."

"And we are in the south tower."

We saw nothing on the upper floors or the main chambers. However, when we reached the main floor I saw a guard at a staircase leading down. As I approached him he put his spear across the opening. Wulfric growled, "Unless you want me to put that spear somewhere painful move it!"

"The Castellan said no one is allowed down these stairs."

I laid my hand on Wulfric's chest, "And why is that?"

"We have some prisoners who are to be tried for murder and they are dangerous."

"As are we, my friend, still we need not see prisoners eh? Come Wulfric we will take a turn around the ramparts before we eat. Carry on sentry. Your sense of duty is commendable; I would not try to stop Wulfric here doing anything! You are a lucky man."

I waited until we were alone on the walls looking south towards the town. "Baron, that is suspicious. Why should we not see prisoners awaiting trial?"

"Because those prisoners are four priests from the Archbishop of York and they do not want me to talk with them."

"Why not?"

"I am not certain but we shall visit there this night when everyone is asleep. However, just to make sure no harm comes to them I want the four of you to take it in turns to pass the sentry. I do not want them spiriting away. If there is no guard there then they have got rid of them too. John and Leofric I want you to watch the sally port yonder," I pointed to the wall.

"How do you know that the sally port is there, Baron?"

"Because it is how we gained entry when we retook this castle. Tonight I will play the fool and let our hosts think that they have duped me."

That evening I pretended to drink too much and to become drunk. I was stone-cold sober. I kept my wits about me and watched as Hubert and the Dean passed secretive looks between the two of them. I had already warned John and Leofric of my plan and they played their part and helped to carry me to bed. Once in my chamber, we quickly donned our armour. I sent John to find Wulfric and warn him to be ready. We put pillows beneath the covers to give the appearance that I was asleep within.

John had only been gone a short time when I heard the sound of footsteps on the stairs leading to the tower. I doused the candle. Drawing our swords we stood on either side of the door. The blanket was already crumpled and my fine tunic lay upon it. The door slowly opened and a chink of light appeared and shone across the bed. Two swords entered. The men who held them hacked and slashed at the bed. The third man stood at the door. I did not know how many there might be and they would soon realise that it was a pile of bedclothes they had killed. I brought my sword around in a mighty sweep and took one of the assassins in the neck. I reversed my sword and stabbed the man at the door; he tried to stop my sword with his hand. Leofric slew the last surprised killer. He was busy watching his comrades die when Leofric's sword pierced his side.

"Watch the stairs!"

I lit the candle. The three men were all guards from the castle.

"Someone coming, Baron!"

I had my bloodied sword ready to face the new foe when John ran up the stairs. Leofric pointed with his sword. "They tried to kill the Baron."

"Did you see Wulfric?"

He nodded, "He said no one had left from the guarded door."

"Follow me." We began to descend the stairs. We had just reached the bottom when I saw Hubert and four of his guards. They were heading for the warrior hall.

He almost snarled when he saw me and my bloody sword. "Kill them! Alarm! Treachery!"

Guards erupted from the warrior hall. I heard the clash of metal from within. "Put down your swords I represent King Henry!"

"He lies! He is here to kill me!"

The guards were confused. One of them made a half-hearted attempt to stab me. I used one of my mail mittens to deflect the blow and then punched him on the nose with the crosspiece of my sword. He fell to the ground. Wulfric and my other men stood at the doorway. The sentries were not warriors; the men they faced were. The half a dozen guards looked at us surrounding them and then dropped their weapons. Hubert pushed two of them towards me and fled.

"Wulfric get down to the stairs and find out who is down there. Make sure the Dean is secured! John and Leofric, come with me."

We raced out of the gate. I heard the sound of hooves as Hubert galloped towards the gate over the bridge. "Open the gate!"

"Stop the Castellan. He is a killer!"

Leofric ran towards the stables as John and I followed the Castellan. He reached the gate and I saw him speak with the guards. They closed the gate and the four of them stood before it with weapons drawn. "Open the gate!"

"I am sorry, Baron, but the Castellan said you have gone mad! You are trying to kill him."

"I have no time for this. I do not want to kill you but believe me, I will unless you open the gate. I am the Baron of the North and I answer to the King alone! Now open this gate or so help me your wives will be widows in a heartbeat!"

Leofric appeared with three horses. None had a saddle but that did not matter. The guards looked at each other as we mounted. "Well?" The gate opened. "And let no one else leave. Wulfric, my sergeant at arms commands until I return."

We had flushed out the traitors but I did not have them in my grasp. Unless I caught Hubert then I would have no proof of this conspiracy.

Chapter 9

I slapped Scout with the flat of my sword and gripped with my knees. It was many years since I had ridden bareback. If I was to catch the traitor then I would have to remember how and quickly. I turned north as soon as we crossed the bridge. Hubert would not be foolish enough to head south. There lay only danger. He was Gospatric's man. I knew that now. He would head for the border. Scout was a fast horse as were those of my squires. It was dark and the Castellan would have to use the road. Anything else would invite disaster. We kept a steady pace. Once we had travelled four or five miles the road straightened out and I saw him as a moving shadow just ahead. I saw a flash of white as he turned his head to spy us and then the shadow disappeared. I did not panic. He had spurred his horse and that was a mistake.

We maintained our pace, "Be ready to go left and right on my command. If we can I want him alive. He has names in his head and I want them."

The road dipped and I saw the shadow at the bottom of the hill. We were gaining once more. He turned again and made the same error. He spurred his horse on. Scout was using the ground eating stride which gradually pulled him back to us. When we next saw him his horse was spent. He laboured up the hill as he headed north. His face turned as he spied the three of us and heard the thundering of our hooves on the cobbles. He panicked as we closed with him and tried to head off the road and through the trees. It was a mistake. His tired horse missed its footing and the Castellan was thrown from the weary beast. I heard a cry and a crack and he lay still.

I dismounted and walked into the trees. I did not want to risk the same fate as the traitor. He was not moving but he was alive. He opened his eyes. I could see him struggling to breathe.

I could see from the way he was laying the injury he had suffered. "Your back is broken Hubert of Durham. You are going to die. I can make your passing easier or I can leave you here for the wolves and the fell beasts of the night. It is your choice."

Leofric had the Castellan's terrified horse and was calming him.

"Who is your master?" I saw him wince as pain wracked his body. "Blink once for no and twice for yes. Do you understand?"

Two blinks.

"Is it Gospatric?"

One blink.

That surprised me. Was he lying? I tried another name, at random, "The Fitzwaller family?"

Two blinks.

"Who else was involved? Stephen of Blois?"

There was a slight pause and then two blinks.

I wondered why the Castellan was heading north. "Does he have allies in the north?"

Two blinks.

I was about to give more names when he opened his mouth and then fell still. He was dead. I turned to the squires. "You heard and saw his responses?"

"We did."

"Then put his body on the horse and we will head back to the castle. I wish he was not dead for I would like to have had him write out a confession. I fear the King will not believe me."

By the time we reached Durham the first faint light of dawn was in the east. Roger of Lincoln was waiting at the gate. "Wulfric was about to send out a party to search for you, Baron."

I smiled, "I take it he has control of the castle?"

"He does. We found four priests in the donjon beneath the castle. They had been badly treated. William of Deal is caring for them."

I handed the reins of the horse which carried Hubert to one of the guards. "Take your Castellan and bury him. He confessed his sins to me before he died. He can be buried."

I dismounted and walked towards the Great Hall.

"Where is the Dean?"

"He has barred himself in the cathedral and claims sanctuary."

"Then he can stay there until I am ready for him." I was weary but I found new energy for I had found at least three of the traitors. The four priests had been beaten and whipped. They looked terrified. "I am sorry that you had to suffer, I was too slow in coming here."

One of them, I later found that his name was Michael, spoke. "No, Baron. Our fate was sealed the moment we stepped through the gate. The Dean and the Castellan had us bound and thrown into the donjon. When we had travelled north with the Bishop we spoke of many things. We knew the Bishop's mind. He did not trust the Dean. The Archbishop selected us for we knew Durham. All of us had served here as novices. We knew the Bishop well. He was a good man. We heard the Bishop remonstrating with them both as we were taken off. We were told it was to be taken to our rooms but were struck and then thrown into the cell."

I turned to Wulfric. "Are there any here whom we can trust?" they hesitated. "You must have formed an opinion."

"The ones you slew appeared to have been the ringleaders. When you left we questioned those who laid down their swords. They were as surprised as any. Perhaps they can be trusted."

"Fetch me one to question." As he left I said, "John, ride to Stockton. I want ten men at arms here as soon as possible and Tristan of Yarm."

He knew better than to question me, "Aye my lord. It may take some time to bring Sir Tristan."

"It matters not."

Wulfric brought in the man who had been first to lay down his sword. I decided to be blunt, "When did you know of your master's treachery?"

"We did not..."

I leapt at him and grabbed a handful of his tunic. "You lie! You knew that the Bishop was murdered did you not?"

"The Dean said he was a heretic and would poison our minds. We..."

"So you knew! There is the lie and for that, I could have your life! Would you like to be hanged, drawn and quartered?"

"No Baron!" He dropped to his knees. "We obeyed orders that was all."

I decided to use deception, "It was Gospatric who commanded the Castellan?" He looked blankly at me. "Stephen of Blois then?" Once again it was as though I was speaking a foreign language. I nodded, "Rise, I believe you. Now tell me whom I can trust from the garrison. Speak truly and you shall live."

"Old Cedric has been here the longest. He was the Sergeant at Arms but Sir Hubert demoted him and put him in charge of the stables."

I vaguely remembered the man. He had always commented kindly on Scout. I turned to Wulfric, "Have someone find him and fetch him hither." The man I had questioned was shaking. "Sit. I keep my word. If you have spoken truly then you shall live but it is treason not to mention the murder of one of God's servants."

"I know, Baron, and many of us were unhappy. Sir Hubert had men who inflicted beatings and worse on those who questioned what we did."

It all made sense now. No wonder Fitzwaller had passed through the land unseen. Sir Hubert had chosen to turn a blind eye. He had lied to me and I had believed him. I was angry. I would that he had suffered more at the end. It all served his master's plans. He was not working for Fitzwaller but with him and they were both serving the same leader. I dare say that Gospatric was part of the plan too. Old Cedric was brought in. To my mind, he was not that old. He had a few grey hairs but that was all.

"You are Cedric and you were Sergeant at Arms?"

"Aye, Baron."

"Then why do you work in the stables now?" he hesitated, "Come, man, I tire of this prevarication. Know you that Sir Hubert is dead along with his three henchmen and I am here on the King's business. Speak."

"I was Sergeant at Arms and a good one, Baron, but I questioned Sir Hubert and the Dean o'er much for their liking. I spoke my mind."

"You were lucky not to have paid with your life."

"I know."

"Did you know that the Bishop was murdered?"

"I heard a rumour that he had been killed to silence him but I was kept in the stables. I was shunned." He flashed an angry look at the man who had spoken to me. "And the Dean; what of him?"

"He wished to be Bishop. I heard that he was promised the Palatinate when the King died."

This was treason indeed. "I would make you Sergeant at Arms again, Cedric. Will you accept?"

His eyes brightened, "Aye my lord. Readily."

I pointed to the fellow before me. "You know your men better than I. Go with Wulfric here. Any who you do not trust will be disarmed and sent hence."

Cedric nodded and hauled the shaking sentry to his feet, "You, come with us!"

I was tired but I still had much to do. This nest of vipers had to be cleansed. Then I remembered the Bishop. He was to have been buried this very day. "Leofric, fetch me Father Michael."

When I was alone I heard the sounds of the castle coming to life as Cedric and Wulfric scoured the castle for Hubert's men. I would need to send a message to the Archbishop. I suspected that Michael would be the new Dean but I still did not know how to deal with the old one. He had claimed sanctuary. He could stay in the cathedral untouched. I did not like that idea. Father Michael had cleaned himself up and had his injuries tended to. "The Bishop was due to be buried today in the chapter house. Can you perform the funeral rites?"

"It would be my honour."

"Let me know when you are ready. Those in the castle will do him honour." He turned to go. "And the Dean has claimed sanctuary. What can we do about that?"

"I fear nothing. It is sacrilege to forcibly take someone from a church if they have claimed that right," he paused and shook his head, "no matter how heinous the crime."

"Who will be in the church?"

"There may be a priest in there but if there is then he will be a confederate of the Dean."

"And he would have heard the Dean's confession."

"He would. In the eyes of God and the Church then the Dean has been absolved of his sins."

"I thought so. Let me know when all is ready," I rose, "Come Leofric, let us find some food."

As we went he asked, "If Durham is not safe then the whole of the valley and the south are in danger."

"And that is why Stephen of Blois used Hubert and the Dean. It explains why there were never any men from Durham who could fight with us. He sent one knight and four men at arms the last time. All of this makes sense. Durham's lands were never touched. It was always my valley and the land on the borders. I was a fool. I have no doubt that the priests who were sent to aid us were the ones that the Dean wanted out of Durham. They may even have hoped that they might die, along with us. It must have caused them more than a little annoyance that we returned successfully each time we travelled north to fight. Do not worry, Leofric. I am here now and I can put in place measures to prevent this from happening again. I will need to find time to write to the Archbishop and the King."

"Will you tell the King about his nephew?"

"Without proof, I dare not. It would anger the King. He already thinks that I have become so jealous of him that I make things up. I will find proof, fear not."

We went down to the kitchens where the servants scurried fearfully into the corners. "Fear not, you will be safe from my anger but we need food!"

I felt better after the bread and soup we ate. I was not concerned with the taste but I knew that I was more likely to be bad-tempered if I was hungry and I needed a cool head.

"Thank you. There will be extra men arriving this afternoon. You had better prepare better food for them!"

"Yes, Baron."

I emerged into the light of the green before the Cathedral. The Dean was safe in there and I could not lay a finger on him nor ask him a question. He could give me the proof the King might believe. One of the York priests hurried over to me. "We are ready to inter the Bishop."

I held up my hand. "I will join you in a very short time. I have one more thing to do first."

I went to the warrior hall. Cedric and Wulfric had two groups of men. One was smaller than the other. "Well?"

Cedric pointed to the smaller group of eight men. They looked sulky. "These are the ones I do not trust."

One stepped forward, "I protest, Baron! This man was reduced to the stables by Sir Hubert. Why do you listen to him?"

Wulfric fetched him a clout about the head. "Watch your tongue else you lose it!"

"This man is loyal and is returned to Sergeant at Arms. You will lay down your weapons and leave this castle. My men have your faces etched in their memory. If we see you again then you will die. I am giving you the benefit of the doubt in honour of Bishop Flambard's funeral. Thank him for your lives but make no mistake you are now marked men!" I nodded to Wulfric. "See them out and then join me at the chapter house. It is time to bury a great man."

Leofric walked next to me as the eight were followed to the gate by Wulfric and the others. "Should you not have put them to the sword?"

"Possibly but sometimes you have to give people a second chance. They may serve another lord. If they have any sense they will head south and make a new start. It is what I would do."

We had buried the Bishop and were walking the walls to check the security when my men returned. "Wulfric, these men will form part of the garrison until the new Castellan appoints his own men."

"Aye Baron."

"New Castellan?"

"Yes Cedric, Tristan of Yarm will hold this until I have had time to find a new lord to hold this most precious of palaces. I would rather take my time and make the right decision than end up with another Hubert."

He nodded, "And the Dean?"

I turned to Father Michael. "You are a man of the church best that you speak with him. He might be less fearful. We will move away so that he might open the door."

We headed back to the castle. I felt happier with the lost men replaced. I would have to stay here for a while in order to give advice to Tristan and then I would need to visit Sir Hugh and the rest of the border lords. They would need to know what had happened.

"Leofric, I need to write some important letters, see to it that I am not disturbed." This was when I missed John. My steward had been my clerk and it was some time since I had had to write my own letters. I thought about each word that I wrote. I made sure that I used facts and not conjecture. I just wished that it had been a third party and not my just squires who had heard Sir Hubert's confession. Although even then they might have said that it was extracted under duress. My hope now rested upon the Dean. If he confessed then all would be well. It took half a candle to write the two letters which I then sealed. As I emerged Leofric said, "My lord, John and Sir Tristan have arrived."

Sir Tristan had brought his squire, Ralph, with him. "Ralph take your master's horse to the stable. John, show him where it is." I wanted to speak privately with Sir Tristan.

"Aye my lord."

When we were alone, he looked at me expectantly. "The Castellan, Hubert and the Dean have been proved traitors. The Castellan is dead and the Dean has claimed sanctuary." He nodded, "I would like you to be Castellan until I can appoint a permanent lord."

I had genuinely shocked him. "My lord! You wish me to take charge of this mighty fortress?"

I nodded, "It is a grave responsibility but it will hold you in good stead for the day you are given your own manor. I am leaving Wulfric and ten of my men at arms here but I need a knight I can trust and I can trust you. All that I need you to do is to hold Durham. I doubt that there will be any attacks but I intend to take to the field in any case and make a presence in the north. We did so this time last year and it kept the peace. I hope it will do the same this time."

"I am honoured, Baron and I will do the best that I can."

"That is all that a man can do. Come I will show you the castle."

The longest of days finally ended. I dined with my squires, Wulfric, Cedric and Tristan. I wanted them to know about my plans. "I will send my letters as soon as I reach Stockton but it will take months for the King to learn the news. You are the three men who will hold Durham until you are relieved. I will visit as often as I can. When I am not available then I will send your father and Harold. It is important that any spies see us controlling this land. At the first sign of weakness, they will pounce."

I could see that Tristan was still worried about the responsibility. I smiled, "You need not collect taxes, nor hold court. The church I will leave in the hands of Father Michael. Cedric knows the castle and Wulfric here knows men. The ten warriors I leave with you are the best that I have. You may not be fully garrisoned but you can hold this mighty fortress with half the number you have."

He smiled, "I am resolved, my lord. We will hold it."

"Good man."

I slept well. Leofric and John were in the antechamber and I was exhausted. When I heard the cry in the night I awoke quickly from my deep slumber. Grabbing my sword I ran to the main hall. Wulfric stood there. "Baron, the Dean and his priest have escaped. They have slain Father Oswald."

I regretted now that I had not forcibly taken the Dean. It would have been sacrilege but a fine priest would still be alive. "How long ago?"

"I know not. Father Michael wondered where the priest was and discovered him. The sally port is open. The guards saw nothing."

I nodded. "Bar that sally port! I realise the horse has bolted but we need the castle more secure." I could see that Wulfric was upset. "It was not your fault, Wulfric. He will pay, fear not."

As I went back to my chamber, I realised that the Dean would flee directly to Gospatric. They would know how thinly Durham was held. I would have to bring my men north once again.

Chapter 10

I sent one message to the Archbishop with one of Dick's archers but I was fortunate that Olaf was in port and he was about to sail to Harwich and then London. He had come back for one last cargo as the river had yet to freeze. Stockton's thriving economy meant more goods for him to transport south. "Olaf, it is vital that this gets to the Tower as soon as possible. I have addressed a letter to the Constable but inside is a letter for the King."

"We will fly like the wind, Baron!"

My riders summoned my knights and their men at arms. I left the rest of my men at arms under the command of Edgar. I would not leave my home undefended at such a time. Adela was more worried about Tristan than she was about her own safety. "It is a grave responsibility for one so young."

"We all have to learn and he is a good fellow. If there is danger here then have Alf call out the fyrd."

"We will be safe. Look, William has almost finished the gatehouse."

I had noticed it when I had arrived. There were now two low walls that divided my bailey into two. If anyone breached my walls they would not have easy access to the gate of my keep. "Good, he has done a good job. I will leave Aiden this time. He has a nose for danger. Let him keep watch."

I noticed the sadness in her eyes and I cuddled her, "I keep thinking of poor Wulfstan and Faren. When you were last away it was he protected me and..." She burst into tears. I saw William looking fearful.

"You will have to look out for your mother now, son. I go to war again."

He held his wooden sword. "She is safe with me, father."

This time I led my whole conroi into the bailey of Durham Castle. It was a message to the spies who would, no doubt, report to Gospatric. It told them that this land still belonged to King Henry and was protected by me. Tristan seemed happier after a few days in command. His father looked proud and Harold looked envious. Here we had a Great Hall in which to dine and I used it to speak to my knights. Wulfric and my men kept the doors guarded so that we would not be overheard.

"We thought it was dangerous the last time we came north; I have to tell you that this time will be perilous beyond belief. Thanks to the treachery of those who lived here we have fewer men with which to patrol the north. The rebels know our weakness and will, I have no doubt, exploit it. This time we cannot sneak across the border and cause mayhem. We go to show them that we are not afraid of them. We go to show our people along the wall that King Henry has not forgotten them but we go, most importantly, to stop our people suffering raids this winter."

I had not meant it to be a rousing speech; I was just speaking the truth and telling them what to expect but they took it as a call to arms and they banged the table and applauded loudly. I sat and Edward said quietly, "Good speech; you could have been an orator!" He made me smile; not because of his words but because my right hand was back.

We had brought many spare horses, arrows and weapons. I left these at Durham. We would not have as far to go to re-supply. I took Father William with the Pyx and the banner. He was one of Father Michael's priests and he was keen to help us. More importantly, he was a warrior monk. He had been a knight before he took holy orders and he carried a sword. It was another mark of the differences this time. We headed for Hexham. Sir Hugh had been informed of the Dean's escape but he and his men had not seen any sign of him.

"If I had known of the problems further north then I would have had the Tyne crossings watched. I thought we had bought peace at Bamburgh. I can tell you this; the bridge at the New Castle is now watched as closely as any and he did not cross there."

"I wonder if he had friends at the Abbey here."

He shook his head, "The Abbot is a good man. He would have told me."

I kept my counsel. The Dean and Sir Hubert had fooled me easily enough. "Then where do you think, Sir Hugh, that he would have gone? My men found signs that the two killers had headed north. If they did not cross the Tyne then where would they go?"

Sir Hugh quaffed some ale and, after wiping his mouth said, "Dumfries. That is where Gospatric and his rebels have their estates. It is fine hunting and they have good, well-sited castles." He laughed, "You have bloodied their noses too much on this side of the land. The ransoms we took mean that there is not a manor east of the divide which is not reduced to poverty. I have heard that most of the knights who were ransomed have taken the cross in the hope of riches."

"Where is the nearest castle then?"

"Gilnockie on the Esk. It controls the road north and the road to Dumfries. I chased some cattle thieves there last year. The castle is well sited and the bastards got away with thirty head of cattle!"

"How far away is it?"

"Forty miles or so."

"Then we head there. I want prisoners so that we can discover where the Dean has fled and I want to show Gospatric and his rebels that they are not forgotten. If we are to defend our land then we have to go on the offensive."

Sir Richard warned, "But it is in Scotland!"

"The King commanded me to prosecute the war until our borders were safe. We destroy Gilnockie!"

Sir Hugh laughed, "But you have never even seen it."

Sir Edward said, "It matters not to the Baron. He will devise some plan when he sees it."

"However, Sir Edward, we will leave half of Sir Hugh's men here to guard our backs. I will not leave this back door into Durham unguarded this time. We will leave in the morning so that Dick and his archers can scout it out for us. We leave our warhorses here we shall not need them. When we reach this castle, we will fight on foot."

As we rode, I discussed with Edward our plans as well as the motivations of Stephen of Blois. "You will have to be careful with this Stephen of Blois, Baron. When I was at the wedding his brother, Theobald, was favourably viewed by the King. I heard that they are also possible heirs for the King should he not have issue himself."

"Then he is not enamoured of Geoffrey of Anjou either?"

"It is expediency from the king, no more. He is a gambler and he is betting on the first horse to win, however, he has a contingency plan should that go awry."

"Blois is very close to France. King Louis is a cunning man. He is no warrior but he knows how to plot and suborn. It would not surprise me to discover that he was behind the problems we are having." Edward nodded, "Do not be like the King, Edward. My motivations are not personal. It is true I do not trust this Stephen of Blois; after all, you and I know that he tried to capture the Empress but it is the trouble he fosters and ferments here which is of more concern to me."

"You are right. I had forgotten the Red Knight. Perhaps the time I spent at the King's court addled my brain."

I laughed, "My father always said that courts did that. That is why he surrounded himself with down to earth warriors like Wulfstan and Osric."

"And you have done the same now."

After reaching the small village of Hautwesel we rested to allow Dick and his archers to range ahead. I took the opportunity to tell them what Edward and I had formulated between us. "From what I have learned this is a wooden castle which nestles in the bend of the Esk. We will use our armour to gain entry. While the archers secretly cross the river to attack that side of the castle we will march to the gate and force it."

"That is dangerous."

"It is not safe, Sir Roger, I grant you that but it is not as hazardous as you might think. The only danger will come if they have a bridge that they can retract. If they do then we will have to change our plans. I am guessing that they have made the entrance so that there is no direct approach and a ram cannot be used."

"I hope your guess is right, Baron."

We headed west after the horses had been rested. We were the smallest conroi I had led for some time. With just ten knights and less than sixty men at arms, we hardly made a mark on the landscape. I was hoping that this castle would have a small garrison and trust to the arms and weapons of my men.

Dick and his men were awaiting us at the huddle of huts that would become, some years later, Catlowdy. Dick and his men had not harmed the villagers who hid in their homes fearfully.

I dismounted with my knights and Dick used an arrow to draw the castle in the soil. "It is a slightly bigger castle than you thought, Baron. It uses an ancient fort for part of its defences. There is a double ditch that surrounds it but no stone was used in its construction. The path which ascends the hill twists and turns towards the end so that those on the walls can hurl missiles at advancing enemy warriors who have to climb up an earth ramp. It is like the one at Bamburgh but less sophisticated."

"Is there a bridge which can be withdrawn?"

"No, Baron."

"And is there cover for you and your archers on the riverside?"

"There is. My better archers can use the small hill which is across the river from the castle. The range is extreme but they can send arrows within the walls. The others can ford the river and use the shelter of the lower ditch. The old fort must have had three or four ditches at one time."

"Good. How long will it take us to reach it?"

"No more than an hour."

"Good, then we camp here and leave an hour before dawn. Send two men back to watch the castle for us."

Harold and Richard joined Edward and me after we had eaten our frugal meal. As a conroi, we had fought alongside each other enough times for friendships and alliances to be formed. It was no bad thing. Most of my knights listened to the stories of Sir Hugh who was a larger than life character in every sense of the word. He regaled them with his adventures and an easy atmosphere prevailed. That was important. I had seen camps where rivalries and tensions led to bloodshed the night before a battle. That was not a good thing.

"Why did you choose Tristan to be Castellan. Baron?"

"You think I should have chosen you, Harold?"

"Oh no, my lord! I am the last person who should be Castellan. I could not even hold on to Elton. I was not thinking of myself but Tristan. You have given him great responsibility."

"Aye, and you should know that I considered you as well Harold. My choice was made because you have had the experience of being the lord of the manor. Tristan's time will come. This will stand him in good stead."

"I lost my manor!"

"No, you did not. You were serving me and the King and your home was raided." I threw the bone I had been gnawing into the fire. "What will you spend the winter doing?"

"Baron?"

"Will you sit before my fire and feel sorry for yourself?"

He coloured. "Do you think so little of me that you would say those words to me, Baron?"

"Then answer me."

"I will build my home and make it stronger."

"Why?"

"So that it will not be taken again so easily."

I smiled, "And that is the reason I chose Tristan. He will live in Durham. He cannot make a castle as mighty as that one but he can learn from its construction. When he is given a manor, and it will not be long coming, then he can use those ideas. You will do the same. When you next leave your manor to obey my orders you will have left in place a manor which can be defended." I pointed to the north. "These Scots and these raiders will never stop coming south to take what our people have earned. Ten generations from now our descendants will still be fighting off the Scots. They have the same problem in the east. Miklagård is mighty but each year the Emperor has to despatch troops to the borders to send back the hordes who come to take what they covet."

Sir Richard shook his head, "Then the only way to stop them coming is to become as poor as they are."

"I am afraid so. I have read books and it is ever thus. Our fathers took risks and they built up something valuable. Others do not want the hard work they merely want to take."

Sir Richard had been listening to our conversation from the moment we had mentioned his son by name. "And that is why you will destroy this castle."

"It is, Sir Richard. It tells them that my arm is long and even though my home is many leagues away I can swat them like a fly if I choose." I saw Harold take all of what I had said and reflect upon it. That night he changed and he became stronger. He became the Harold of old. He became the Harold who had survived in Sherwood forest against all the odds.

We left while the night was still black. There was a mist that covered the ground. It was the sort of mist which would be burned off by noon the following day but which would cling to the ground and deaden sound. It worked in our favour. Dick led his men along the eastern side of the river to their point of attack. We swam our horses across the Esk. We only had a few paces to swim for we crossed at a bend in the river where there was a beach and a single farm. According to Dick, the castle was just two hundred or so paces to the north but the night and the mist hid it. We left the horses with three squires. Two men at arms guarded the farm. If things went wrong we could shelter there and use it for our defence.

We moved north through the mist. I counted the steps so that when I reached two hundred I held up my hand. I waved Leofric forward and the lithe squire disappeared into the mist. I turned and motioned the men into position. We were using a version of the old Roman testudo. Edward, Hugh and I would be the front rank. The other seven knights along with Leofric and Gille would form the rest of the block. Edward's men at arms would lead the others in a similar formation. John and the rest of the squires would remain with the banners to give the illusion that we had reinforcements to bring to the fight.

Leofric appeared and held up his hands five times. We were fifty paces from the castle. He took his place and we began to move through the eerily dark land. Had there been no mist then the sun might have appeared sooner however the sky remained dark and dank until well after the sun had risen. My hauberk would need work from John; I could almost feel the damp creating rust. I heard voices and I slowed a little. It was the sentries on the gate. I noticed that the land rose gently at first and then steeply the closer one came to the castle. I heard the voices of the sentries above us but we were hidden in the mist. I could not understand their words but it sounded like typical sentries' conversation. The path became even steeper and then suddenly turned. I saw the wooden bridge over the ditch. We were on the ramp.

We had been fortunate or perhaps my men had been well trained. There had been no sound until that moment. I heard a clang from behind as two swords accidentally touched. Above us, I heard a shout of alarm. I lifted my shield above my head and led my men across the bridge to the wooden gate. It was a well-made gate. Sir Hugh's shield was held by Edward and me as he took his axe and began to hack at the gap in the centre of the gate. In our own castles, we had learned that a single bar was never enough to stop an attack. The Scots were about to learn that lesson the hard way.

I felt a jar as stones were dropped onto our shields. The fact that our three were interlocked gave us greater strength and we held. I heard shouts from within the castle and then cries. I could not see but I knew that Dick and his archers were loosing blindly into the heart of the castle. Any hits would be lucky but with the garrison racing to the walls inevitably some would be hit and confusion would reign. Men would have to run with shields held up and there would be collisions and crashes. An enormous rock was dropped which made both Edward and I sink a little. I angled the shield and the rock slid into the ditch.

Behind me, I heard Sir Roger moan, "Come on Sir Hugh!"

The mighty knight laughed, "Do not worry little man; it is almost through." It was as though the words gave added strength for he suddenly said, "Push and it will break!"

"One, two, three, heave!"

The weight of twelve knights and squires was enough and the door splintered open when the almost severed bar shattered. I barely had time to bring my shield down as a spear was thrust at me. Sir Hugh hurled his axe to impale the spearman in the head. He grabbed his shield from Edward and drew his sword. I took the blow from a war hammer on my shield; Alf would need to do some work on my shield when I returned from this campaign. A war hammer needs two hands and I slid my sword through the middle of the warrior who had no shield to protect him. The three of us had cleared enough space for Sir Richard and Sir Roger to join us at the front and with Sir Hugh in the middle we began to plough our way through the garrison. The bailey sloped up towards the keep and I saw the Scottish knights gathering before the wooden tower ready to meet us man to man.

The men we cleared were the sentries who had been sent down to slow us down. The knights and the men at arms had armed themselves and wore armour. They would not be as easy to defeat. We moved steadily through the bailey. Our foes awaited us. I did not recognise any of the shields save one. Ahead of me, I saw one of Gospatric's sons, Ralph. I had met him once before. "Remember we need prisoners if we can get them."

We marched rather than ran towards them. There was no hurry. The walls had been cleared and I knew that Dick and his archers would be fording the river to add the weight of their arrows to our attack. Behind us, the men at arms were forming up for the second assault and I knew that our squires would have mounted the gatehouse to flaunt our flags before our foe. It would demoralise them.

A huge warrior with a mighty sword faced me. It was a sword that would have needed two hands from many men. He swung it at me and I blocked it on my shield. There was an ominous crack. The stones and the blows I had suffered up to now had weakened it. He braced himself for a blow to his shield. Instead, I stabbed towards his legs. His hauberk only came to his knees. I saw him wince as my sword sliced into his shin and along his calf muscle. I punched my damaged shield at him. The shield cracked in two but the hand holding the sword was hurt. Dropping the ruined shield, I now used my quick hands and feet to pivot around and I hacked, two handed, into the back of his knees. He was already weakened and he crashed to the ground, dropping his sword. I put my blade to the back of his neck. "Yield or you die!"

"I yield!"

He had no choice and I picked up his sword and held it aloft. I heard the groan from the men before us. I jabbed it into the ground and lunged forward at the man at arms who faced me. He had seen me defeat his leader and he half-heartedly blocked the blow to his head. It glanced off his helmet and knocked him to the ground. As he lay there I pierced his forearm. He was not dead but he was out of the fight.

He shouted, "Quarter!"

Around me, I heard the cries of knights surrendering and asking for quarter. I wondered why for they still outnumbered us and then I looked behind me. The walls were lined with archers. It would have been a massacre had they released their deadly missiles.

"Gille, Leofric, search the keep and seek any priests."

I turned and walked back to the man at arms whose arm I had pierced. He was tying a tourniquet about it. I stood above him, "I could have killed you."

He spoke Norman but he had a guttural Scottish accent to it, "Aye I know. What do you expect, gratitude?"

"No, information."

"And if I do not give it to you?"

"Then I will take the fingers of your right hand. You will live but you will lose your livelihood. What will you do then? Become a farmer?"

"What do you want to know?"

"Did two priests come through here in the last few days?"

"That is all you wish to know?"

"It is. Tell me and you shall be freed."

"Aye, yesterday. They were on their way to Dumfries. It is lucky for you that they did for the Earl himself escorted them there with ten men. You would have not breached the gates else."

I nodded, "Then perhaps God is on our side and not yours." I turned. "This one may walk free."

"You are letting me go?"

"I gave you my word and I am never foresworn." He jumped to his feet and, grabbing his sword, ran gratefully from the castle. It suited me for he would go to Dumfries and tell the Earl and the Dean who had caused this disaster. I wanted them to fear me. I saw that Gospatric's son had been slain by one of my knights but we had four knights for ransom including the giant I had captured.

"Sir Hugh, we will take these for ransom. Disarm the men at arms. Sir Edward find the horses and take the supplies from the castle. Sir Richard make the walls and the keep ready for burning. This is one castle they will not rebuild in a hurry." I turned to the giant, "What is your name?"

"William of Hawick."

"And your castle is there?"

"Aye. Tell me, Baron, why do you make war on us here?"

I poked the body of Gospatric's son with my foot. "So long as you harbour traitors and rebels then I will make life difficult for all along this border."

"King David is becoming tired of this, you know. He will write to his brother in law, your King."

"And if my King tells me to cease then I will do so. He is in Normandy and it will be a long winter for your folk. Where is your squire?"

He turned, "Angus." A smaller version of the giant strode up. "The Baron has a task for you."

I smiled at the bluntness of the knight. He was an enemy but I liked him. He reminded me of my father's oathsworn. "The ransom for your father is fifty gold pieces." I glanced at him. He nodded. "Bring it to Sir Hugh's castle at Hexham." The squire hesitated, "He will be well cared for. We have a priest who will see to his wounds. They are not life-threatening."

As the horses were led from the castle with their supplies so squires were sent back to their manors and their families for ransom. Finally only the twenty or so men at arms and foot soldiers remained. The two who were men at arms had had their armour and weapons taken. They looked sorry for themselves. William of Hawick asked, when he was helped to the back of his horse, "What will happen to them? Will you kill them?"

"I should but I will not. They are free to go. I daresay they will find another lord."

He nodded, "Make for my castle in Hawick. I will take you all to my household if you have a mind." Most brightened at that and I realised this knight was no rebel. He was a patriot fighting for his own country much as I fought for mine. He nodded at me. "You are an honourable knight and when I capture you I will offer the same courtesy for you and your men."

I nodded. I liked such honesty.

As we left the castle fires began to flicker around the fat soaked walls. Hay had been strategically placed so that, by the time we had crossed the river and were heading east we saw the huge column of smoke rising into the skies. The Earl of Dumfries would soon send men but by then we would be close to Hexham and safety.

Chapter 11

I used our time at Hexham wisely as we waited for the ransom. Dick and his archers patrolled the lands around the wall. The Scots investigated the ruined castle but discretion prevailed and they returned to Dumfries. We had done well from the raid and many of the supplies were sent south to Durham where we would divide them up. I went to Otterburn, Alnwick, Morpeth and Rothbury with my knights to show that we were once again ready for war. We took the perishable supplies we had captured and gave them to the four settlements along with some of the spare weapons. It was little enough but it was gratefully received. I was letting the people know that someone cared.

Speaking to the captured nights I also discovered that Gospatric and his rebels were not popular amongst the Norman knights of Scotland. They were seen as a burden on a land that struggled to feed itself. The fact that they all had rich lands south of the border aggravated the situation. When I asked about the two priests I was told that they were only passing through the land and were heading for a port on the west coast. That set me to wondering. I knew that the King had had issues with the Pope, as had the Empress; could this be a greater conspiracy?

The ransoms were paid by the first week in November. I said farewell to William of Hawick and, with a quiet frontier and a blanket of thin snow on the ground, we headed south to Durham. Our war horses and extra supplies had not been needed. We divided the spoils of war at Durham and we left Tristan and Wulfric to winter alone. Wulfric would rather have been with us but he knew how to obey orders. The only news we had had was that Father Michael was the new Dean of Durham. For the first time in many years, we had a churchman whom I could trust and I would sleep easier.

The last four miles of our journey home were the hardest for a blizzard descended upon us. I called in at Norton if for no other reason than to speak with Osric. He was now my only link with the past. I sent my men home and kept just John with me. He looked frailer each time I saw him but the smile in his eyes showed me the man who lived within. Father Peter spent much of the day with him and it was Leofric the moneyer who acted as Steward. Osric was held in great esteem by the people of Norton and along with Father Peter was the heart of the village.

I told Osric of our exploits. He chuckled when I told him how we had breached the walls. "I should like to meet this Sir Hugh. He sounds like he would have made a good Varangian. It takes a powerful blow for an axe to break through a gate."

He frowned, however, when I told him of the treachery and treason. I did not mention Stephen of Blois but I did tell him of Fitzwaller, Sir Hubert and the Dean.

"I told your father we should have killed that boy when we had the chance."

"It was the King who forbade it. He wanted the ransom."

"That is the problem. Sometimes the ransom is more trouble than it is worth. Kill them all I say and there will be no blood feud." He shook his head, "Poor Wulfstan."

I looked at Father Peter who shook his head. He had already told me that Osric's memory failed occasionally. He spoke of Wulfstan as though he had just died. He asked John of his exploits and then, inexplicably, fell asleep.

As we left I said, "Thank you for looking after him, Father."

"He deserves it. He and the rest of your father's oathsworn gave their lives for Norton and its people. We will always honour their memory. They are remembered in our prayers each Sunday."

We rode in silence the last few miles home. That was something they would not have had if they had stayed in the east. They would have been forgotten and had no purpose in their life. Here they had been valuable and vital. They had shown that old did not mean useless.

My gate slamming behind me was a reassuring sound. I could not help turning, as I led my horse through, to watch the two bars slide into place. There was no gap here through which an axe could penetrate. Even so, I knew I would need to make the gate a stronger feature. We had gained access to the Scottish castle too easily.

Once back in the embrace of my family I enjoyed a few weeks of peace. Winter's icy grip tightened about the land but we had prepared well for it and were both comfortable and well supplied. Our cows and goats provided milk throughout the winter and the dried logs gave us heat. The long nights did not cause us hardship as I knew they would elsewhere. The frozen land would be as effective a guard as a hundred men at arms. No one would risk the cold to raid.

Hartburn was still an empty manor. A few farmers had settled the land but there was no lord to watch and to guard it. I had thought to give it to Tristan but he would be at Durham for a while. It was Adela who gave me the solution. She was the most thoughtful of wives and she knew me better, I think than I knew myself.

"There is an answer to this, my husband, which is as plain as the nose on your face. Harold should be the Lord of Hartburn. You know you want someone there who is close to you for it is the nearest manor. Elton is closer to Yarm and when Tristan returns he would, as Lord of

Elton, be closer to his father. For him, there would be no sad memories as there will for Harold. Hartburn would be a new start. He could choose a different site for his hall."

I stood and kissed her. "You have given me all the answers I needed and more." To some men their wives were an adornment and a mother for their children; Adela was a partner in the manor. I could not run it without her.

Harold still stayed with me and I took him out the next morning for a ride. I was Baron of the North and I could command. I could order him to be lord of Hartburn. That was not my style. We would talk. The air was so cold as we rode our horses along the hardened ground, that it almost burned our faces and we spurred our mounts to make them sweat. Their body heat soon warmed us up. I rode to the ridge which rose to the west of Hartburn and divided Hartburn from Stockton. Wulfstan had built his manor to the east of the demesne. I had always wondered why, for I preferred this site. A small stream meandered down a shallow valley but the ridge commanded a fine view all around. The land fell away gently to the north and the west. Most importantly it was closer to my castle. The only drawback that I could see was that it did not command the track which headed to Elton. From the ridge, however, the greenway was still in view.

We reined in and sat in silence. The heat from our horses and our mouths appeared in the air before us. "What do you think of this place, Harold?"

He surveyed the land. "It is a good place for a farm." He pointed to the stand of willows which lined the stream. "Old Tom had his farm on the other side of that stream and he used those willows for his arrows."

"Aye, he did. But what think you as a site for a manor house?"

"It is an excellent choice. I often wondered why Wulfstan chose the land to the east."

"I think he liked the fact that it was flatter and he had an easier task to build his home."

"And that got him killed, Baron, for it was harder to defend. If I had been the lord of the manor then I would have chosen here. This side is protected by the stream and it would be easy to dig a deep ditch on the western and northern sides."

"Then you can do so, Harold, Lord of Hartburn."

His mouth opened and closed like a fish. "But, what of Elton?"

"In your heart, Harold, would you choose to go back there with all its dark memories?"

He shook his head, "No Baron, but what of my duty? What of the people who survive there. They need a lord."

"And they shall have one. Tristan will be rewarded for his duty at Durham and he will make a good lord will he not?"

His face brightened. "He will be a good lord." He looked around the land with a keener eye now that the issue of Elton had been dealt with. "Truly it is mine?"

"It is, Harold. When the days become warmer then you can bring your men and begin work." Harold had used his coin well and he had his own conroi. It was small as yet but they were doughty men. The manor of Hartburn was a richer one than Elton had been for it was larger. Only Norton and Stockton were bigger. He had learned lessons from the raid of Fitzwaller. He would build better and stronger. We rode back some time later and the smile on Harold's face warmed my castle once more.

It was as though, here in the far north of the kingdom, we were cocooned by the cold. No news came to us. In many ways, it felt as though I had my own small kingdom. Although the grip of winter was still upon the land I still had judgements to make and disputes to arbitrate. Until there was a new Bishop of Durham I would be the one who made decisions. I had no idea what was going on in York let alone London or Rouen. No missives came to give me orders and I began to enjoy my power.

All of that changed just before Easter when two ships sailed into my river at dawn. The pennant flying from the masthead told me that it was King Henry himself. We had been warned that ships were coming by calls from the sentries in my tower. Adela quickly began to organise accommodation. When word came that it was the King then all of her plans were thrown into disarray. "We have no room to house the King's retinue! We are a small castle!"

"Do not fear, my love. The King knows the size of my castle. He can have our chamber and his man can camp." My confidence was surface deep. King Henry normally warned his lords of a visit. This smacked of something else and that normally meant trouble for me. I had my guards present themselves at the gate in two lines to greet the King. Adela was still making my children presentable when King Henry stepped ashore. Robert of Gloucester was not with him but I recognised the Archbishop of York. There were just ten men at arms accompanying him. It seemed a small retinue. Adela pushed the children next to me and she curtsied just in time.

"Welcome your majesty. My castle is your castle."

"Thank you, Baron and your lovely Baroness. I realise I have come unannounced. Pray rise, Baroness, we will not tarry long here."

He began to walk into my castle followed by his retinue.

The Archbishop smiled at me, "This is the first time I have seen your castle, Baron. It is one of the few made of stone north of the river is it not?"

"It is your Grace. I know it is not over large but it will do for a minor baron such as I."

King Henry stopped and laughed, "Do not do yourself a disservice Baron. You are as important to me here as my son in the Welsh marches. Perhaps more so for the raiders in the north appear to be more dangerous."

My steward John had quickly organised some food and brought out some wine. When we reached my hall he had my servants and slaves ready to present our guests with both. I noticed that, despite having just stepped from a ship, the King and the Archbishop had very healthy appetites. One or two of the King's knights had entered the castle. I vaguely recognised their surcoats but they came from Normandy and I was not familiar with them. The rest remained in the bailey.

I was introduced to one, Sir Gilbert de Bois and his cousin Guillaume de Maine. They were from Normandy. Both were a little older than I was. Their scars spoke of battles.

When he had finished eating the King stood and, taking Adela's hand, kissed it. "Thank you for your hospitality Baroness but I promised you I would not stay long. Baron, I need you and ten of your men to accompany us to Durham. You have spare horses?"

"Yes, your majesty. How many will you require?"

"Just twelve."

I turned to Leofric, "Have horses saddled and tell Edgar to prepare his men to ride."

We had not ridden much further than Thorpe when the King waved back all of the men who accompanied us save for the Archbishop.

"I have need to speak with you privately. The Archbishop knows my mind on this matter." I nodded, "We ride to Durham for Sir Gilbert de Bois is to take command of the castle until we can appoint a new Bishop. The selection is proving more difficult than I imagined. The Archbishop has confidence in his new Dean and Sir Gilbert is more than capable of ruling the palatinate for a short time. Who commands there now?"

"I left my young knight, Sir Tristan of Yarm, with my best men at arms. There has been no trouble."

"Good. You do seem to attract sound men." He hesitated and then sighed, "Firstly Baron I am more than pleased with your work protecting my borders and preventing raids on my people. This has, I understand, been a quiet winter and there have been neither raids nor atrocities."

"I merely carried out your commands, my liege."

"And you have done it well." He paused, "Perhaps too well."

"Your majesty?"

"You know that King David of Scotland is the brother of my late wife." I nodded. "He is less than enamoured with your attack on his lands. He was Prince of the Cumbrians before he became king and the castle you destroyed was on his land. He feels aggrieved at your actions."

"But I just did as I was commanded."

"I know and I am pleased that you carried out my instructions. Some think you were overzealous and that I must be seen to punish you."

"But…"

He held up his hand, "You are from the East you should know how these things work. Publicly I will punish you but it is all for show so that King David becomes my ally and I can deal with the rebels in Maine. The Scottish King visited me in London and he agreed that if you were punished he would guarantee that no one would raid our northern lands neither Scot nor rebel and he would send knights to fight for me in Maine."

I could not believe this. I had done as I had been asked and I was to be publicly punished for it. "Yes, your majesty. I am your liege man and I obey you in all things."

"Good man, I knew I could rely on your discretion! Now the Archbishop is not only here to speak with Father Michael he has conceived a plan which will see you punished but also allow you to perform another service for your King." I was not excited by that prospect either for it seemed that I was being used as some kind of pawn in the King's machinations and following the King's orders was not as straightforward as it might have been.

The Archbishop spoke. "You will abase yourself in Durham before the tomb of St Cuthbert and beg forgiveness for the sacking of the Scottish castles you attacked. "

"That is not so bad, is it Baron?"

"I suppose not."

"And then you will endure a short banishment."

"Banishment!"

"It will not be a real banishment but it will be something which King David will believe and our alliance will be strengthened. You will travel to Constantinople. I will take your family back to London where I can protect them." I was not fooled, they would be hostages to my good behaviour. "Your knights will continue to protect the valley and you will leave a garrison at your fine castle. All of that is for public consumption. However privately you will deliver to Emperor John Komnenos certain letters and treaties from me. I wish to ally myself with him. Now that my daughter is no longer Empress of the Holy Roman Empire I need a powerful ally and the Pope is not particularly friendly towards us at the moment."

My shoulders slumped. "But my family!"

"I swear before the Archbishop here that your family will be safe. We will tell King David that you have been sent to Jerusalem on a pilgrimage to absolve you from sins."

The Archbishop tutted, "I could not countenance such a lie."

"It is I who will do the lying. A King will do all that he can to protect his kingdom. And when you return with the treaty signed then I will reward you with an Earldom." I was silent. "This is important and I am relying on you. I know it will blacken your name but you are the only man who can do this task for me. You speak Greek and you know the Empire. Who else could I trust but one of the Knights of the Empress?"

He was using my devotion to the Empress as a bargaining chip. But I knew when I was beaten. I had no option. I had to obey. "I will do as you command sire."

"Excellent and I will confirm the titles and manors of your knights for they have served me well. We will stay but one night in Durham. The other ship which waits at your home is the one which will take you east."

"I leave tomorrow?"

"You leave as soon as we return from Durham. You will have little time for goodbyes and for that I am sorry. I have made many sacrifices for England and Normandy and you shall do the same. We are nobles and we have responsibilities."

I wondered if my father would have returned to his home in England had he envisaged this would result from such action.

The sentries at the castle were as surprised and shocked as mine had been when we rode through the gates. Tristan seemed particularly flustered but King Henry showed me his human side. "Sir Tristan, the Baron here has told me of your efforts on our behalf and you will be rewarded but your tenure is now ended. Sir Gilbert de Bois will take over and you shall return to your home in the south on the morrow."

The Archbishop said, "Dean, come with us to the Cathedral for the Baron has a duty to perform." He led the three of us across the green to the cathedral.

As we did so I asked, "What do I say, Archbishop?"

He spoke quietly so that Dean Michael who followed us would not hear, "Just ask God and St. Cuthbert to forgive you for disobeying your King and attacking the Scots."

"Is that not a lie?"

"You did attack the Scots did you not?"

"But I was obeying the King's command!"

"The King commanded you to protect his lands so this is not a lie. Perhaps you did not completely understand your orders eh, Baron?"

I could not win and I resigned myself to the humiliation. I knelt before the altar and bowed my head. I was keenly aware of the priests who were watching me. Even as I said the words I was thinking how clever King Henry had been. The priests would report my words; perhaps one of them was a spy. The presence of the King and the Archbishop would add credence to the story and King David would be convinced of the truth.

"I beg Almighty God and St Cuthbert for forgiveness for the sin of disobeying my King and attacking the Scots."

As we left the cathedral and headed back to the gate the Archbishop said, quietly, "We have heard that the Dean and the other murderous priest have gone to Rome. They are beyond our grasp. Perhaps that is all for the best eh?"

I knew it was not. The Dean still knew who was behind the plots. One day I would bring him to justice. It was through him that Wulfstan had died. I did not forget and I certainly did not forgive.

As we rode back the next day with the King and the Archbishop protected by my men I rode at the rear with Tristan. He was as confused as my men were. The tale had spread of my confession. "But Baron you did not disobey orders, you were commanded to do as you did."

I shook my head, "I must have been mistaken and perhaps I was overzealous. It matters not." I smiled, "And you are to be Lord of Elton. You have served me well and I reward those who do so."

"It is a bitter taste, my lord. I would that you had not been punished."

"You will learn, Tristan that we are not always in command of our own destinies. Sometimes Kings play for higher stakes and the search for a safe throne is important." I changed the subject. "John, my steward tells me that the clay of the river is perfect for making tiles. He is seeking a tiler to come to Elton and begin making them. It will not only be a good source of revenue for you it will make our homes better."

"Thank you, my lord. And, may I ask, can I build my manor anywhere I choose, in Elton?"

"Of course."

"Then I will site it closer to Hartburn. I would not have the memories of the dead coming to haunt me."

We reached Stockton by noon and I had the heartbreaking duty to tell Adela that she, my family and her ladies would be travelling with the King to London. I could not tell her the real reason for I dreaded her revealing it to King David should he visit. I had to carry out the lie and tell her what the Archbishop had concocted. I was to go on pilgrimage. Nor could I take a large retinue with me. I was able to take just my squires, Wulfric, Roger of Lincoln, Dick, Griff of Gwent and Ralph of Wales. When we were aboard the ship then I could tell them a little more.

Harold, thankfully, and Edward were at my castle. While Adela gathered her goods and my squires gathered my luggage I had time to speak with them briefly. "I am to go to the east." I held up my hand, "There is no time for questions. I leave you two to watch my castle. My lady and my family will be guests of the King."

"Hostages you mean!"

"Peace Edward. When I can explain then I shall until then trust me as I now trust you. Harold, build your manor and Edward you shall be Sheriff while I am abroad. Tristan will build a hall at Elton. The Kings thinks that six months should suffice. I will return and, in the fullness of time then all will be revealed. Look for me at harvest time." Edward's face was a mask of both confusion and anger. We were interrupted and all discussion ceased.

"Baron! Your ship and the tide await!"

I turned and saw the King impatiently pointing to the ship, *'Sign of the Cross'*. I clasped their hands, "Farewell!"

Adela was tearful as was my son. Thankfully my daughter was too young to understand. "William, you must look after your mother until I return." He nodded and I saw him fighting the tears. "You will be staying in the finest castle in England." I kissed Adela and then whispered in her ear, "The King swears you will be safe but trust no one and keep a knife close to you."

"I will, my husband, and I know that when you return I shall understand this." She smiled, "We will treat this as an adventure; won't we children."

"Baron! I have said I will watch over your family and the tide is turning. We must all leave now!"

I kissed her again and then went to the tiny ship where my men were waiting. I had no sooner stepped aboard than we cast off. My men stood on the ramparts beneath my fluttering banner and I wondered when I would see my home again. Wulfric, Roger, the squires and myself had left our hauberks at home. There was little advantage in them at sea but we took our helmets and shields for who knew when they would come in handy.

Part 3 Miklagård
Chapter 12

The captain of the cog was a little Welshman called Dai. I had not known that when I had chosen Griff of Gwent and Ralph of Wales to accompany me but it proved to be a clever move. He could not do enough for us. That was just as well for the ship had limited accommodation. The cog was a simple ship developed from the Viking knarr. There was no deck. There was a small wooden tower at the bow and the stern which could be used for defence but both were too small for us to use as chambers. Instead, we slept in the bottom of the ship on the planks which normally held the cargo. We ended up using a spare sail to make a shelter between the bow castle and the mainmast. The sides of the ship were high and that made life a little easier for us for it would take a mighty wave to wet us and we would be sailing close to the coast. The captain did complain that we had no cargo and he would not make much profit from the journey but I suspected he had been well paid by the King. Being flat bottomed the cog had to hug the coast. That was not a problem sailing around the Empire and Normandy but once we crossed into the Mediterranean then we would have to watch out for Barbary pirates.

Dai was happy to have the archers aboard and spent many evenings explaining to my three archers what they should do if we were attacked. Of course, John and Leofric were also fair archers and five men each armed with a war bow would give us an edge in battle.

That first evening, as we hugged the east coast of England I explained to my men what I could of our mission. "We are not going to Jerusalem as you may have heard. Instead, we are going to Constantinople, Miklagård. It was my home and I know it well. You will enjoy life there. Once there it will be my responsibility to speak with… well, let us just say I will be in the palace and then it will be up to you, Wulfric, to take charge of the men." He nodded. They would be well cared for.

"If you have coins then there will be a chance for you to become rich men. They have fine spices in the city and they do not cost as much as in England and Normandy. If you use your coins well then you could sell them in England and make a small fortune." I saw that they brightened at that. "However it will take a long time to reach the fabled city. We will only eat hot food when we find a port and that will only happen rarely after the pillars of Hercules. You will become bored. Believe me, I know, I did the reverse of this journey. To alleviate the boredom and to stop us from becoming soft we will practise each day with wooden swords and we will wrestle. If needs be we will help the crew. The sooner we get there then the sooner we get back. I promised Edward we would be back by harvest time but that depends upon the wind and how hard we work."

They did not let me down. Wulfric had them up at dawn practising before he allowed them to eat. After the stale bread and cheese Dai showed them the oars we would use if becalmed. There were slots in the side through which they would be pushed. Although we had a fair wind we made the men practise with them. It was better to practise when there was no urgency than wait until we were under attack. And so we developed a routine. Practise, eat, row, eat, practise, sleep. It made the days fly by.

By the time we crossed through the Channel and passed Normandy the weather had improved a little and the winds had picked up. It meant we could no longer practise rowing and we wrestled instead. It took a week for us to reach the Loire. We had stopped three times. Dai replenished the water and the beer barrels and we took the opportunity of having hot food. It tasted better just because it was hot.

Once we were south of the Loire then we were in unknown lands. We passed Aquitaine where we were regarded with suspicion before we entered the waters of the Moor: Lusitania and al-Andalus. The Moors had been driven from the northern Christian Kingdoms but we dared not risk an encounter with them. This land had been Christian but the Arab and the Moor had come and reached the pass of Roncesvalles before Roland and his horn had thrown them back. Had we been taken then the documents I carried would have meant we would have been treated as spies and forced to row in their ships as slaves.

Frustratingly the winds died when we were halfway down the Iberian Peninsula. We rowed. In the end, it proved a blessing for it kept us all occupied and built up our strength. When the voyage was over I had more strength in both of my arms and the rowing put weight and muscle on John and helped him become a giant of a man. He had been steadily growing but in that first month, he grew a hand span in height and became bigger even than Wulfric. Wulfric found it amusing, "You will need much gold, Little John if you are to be able to have a hauberk to fit you!"

I had laughed too. "They make finer, lighter armour in the east, Wulfric, so you may all decide to use your coins to buy better hauberks."

I noticed a real change in Dai once we entered the calmer waters of the Mediterranean Sea. I stood next to the steering oar as he peered nervously to the south. "Barbary pirates?"

"Aye, Baron. This is their home and they are fast as well as having so many men on board that your archers do not have enough arrows to slay them all."

"Then we have to trust to God."

He held up a crucifix. "I kiss this each day and pray to the Almighty to watch this Welshman who is far from his home. You should pray too, Baron."

As soon as we passed in what the Romans had called *Our Sea* we noticed a pronounced rise in the temperature. It became almost unbearably hot and yet it was not even high summer. I was the only one who was in any way accustomed to the searing heat and the relentless glare of the sun. Soon the sail awning became the place where my men huddled to get some relief from the sun and a little breeze from over the strakes. However, the proximity of Africa meant we had to keep a better watch and with the crew having to work harder to catch whatever breeze there was that task fell to my men. Over the next days, their fair skins changed to red and eventually a nutty brown. The sailors showed them how to make a square of cloth become a sort of hat to protect their heads.

John and Leofric were the youngest of my men and they were fascinated by the smells which drifted towards us whenever we neared land. Fortunately, the calmer waters meant we could sail further from land but whenever we did near land I was assailed by questions. When they glimpsed their first palm tree it resulted in another round of interrogation. In truth, I did not mind. When my son was older I would bring him back to the place of my birth and he would ask the same questions. I had always taken the smells and the vegetation for granted. Having been in England for some years I could now understand their curiosity.

We pulled in at the port of Syracuse on the island of Sicily. We were desperately short of water and there was no beer left. The King had provided some funds for such emergencies but Dai was worried as we neared the port. "This is a Norman Dukedom now. Roger Hauteville is now Duke of Apulia. They say he wishes to be King. We should tread warily here, Baron and I would not let your men ashore. It may be dangerous."

It rankled to be told what to do by this diminutive Welshman but it made sense to heed his advice. "We will just let the men put their feet on the stone jetty, captain. How will that do?"

He smiled, "That will suffice but I have to warn you, Baron, your men will get no beer here. It is Sicilian it is wine only."

I was used to that. "Fear not, Captain, we will water it down and it will be a good substitute."

The Moorish buildings we saw were also a shock to my men as was the dress of both the men and the women. There were many in flowing robes and the dark skins of the Arabs and Moors came as something of a shock too.

"Baron, do we go ashore?"

"No John. Wulfric, the men can walk on the jetty next to the ship but I do not want them out of sight of the ship."

"Aye Baron." He turned, "And I will fetch a clout to any who is further from me than I can spit! And with no beer for days that is not far."

I smiled at the men as they stepped ashore for the first time in many days. I had experienced this before. The ground felt as though it was moving and they stared at each other as though they had been enchanted. They felt drunk and had drunk naught. Although none of us wore mail my men looked markedly different from the locals, even the Normans we saw. The flowing garments which I had once worn were far more comfortable in the heat of this land. Dai and his First Mate scurried off to buy more supplies. I cast my eye over the defences. As in the Byzantine Empire, this was a land that had been built by Romans and that was still in evidence. The Moors had added to the defences and now the Normans had left their mark. It made my small castle look pathetically inadequate in comparison. Then I reflected that they needed more protection here. It was not only the Moors and Arabs who were enemies, the Empire and the Normans were also implacable foes.

Suddenly a glint of light caught my eye as a column of men at arms came towards me. I said hurriedly, "Wulfric, I will speak. Get the men aboard as surreptitiously as you can."

"You want that I should arm them, Baron?"

"No but have Dick, the archers and my squires go to the bow castle. You guard the gangplank."

I waited for the men at arms to reach me. My men slipped aboard in ones and twos so that by the time the knight approached me I was alone. He was just a little older than me but I could see that he had lived most of his life here; he had the olive skin which marked a native of Sicily. "Who are you Norman? I do not recognise that livery."

"I am Baron Alfraed of Stockton and the captain of my ship is buying supplies here in your city. Have we caused some offence?"

"I am John of Palermo and I rule this city on behalf of Duke Roger. We are suspicious of all such as you; Norman knights who land unannounced. Where do you voyage?"

"King Henry and the Archbishop of York have ordered me to go to Jerusalem to pray there. I am on Holy pilgrimage." The lie almost stuck in my throat. I noticed that Dai and his men were returning laden with barrels and boxes. That was a relief. They began to load the ship and stored the goods at the steering board end of the cog.

For the first time, the aggression was replaced by curiosity. "What was your crime?"

"Who said I committed a crime? Besides what passes between a King and his vassal lords is of no concern to anyone else."

This did not please John of Palermo. "You are a visitor here and I could impound your ship and imprison all of you."

"But we have committed no crime."

"This is neither England nor Normandy. We bow the knee to no man and all who land here obey our rules and laws!"

I remembered now that Dai had told me that the Duke wished to be king. "And I bow the knee to no man save King Henry so we shall leave."

I had seen that the goods had been loaded but as I turned I heard the rasp of swords being drawn. "I think you are spies and I impound your ship in the name of the Duke!"

"I think not! Dick!" Suddenly my archers had their war bows aimed at the men at arms and Wulfric appeared at my side with his axe. "Those war bows are held by the finest archers in England, John of Palermo. If I give the command then you and four others will die. Wulfric and I will despatch the rest. You will die for nothing because I am no spy. Sheath your weapons and we will depart."

I saw him glowering and glaring at my archers but they were less than twenty paces from him.

"Dick, give them a warning!"

An arrow thudded into the ground between the knight's feet. He was wise enough to realise that he and his ten men stood little chance. "I will remember this, Baron Alfraed, and your name will be recorded so that one day you and I will meet again and then you will die."

I nodded, "Many men have made that promise and yet I live still. Do not fret, John of Palermo, when we meet again I will give you satisfaction." Out of the corner of my eye, I saw that there was just one rope holding us to the stone jetty and I backed up to the ship. "Farewell!" The rope was thrown aboard and we began to edge away from the wharf.

Wulfric grunted as I stepped aboard. "Another friend for us to avoid, Baron!"

I went to speak to Dai. "You did not say they were so belligerent."

"That is why I warned you to stay aboard the ship."

I glared at Dai. "My men were aboard the ship! I hope you have thought this time to buy enough supplies for the whole voyage?"

"I have."

I pointed to the empty hold, "It seems to me that you could have filled the hold with supplies for us and avoided having to call in here anyway!" I knew now that he had been parsimonious and was trying to save money.

"You are correct Baron and we will not need to land again."

"Good!"

Once we had passed the heel of Italy we were in Byzantine waters. That did not make our lives much safer but at least, if we were approached, we could use our letter from the King to give us access to their ports. As it transpired we had a peaceful if rather a hot journey. As we approached the city, whose walls seemed to rise almost to heaven, I took over the navigation. "It will be better for us if we use the Langa harbour to the west of the city. It will save us sailing around to the Golden Horn and it is close to both the Forum Bovis and the Forum of Arcadius. You and your men will be able to buy goods there to sell back in England."

He gave me a sharp look.

I laughed, "Do not worry, my friend. I have merchants in my town and I know that they are always looking for a profit. I will not tell the King if you use his hired ship to make a little profit for you."

"Thank you, Baron."

My men were awestruck by the sheer size of the walls of Theodosius. Each wall was as tall as my whole keep; in places, they were bigger. Once Dai knew where to point his ship I turned to Wulfric. "Have the men put on their leather hauberks and surcoats. Keep them on board when we land. I will just take Leofric." His face fell. "Do not worry Wulfric, you and the men can explore this fabled and fabulous city later but I need to spy out the lie of the land. We do not want another Syracuse, do we?"

It was as I had expected; there were ships in the small harbour but not too many. We easily found a berth at the western end of the harbour. As we tied up one of the Greek officials strode up to us. The whole of the city was run by clerks. There were rules and regulations for everything. He came up to us and began to speak in poor Norman. "Who are..."

He got no further. I held up my hand and spoke in Greek. His face brightened immediately. Until I had spoken we were barbarians. My Greek told him I was still a barbarian but a civilised one. "I am Baron Alfraed of Stockton and I am here as the representative of Henry

Baron of the North

Beauclerk, King of England and Duke of Normandy. I have letters for the Emperor."

He nodded, "Thank you, Baron. If you wait here I will send a message to the Palace." He waved his hand and a slave came over from a small building with a glass amphora and a goblet. "Pray enjoy some iced wine while you wait."

I took the wine and he scurried off. I was going to sip it but as soon as the icy liquid touched my mouth I downed it in one. The slave cocked an eyebrow but said not a word. I held out the goblet and he refilled it. I took it back on board. Wulfric and my men awaited me. "They are sending to the palace. Here Wulfric, try this."

He looked sceptically at the liquid which had the appearance of yellow water.

I laughed, "It will not poison you. It is iced wine."

He sipped it and then, as I had done he downed it in one. "That is a fine drink, Baron. I would prefer beer but on a hot day like this, then that will do."

"Leofric, we will just need our swords and the letters. I am afraid that I will be speaking Greek but do not worry. I will tell you if there is anything you need to do. Keep your eyes and ears open. Watch for those who wait in the background. I shall ask you later what you see."

The afternoon drew on and I wondered if this was a case of politics and we were being kept in our place waiting under the hot sun. Eventually, a column of Skutatoi with Imperial shields and led by an officer descended to meet us.

"Baron?"

"Yes."

"You are to come with me to the palace." He was a young officer and his eyes flickered nervously to my men.

I looked around and saw them with his eyes. They looked like fierce barbarians. "I will just need my squire. The rest of my men will wait here."

He looked relieved. "If you will follow me; it is not far."

As we walked I said, "I know, I lived here for many years."

"If you have come from England then you have travelled far. Were you not attacked by pirates?"

"No, God smiled upon us and we had a peaceful journey."

He nodded, seemingly satisfied, "The Emperor is not here. He is in the northwestern part of the Empire. The barbarians have invaded us once more. You will be speaking with the Kometes."

We entered the inner sanctum through the Contoscation Gate. Had we landed at its harbour we would have had a shorter wait and walk but I saw, as we passed it, that there were no spare berths. I had made the right decision. The Hippodrome looked as though it had not been used for some time. Scrubby grass grew at its entrance. When I had been growing up there had been races there every week. The Empire was not what it had been. The presence of our escort assured us a rapid entrance to the court. Our guide gave a slight bow. "We will wait outside, Baron."

Kometes Choniates looked to be as old as Wulfstan. He had the look of a warrior. His severely cut beard barely hid the scar running along his face. His eyes narrowed and he frowned as we approached. "I do not have much time Norman. It is only because you speak Greek and I am intrigued that I have granted an audience. My clerk was impressed with you."

"Thank you, Kometes."

"Where did you learn it?"

"Here. I grew up here."

His frown deepened. "Here, in Constantinople?"

"Here in the Palace. My father was Akolouthos of the English Varangians."

Had I slapped him I could not have shocked him more. "What was his name?"

"Ridley."

He suddenly smiled, "I knew him and Alfraed too, his predecessor. They were fine warriors. How is your father?"

"He died in England fighting the Scots."

"Then he is lucky. That is how most Varangians wish to die; in battle. Were you chosen for this reason; because of your father?"

"I was chosen because I speak Greek and I have done some service for King Henry and he trusts me."

"Then your King is shrewd. The Emperor normally hurls Normans into his dungeons and lets them rot a while. I am afraid, however, that he is on campaign. You may have to wait for months to speak with him."

"I have urgent business back in England, Kometes. Could I not visit him on the battlefield?"

"You could but it might be dangerous."

I laughed, "I am a warrior, Kometes, and danger is ever-present. My men and I will survive."

He nodded, "How soon can you and your men be ready to leave?"

"If you have horses for us then as soon as my squire goes back to the ship for my men. We are ready."

"Then send him for I have an Allaghia of cavalry leaving for the front. You can travel with them."

I nodded, "Leofric, come with me." I took him outside. I explained what I wanted him to do.

The young officer smiled, "That was quick."

"Would you escort my squire to my ship? He and my men will be returning to the palace. We leave with the Allaghia."

"You are going to join the Emperor?"

"So it would seem."

"Then I envy you for I am stuck here. I would be with the real soldiers."

I returned to the Palace where the Kometes was finishing a document. He put his seal upon it and then handed it to me. "This is a pass which will allow you and your men travel through the Empire. Do not lose it. Normans are not popular here nor are Franks. The First Crusade showed us the mettle of your colleagues."

"Not all of us are like that, Kometes."

"Perhaps. When you return I would speak with you a little more."

"My ship will need to wait in the harbour."

He laughed, "It is so small that it will not cause us distress but it is a mark of your courage that you travelled so far in such a vessel. I would not sail across the Golden Horn in it."

"It served us well."

"Come I will take you to meet the Turmachai. He may not be happy to have passengers with him."

"We will not slow him up. I only brought a handful of my men and we travel light. All my followers are horsemen." He nodded and we moved out of the palace towards the stables and the barracks. "Your man said it was the Magyar you fight. I thought their land was far to the north."

"It is but their king, Stephen, has become emboldened of late. They have encroached as far as Braničevo."

I had heard of it. "That is close."

"The Emperor hopes to stop them before they reach Serdica. The Tagmata will travel quickly. The commander hopes to be there in seven days."

"He will be travelling quickly then."

"He is young and he is keen to make a reputation."

As we approached the stables I saw and heard the noise of men preparing horses. They were Kataphractoi. They looked to be dressed in a similar fashion to our men at arms save that the hauberk only came to the waist and they had an oval shield. Their lances were slightly longer than ours and their helmets all had an aventail attached. The armour was lamellar and not mail.

"Turmachai." The leader turned around. "I have some Normans to accompany you."

The young man's face fell. There was something familiar about him. As he approached, I realised that I recognised him.

"They had better not slow me down!"

"Basil Nikephorus, the day that I slow you down will be a first!"

His face creased into a grin, "Alfraedus! Is it you? I thought you must have died in the wild lands of the west, slain by a barbarian."

"No, my friend, I have prospered."

We embraced, "But you have not bathed! You smell of... what do you smell of?"

"England and I have been at sea for many days. I could bathe, my friend, if it offends you but it will delay our journey."

"No, I will ride upwind of you."

The Kometes laughed, "I can see that you two know each other. I will send your men Baron and then speak with you when you return."

"Thank you for your kindness."

"Your father was a good man. I would he commanded the Guard now."

"Baron eh? And how many barbarians do you bring with you?"

"Just seven and pray do not call them barbarians. They are sensitive."

"Well then, let us pick you out some horses. The Kometes told you that we travel quickly?"

"He did. And my men are as good on the horse as you or I."

He looked sceptical. "Come." As we walked down the stables he asked. "How is your father?"

"He was killed."

"I am sorry and are you married? Have you a family now?"

"I am and I have a son and daughter. You?"

"I will marry when I have made my reputation. We will drive these Magyar back to their plains and I will enjoy the glory of my victory." It would have been churlish of me to point out that many things can go wrong in a battle. I had seen that. Instead, I just nodded. He halted at a stall. "This is one of my own string of horses. He is called Caesar."

The horse was indeed a fine one. Slightly bigger than Scout he was a golden brown with a blonde mane. "I will ride him carefully."

"You have no armour and he will think it a joy to have so little weight."

I led him out and mounted him. He was well trained and did not baulk at my touch. I spoke to him in Greek. That would be a problem for my men. They would have to learn a few words of command or they would look foolish. I heard their voices as they approached.

I dismounted and Basil said, "Ye Gods! These are your men? I would have taken them for brigands."

I suddenly saw myself in Basil. That had been my attitude before Wulfstan had shown me the error of my ways. "We have travelled far and had no time to either shave or bathe. Do not doubt these men, my friend. We have fought Scots, Irish, Vikings, Normans, Germans and Welshmen. They have never been defeated."

I noticed smiles amongst the Kataphractoi. Wulfric and my men glared back belligerently. It was time for me to be a peacemaker. I spoke in Saxon so that the horsemen would not hear my words. "Be patient. We look like bandits. When we get the chance, we will wash and we will shave. Just take your horses and mount. We have over seven days of hard riding over rough terrain ahead of us."

Wulfric nodded, "Aye, my lord, we understand."

"And before you mount here are some Greek words you will need for your horses. They do not understand your words either Saxon or Norman." I gave them the basic commands. I saw the smiles become grins as they butchered the words. I just hoped that the horses would understand.

Chapter 13

We made better time than we would in England as we travelled on Imperial Roads. These were like our Roman Roads but were actually maintained. There was still the mansio which allowed us hot food and some shelter each night. My men were treated as officers. That was mainly because they rode with Basil and me. I did not want Wulfric to use his ham-like fists to teach a Kataphractos a lesson.

Despite the urgency, I enjoyed the ride. It afforded me the opportunity to catch up on the politics of the capital and to discover what I had missed. Apart from the baths, it seemed I had missed little. Basil was still trying to get to the place I occupied; a leader of men who would follow you anywhere into battle. The baths and the fine food were something I had missed but I had far more in England than Basil had here, in the east. He had had to buy his commission and this was his first campaign. He had much to learn. I wondered how he would cope on the battlefield.

The journey was good for my men. Gradually they picked up the odd word or two of Greek and mixed a little more with the Kataphractoi. The wariness of travelling with barbarians wore off and the Kataphractoi accepted my men as warriors. One morning I saw that one of the Greeks had been in a fight. Dick told me later that Wulfric had had to put one of them in their place. He did not suffer fools gladly. After that, there were no further problems.

One aspect of the ride which I did not enjoy was the lack of security. I was a guest but I could see that Basil had no scouts out. When I mentioned this to him he laughed, "This is not the wilds of your land, Alfraedus; this is the Empire and we are still safe. We are just days from the greatest city in the world. Do not fear. I keep my men together for it impresses the populace when we go through their towns and villages."

I could not dissuade him but I kept my own men close to me. John insisted on riding with my banner unfurled. I was not certain it would be recognised by any but my squire was determined that all should know the knight who travelled through their land. Leofric was the guardian of our documents. He guarded them as though they were a baby. Each was contained securely in a waterproof leather valise of its own. In addition to that, we each had our shields and even my archers had brought their small bucklers. Their war bows were not fully strung but it would be the work of moments to prepare them. I was pleased that their sharp eyes scanned both sides of the road.

We were six days from Constantinople when Dick's sharp senses came into their own, "Baron! Ambush!"

I shouted, "Ambush!" in Greek and pulled my shield tightly around. It was none too soon for three crossbow bolts smashed into my shield. My three archers had their bows strung and three arrows winged their way into the forest. I had not seen the ambushers but they had.

Basil recovered his composure quickly and he barked out his orders. "Defensive circle!"

It was too late for the four of his men who lay pierced by a number of bolts. Three horses suddenly reared as our attackers targeted the vulnerable beasts. "Basil, you cannot just wait here they will pick us off one by one!"

He hesitated. It was the mark of a novice. His second in command, a grizzled bear of a man said, "The Frank is right! Better to take them on than suffer like this."

"Very well! Left file, hold your position. Right file, clear the forest to the right."

They all turned as one and lowered their lances. That was a mistake. Swords would be better in the forest. "Leofric and John stay with Dick and the archers. Wulfric, Roger, with me!"

I wheeled my borrowed horse around. Caesar had courage. He leapt forward as I pricked him with my spurs. I had my sword ready. I had no idea what arms would be carried by our ambushers but a crossbow is slow to reload and it gave me confidence. I began to swing the sword sideways when I saw a flash of white. It was not a crossbowman; it was a half-naked warrior with a rhomphaia. This deadly curved weapon had been feared by the Romans. My sword was slightly longer and I used my knees to wheel Caesar to the left while I leaned out to the right. The reins were not as long as the ones I used at home and I had less manoeuvrability. We both swung our weapons together but the combination of my extra length and the snorting spitting beast I rode gave me an advantage and the tip of my sword and one edge tore across the man's stomach. His knees crumpled and he dropped the weapon as he tried to hold in the entrails which cascaded out.

I saw a crossbowman aiming his weapon at Basil's back. His second in command shouted a warning and Basil turned. I spurred Caesar and, standing in my stirrups, brought down my sword to split the man's head in two. The ambush had failed and the attackers were fleeing to the east. I remembered that we had left half the men to become targets. "Basil! The rest of the men! Sound recall!"

At first, I thought he had not heard me and then he shouted an order and his second in command, the grizzled Kentarchos, shouted for the trumpeter to sound recall. I knew my men would not know the call and I shouted, "Fall back!"

My men turned and reacted the fastest; we headed back to the road. I saw that the rest of Basil's men had taken heavy casualties. John held the banner above his head and he and Leofric were shouting encouragement to the others. The fact that the Greeks would not understand a word did not appear to matter.

Wulfric and Roger rode to my left and right. Wulfric held his war axe as easily as a clerk holds his stylus. We raced across the road and caught six crossbowmen in the flank; their attention was on the horsemen. Wulfric's axe smashed into one skull so hard that pieces of flesh and bone flew into the others who turned in horror at the apparition before them. Wulfric was too close to me to allow me to swing my sword horizontally and so I brought it down between the head and shoulder of the nearest man. It bit deeply into his body until it ground against a bone. I did not pull but allowed Caesar's momentum to carry me through and drag the sword from the savage wound. His hooves cracked and crushed the leg of one of the men who had not gotten out of the way quickly enough. I reined around so that Roger and I could finish off the last two.

I did not risk further pursuit as there were no enemies before us. Basil's men were busy finishing off the last of the ambushers. I saw that neither Wulfric nor Roger was hurt. I patted Caesar on the side of the neck. "Good boy! Well done!" He whinnied and flicked his head in the air as though proud of his actions. To my great relief, none of my men had been hurt.

We all dismounted to rest our horses and waited for the Allaghia to return. I looked down the line. We had lost ten horses and there were at least twelve dead or dying men. It had been an expensive ambush. Yet, when Basil returned, he seemed elated. "We killed at least forty of them. Your archers are superb; they are so fast and accurate!"

I waved my arm around his dead, "But you have lost too many men, Basil."

He looked confused, "They are soldiers and they died for their Emperor." I shook my head. This was a different philosophy from mine.

The men were buried and the horses burned. They did not do as we would have done and eaten the dead beasts. Perhaps when I had lived in the east I would not have done so either. I had changed.

The best thing to come out of the ambush was that Basil now had scouts riding to the left and right of us in the forest. We would not be surprised a second time. As we rode I asked about the rhomphaia. "It is a frightening weapon, Alfraedus. It is two handed and the men who wield it are fierce warriors. It tears through men and swords. Horses are terrified for the edge can sever a leg."

"But they fight without armour."

"They are susceptible to arrows and crossbows but they charge so quickly that they are a hard target. And, as you saw, they can flee into woods where they are safe." He nodded to my sword. "Your weapon is longer and straighter than the ones we use."

"Aye, we have learned that you cannot use the point to stab a man in armour; it never works. The point is for those, like your Thracians, who deign armour. We prefer the horizontal blow which can break ribs and decapitate infantry or the blow brought from on high. The area between the helmet and the shoulder is vulnerable. If we can then we slice across the face. Your men do not have a nasal. At the very least the blow makes a man recoil."

"You do not use a Kontos?"

"We have a lance but it is not as long as the one you use."

"We used to have bows as well but few could use them effectively and they were discontinued. That is why I admired your archers."

"But they do not fight on horseback. They dismount to use their war bow. They are quick to mount. We find it more effective." We spent the next days discussing how I fought in England. When I had left the east I thought that the Franks, as we called them, were inferior to us. I now saw that was not so.

Serdica was a border fort. There were thick walls and towers. The work begun by the Romans had been extended by the Empire. It was surrounded by the camps of the army and Skutatoi, peltasts and horsemen roamed its streets. I even saw some off duty Varangians. They were the only ones who afforded us a second glance. I suspect it is because they were the ones who recognised us for what we were, English. Basil and I were directed to our bivouac for the night. After leaving the horses with John, Leofric, Basil and myself headed back to the Emperor's headquarters.

Basil was admitted immediately. Leofric and I cooled our heels. The two Varangians who stood guard stared ahead. From their appearance, I guessed they were Norse or Rus rather than English. We had been there some while when one glanced at us and sniffed. It said much that we smelled even worse than two Varangians. I would ask if there was a bathhouse in Serdica. We needed one.

Eventually, the door was opened and Basil stood to allow us entry. "I will see you later at the camp." He looked a little deflated and I suspect his losses on the road had been considered too many. He had been reprimanded.

The Emperor sat at a desk. A single Varangian Guard stood behind him. He had a long axe. Next to the Emperor was a clerk. The room was Spartan in appearance. This was an Emperor who knew his business and that business was war.

"I knew your father, Baron, I liked him. I was sad when he left. Had I been Emperor then I would have made it worth his while to stay." He spread his hands, "It was the will of God. And I understand from my officer that you intervened on the road. Thank you. From what my officer told me you saved more men from being wasted. Would you not consider bringing your men into my army? We can always use reliable and tested warriors."

"It is a generous offer, Emperor but I have a family in England and I swore an oath to King Henry."

He put down his scribe and leaned back in his chair, "Ah yes the oath. I remember your father and those closest to him were great believers in oaths. Harald here fights for a great deal of money but I suspect it buys loyalty. Do you pay your men?"

"I feed them and arm them but they follow me because I am successful." I turned to Leofric and changed my language, "The Emperor wants to know if you fight for me without pay." I knew the Emperor could speak many languages; he had to with such a polyglot army.

Leofric nodded, "We do, Baron, happily!"

"And does King Henry pay you, Baron?"

"No, he gave me a piece of his land to hold but I pay him taxes and guard his land."

"A most interesting system; you pay to protect your King's land and for the privilege of serving him. It would make life simpler if I could do that. You know that Normans are the bane of my life?"

"I do and you know, Emperor, that I am not Norman. Besides my King is not a Hauteville, he has no desire to fight this far east." I turned and took the relevant documents from John, "These letters will attest to that."

He laughed and leaned forward, "I can see that you are your father's son. You come directly to the point and do not waste time. I like that. Leave the letters here. As you will well understand I have more pressing matters than an alliance which may well be irrelevant. However, I promise you an answer within five days. Until then would you like to be accommodated here in Serdica?"

I shook my head, "I will stay with the Turmachai."

"Good and if you wish to reconsider my offer, even on a short term basis then you will be richly rewarded."

"Thank you."

It was a tempting offer. When the door closed I turned to one of the Varangians and asked, "Is there a bathhouse here in Serdica?"

He grinned, "You need it, Frank, that is for certain!" He pointed along the road. "Go to the main square and there is one on the western street."

As we walked in the direction indicated Leofric asked, "Are we not going back to the camp, Baron?"

"No, Leofric. I have had enough of smelling like a farm animal. We will bathe and it is time that you learned a little of the Eastern culture."

It was not a large bathhouse but we were lucky, it was a quiet one. Leofric looked fearful as we were undressed by slaves and then wrapped in towels. The whole experience, from the caldarium to the tepidarium was a revelation to him. When our bodies were oiled and scraped with strigils I think that he thought he was about to be tortured but he endured it when he saw that I was. I had my hair cut, beard trimmed and oiled for the first time in a long time. I felt human again. Finally, when we were both dressed my young squire smiled. "That was an interesting experience, Baron. My body feels... well, different. I sort of tingle."

"Do you like the feeling?"

"Yes, but I did not enjoy the slave's hands on my body. It felt unnatural."

"You could have had a woman you know."

He shook his head, "That would have been even worse!"

On the way back I found a shop which made clothes. If we were to be there for five days then our tired clothes would need replacing. I asked the man to make ten surcoats for me. I used just one size for, apart from John, we were all similar in stature. His apprentice made notes on his wax tablet and I was given a price. It was less than I expected. By the time we reached the camp, it was dark and we struggled to make our way through a town that was filling up with off duty soldiers determined to have a good time. I was pleased we would be outside the town for I knew there would be fights.

It was quiet for two days. Basil went to a daily meeting and his men looked after the horses and their weapons. There appeared to be little communication between regiments. Our new surcoats arrived and, before we wore them and polluted them with our smell, I persuaded the others to bathe. It was Leofric who persuaded them. It was only Wulfric who would not have his beard trimmed and oiled. He glowered and glared at the slaves who were terrified of him. He still looked like a bear when he emerged; a clean bear but a bear nonetheless.

We were camped at the western end of the town. There was a meadow which suited us for the horses had grazing and we were far enough from the water for the biting insects not to bother us. It was also far enough away from the trees so that we could not be surprised by those intent on slitting throats while we slept. However, its open nature meant that it was hot. The smell and heat from the cooking fires were overpowering. It was hard to find somewhere cool. I began to wonder if the Emperor would ever get around to reading the letters and seeing me. I was ready to go home.

A rider galloped in and reined in next to Basil, "Turmachai! The Magyar are attacking! Your men are ordered yonder to the right flank of the army!" He pointed to the north and the road.

"To arms!" He turned to me, "Will you guard our camp for us?"

"Do you not wish us to accompany you?"

"It is not your war."

"No, but you are my friend and your men have been kind to us. Besides if we are not there who knows what may befall you!"

He laughed, "It is your funeral."

"Wulfric! We go to war. Best put on our old surcoats. I would not have these new ones bloody yet."

"Aye, lord!"

When we had mounted we waited for the Kataphractoi. They had armour to don.

"Baron, are these barbarians rich or are they like the Hibernians at home, piss poor?" Wulfric got down to the practicalities of war very quickly.

"I have never fought them but I suspect we may find out soon."

"It is just that I did not see these men searching the bodies after the fight in the forest. Do they not do that?"

"Some do but the Turmachai does not approve."

"I am sorry, Baron, for I know he is your friend but he is a fool. Men will be more likely to fight for a leader if they can become richer following him."

It was what I had told the Emperor.

We rode out in the same formation we had adopted on the road. The Kentarchos rode next to Basil and we rode behind. We rode swiftly without tiring our horses. We could hear the clamour of battle in the distance. I deduced that it was what I had been taught was called an encounter battle. The advancing barbarian army had come across resilient defenders and both sides were feeding men into the fray. There was little planning. I saw many disparate regiments racing from Serdica. We were one of the few companies who were together.

As we approached the road I saw that below us were three regiments. There were two regiments of Skutatoi and Varangians around the Emperor. To the right of the road was a small knoll. It was little higher than the surrounding land but it afforded a good view. I wondered why the Emperor had deigned to use it. Before I could comment on that to Basil, my impetuous friend had spied some of the Magyar horsemen who were so feared. Riding a small pony and armed with a composite bow they were the annoying insects it was hard to swat. They were making for the Emperor and Basil saw them. He stood in his stirrups and shouted, "We must save the Emperor!" They wheeled into line and galloped towards the advancing horsemen.

John and Leofric began to follow. "Hold! We have no armour and my friend is making a mistake. We ride to the knoll and we examine the terrain."

As we headed towards the knoll I saw that the Magyar horsemen were already pulling back on their bows. They sent a flurry of arrows towards the Varangians. The huge shields of the Emperor's guards easily held them. I saw now why they had done this. The regiment of Skutatoi to the right of the Emperor turned to join the Kataphractoi and chase off these horsemen. It was when I reached the knoll that I saw the cleverness of this King Stephen. He had cleverly made two regiments leave their post. He was drawing off the two units which guarded the right flank of the Emperor and I saw a warband of Thracians, armed with the dreaded rhomphaia, advancing rapidly towards him. He only had his Varangians to guard him. Behind the Thracians, I saw huge blocks of warriors armed with shields and spears advancing behind a cloud of peltasts. The Magyar had done their job well and they raced to the north loosing arrows over their shoulders as the two regiments sought, in vain, to catch them.

The knoll was some one hundred paces behind the Emperor. "Dismount! Leofric, plant my banner here and guard the horses. Dick you and your archers kill any who close with the Emperor. You others follow me. We have to help the Emperor. Wulfric, to my right. John, protect Wulfric's back."

The Thracians were ferociously fast and they charged the right side of the Varangians. They attacked the sword and axe side of the Varangians. I watched as their wicked two handed blades took arms from the Varangians and then decapitated the helpless warriors. We moved quickly down the slope unencumbered by mail. However, I was acutely aware that we only had leather hauberks under our gambeson and surcoats. A rhomphaia would make short work of that. The one advantage we had was that we were but four men and, as such, invisible. Their target was the Emperor standing behind his wall of iron and with his eight staff officers gathered around him. They were on their horses and, as such, made a tempting target for the Thracians. The Varangians had locked shields but those on our side were vulnerable. As we ran I saw that many of the Kataphractoi had fallen to the deadly arrows and the Skutatoi were being assailed by peltasts from the flanks. They could not help the Emperor.

It was Wulfric, to my right, who struck the first blow. The axe he held was longer than a sword; he was the only man I knew who could wield it one handed. He swung it around and it took the head cleanly from the shoulders of a Thracian. The head, complete with a surprised expression, flew into the air and landed amongst the others. Still, the enemy pressed and I saw men such as my father had led being butchered by the wicked curved weapon. They were being overwhelmed by the sheer weight of numbers. Thracians were falling but so were the Emperor's bodyguards.

I had no room to swing for Wulfric was by my side but the men before me had no armour and I stabbed forward with my sword; it was more in hope than expectation for the press was so great I could not see my target. When I felt its edge grate against ribs I twisted and pulled. At the same time, I punched forward at the next man. Roger of Lincoln was doing the same to my left. The Thracians were at a disadvantage. It was their left side we attacked and they had to turn to fight us. When they swung their rhomphaia they hit our shields. The blows were hard and numbed my arm but the curve of the blade matched the curve of the shield and we held. When we countered we killed. Every blow they struck resulted in a dead Thracian and we made inroads.

We were making progress but the Emperor was still in danger. John slashed and stabbed at any who tried to get around Wulfric's right and we hacked our way towards the Emperor. My father had told me of Viking berserkers at Stamford Bridge who had held a whole army. I had never understood such reckless bravery but as I saw the men my father had led; the men who had left their homeland to travel the rivers of the Rus to fight for the Emperor being butchered like slabs of meat I began to become angry. It was as though my father was there being slaughtered. All that I could think of was Wulfstan fighting off Fitzwaller's killers and a red mist descended. I began to stab, lunge, punch, slash and head butt with increasing ferocity. When I saw the last of the Varangians who were before the Emperor fall, leaving only his staff officers for defence, I snapped. Yelling my father's war cry of. "Housecarl!" I threw myself, quite literally, into the heart of the advancing Thracians.

My action took me a little way from my oathsworn and it allowed me to swing a full blade. The rowing had made me stronger and the first Thracian who tried to bring his weapon to bear was torn in two by the force of my blow. I did not wait to see the effect. I pushed his dismembered torso towards his companions and brought my sword over my head. I took the rhomphaia on my shield and my blade severed his shoulder and his arm. I was unaware of anyone else. I was swinging, slashing, punching and stabbing at every half-naked body which I saw before me. I ignored the cries from behind me. I was now committed to a course that took me deeper into the enemy lines. I was dimly aware of arrows thudding into bodies as they tried to get at me. Dick was disobeying my orders; he was now protecting me.

Wulfric's strident and commanding voice brought me to my senses. "Baron! Horses!"

I turned and saw some horse archers thundering towards us. The Thracians were withdrawing and King Stephen was trying to end this skirmish with the death of the Emperor. He was sending in more of the dreaded horse archers. It would be Manzikert all over again. I swung my shield around just in time to take four arrows. Then Wulfric swung his axe and it buried itself in the neck of a pony. The pony threshed and fell pulling Wulfric with it. He would have died for a horseman stood in the stirrups with bow ready to finish off the helpless Wulfric. John screamed and, using a dead body as a springboard leapt into the air and brought his sword down on the shoulder of the archer. They both tumbled to the ground.

I ran and punched the next pony in the jaw. Horses, unless they are trained like Star, will not attack a man and my punch made it veer away. I slashed wildly at the horseman's leg and sliced deeply into it below the knee.

I suddenly heard the Emperor's voice, "Baron! Fall back! I command it!"

When Wulfric and John stood, we backed, with Roger, towards the remnants of the Guard. The horses of the Emperor and the staff officers all lay dead, pierced by arrows and the Varangians lay in concentric rings. It broke my heart to climb over the bodies of the fallen oathsworn. They had fulfilled their oath. We reached the dead and dying staff officers and we all fell back towards the Emperor. Had we turned then it would have cost us our lives. As it was we had to constantly raise our shields to stop arrows and to hack at the fierce warriors who tried to end the Emperor's reign there and then. We reached the knoll where the Emperor waited. Dick and the others sent arrow after arrow into those who tried to ascend. I saw that Leofric had tied the horses to the banner and he too was raining death upon these barbarians. Thankfully, Basil and the remnants of the Kataphractoi were now making their way back to the Emperor along with the survivors of the Skutatoi.

"Emperor, take my horse and ride back to Serdica." He looked at me dumbly. "We can fight our way back to the town. You draw their arrows like a flame draws moths." He nodded, "Wulfric take the men and protect him. I will fight with the Varangians."

"But Baron!"

I pointed to his arm. He had been wounded. "Obey me and watch the boys. They have done well."

It was not bravado nor a wish for glory. Basil and the others would reach us and we would soon be reinforced. It was the Emperor they wanted. If he left then the attack would weaken. That was the theory. I found myself surrounded by the surviving Varangians. There were just eighty of them left. One said as I joined him, "You are a mad bugger! You must have some Saxon blood in you!"

"My father was Ridley."

"Then I see him in you. We will drink and talk when we have swatted these insects." He began banging his shield and chanting, "Ridley! Ridley!" Over and over. I felt goose pimples as they all chanted my father's name. I banged my shield too and joined in the chant.

Suddenly a wedge of warriors came at us. They had spears, shields and helmets. They ran the last few paces. I tried something I had never done before. As the leading warrior punched his spear at me, for I was their target, I dropped to my knee and angled the shield so that his spear slid along the leather. I stabbed upwards into his unprotected body and stood as I did so. The sword came out through his neck and I punched my sword so that his body fell amongst those who were following. Those on either side of me took heart as the wedge was disrupted. There were no spears before me and I punched with my shield. The enemy warriors were so close that I could not swing my sword. I punched with the pommel and it tore into the eye of a warrior who fell screaming. I had room now to swing and I sliced at the neck of a warrior who was pinioned by his fellows and my blade tore through his neck.

Unbelievably we were pushing them down the slight slope. The ground was slick with blood and bodies. The wedge fell apart and then Basil and his men struck. Their Kontoi found unprotected backs and the wedge disintegrated as they fled. We stood panting on that bloody battlefield. There were no words for we had no breath. We had turned the enemy. The Kataphractoi were in no condition to pursue and we pulled slowly back to the city. We had lost the skirmish but we had found glory. And I had upheld the honour of Aelfraed and Ridley.

Chapter 14

We were too weary to talk as we dragged our bloodied and battered bodies back into the city. I smiled when I saw Wulfric and my men waiting for me at the gates. They had obeyed me but only just! Wulfric shook his head although my squires looked relieved to see me alive. "Baron, you make protecting you very hard!"

"I am sorry, Wulfric, but these were my father's men and I could not stand to see them slaughtered so."

"Is your father still alive?" I heard the Varangian behind me speak.

"He was slain by Scottish raiders."

The man who had fought next to me nodded his head, "They were ever the treacherous bastards."

Now that I had my breath back I asked questions of these warriors who had walked into the trap."What happened? How did the Emperor get himself in such a situation?"

"Before I tell you that can you tell your name, Baron, son of Ridley?"

"I am Baron Alfraed of Stockton."

"I have not heard of Stockton. Where is it? I come from Winchester."

"It is on the Tees close to the Palatinate."

"I am Harold Hard Spear and I will tell you how we came to be in such a situation. The Emperor is a good general but he is surrounded by idiots. He wanted to view the road to plan our march north. His Strategoi said just to bring infantry." He spat. "Everyone knows that these barbarians use horse archers and infantry cannot catch them. We were viewing the road when they suddenly came at us. We could not turn for fear of being surrounded and we had to wait. We were relieved when we saw the Kataphractoi and then dismayed when they chased the archers."

His friend who had a nasty cut to his cheek said, "Aye, if you had not come to our aid, small in number though you were, then we would have all been slain and the Emperor too. I am Sven Gold Beard and I am from Trondheim. Your archers saved the Emperor. That is what we need; men who can use a war bow."

We would have spoken longer but an Imperial messenger arrived, "Baron the Emperor commands your presence."

I was still a diplomat and I nodded. "I will see you back at camp, Wulfric, and I daresay we shall meet again Harold and Sven."

"It may not be for some time, Baron, for we have an enemy to defeat first."

"Even though you have such depleted numbers?"

Harold spat again, and this time there was blood in the spit, "We only brought half our number. That was the decision of the Strategoi too! There are fifty still in Miklagård. Farewell. We will tell the others that Ridley's son is a man to follow."

As I walked through the streets, which were thronged with the wounded and the curious, a horse nudged me. I looked up and saw Basil. He had suffered a few cuts but none looked serious. "I made a mistake did I not?"

"You did my friend but it was your first command and perhaps understandable. Do not be impetuous. Weigh up the options you have and choose wisely. Had you stayed near to the Emperor then those Thracians would have been destroyed. As it is the Emperor has lost Guards he cannot replace."

He nodded glumly, "You have been summoned?"

"I have."

"Then I will see you at the camp." With shoulders slumped he forced his way through the crowd.

There were ten Varangians outside the Emperor's headquarters. They smiled and gave a slight bow as I entered. The word had been spread already. Inside I saw a physician tending to the Emperor who had not escaped injury. I was discovering just how good the medical services were. We were lucky to have a priest but here there were many physicians who tended to the wounded close to the battlefield and they saved many more lives than our priests. The Emperor gave a wan smile, "I do not know how you escaped injury, Baron. When you hurled yourself into the midst of those barbarians I expected to see your body in pieces. How do you do it?"

"I have had much practice."

He nodded and waved to a servant who brought me some wine. "Will you not reconsider my offer of employment? You outshone even my Varangians."

"Emperor it is in your power to make a regiment of warriors such as me."

"How?" He waved away the physician and I could see that he was interested.

"I was born here and raised here. I am the son of a Varangian and a Greek. Your Varangians have been siring children for many years. They will make perfect warriors for you. They speak Greek, their father's can teach them skills and they are an endless supply of fresh warriors."

"I will give thought to your words. As for King Henry's request; I am happy to form an alliance but I fail to see how it can be of use to him."

"King Henry would make a good Byzantine, Emperor. He thinks three or four moves ahead. I know not why either but there will be a reason and all it cost him was my time."

"I will have my clerks draw up the papers and they will be ready in the morning. We have some wagons returning to the city with the wounded. Some, I fear, will never fight again. It is a terrible waste. Bring your men too for I would reward them. I saw the effect of just four war bows. I thought, from the effect, that it must be a regiment. I could not believe it when there were just four of them. Do you have many more of them at home?"

"I have less than twenty but they are enough. A good bowman is hard to train. I have to begin training them when they are children. It is an investment."

"Ah, I see now where your suggestion began. I will see you in the morning. I have much planning to do if I am to turn this setback into a success." The Emperor would work long into the night. He and King Henry had much in common.

There was a nervous air in the city that night. The bold attack had stunned the population. There had been no disguising the losses as the wounded had returned to the city. Victorious warriors sing and are full of noise. We had returned silent and without joy. I made my way through the streets to the camp. The fact that I rode Caesar again made my life a little easier. The crowds parted at our approach. The camp too showed the change in circumstance. The sentries were more alert and questioned me closely. I did not mind; we would be safer that way.

Leofric took Caesar away and my men made way for me at the fire. John found me a bowl of food. It appeared to be a stew of some description. Thankfully the darkness hid the colour and the content. Sometimes it was best not to know what you ate and just fill the void.

As my squires pulled off my surcoat Wulfric tut-tutted. "Look at that leather hauberk, Baron. The blades almost cut through it. The surcoat is ruined but I have never seen hide suffer so."

"Then it is as well that we have no more fighting. We soon go home."

When I had eaten Dick said, "I have spoken with some of the Greeks. They thought they would have an easy victory today."

"They are new to the battlefield, Dick; they will learn."

"The battlefield is an unforgiving teacher, Baron, and those horse archers are good."

That interested me for Dick rarely had time for any other weapon than the war bow. "You think their weapon is a good one?"

He was wary. "It is effective and they are skilled. I watched them turn in the saddle and release when their ponies were galloping. Our bows would have a longer range but they move so quickly that it would be harder to hit them."

"Then how would you fight against them?"

He looked into the fire and then threw a small log into the inferno. "I would use archers behind long shields planted in the ground. Their ponies could not breach the shields and the longer range of our war bow would rain death." He nodded, "And you would need many arrows."

"How is your supply?"

"We will go to the field tomorrow and see what we can salvage. Some of the enemy arrows may do."

Wulfric asked, "We fight again then, Baron?"

"I do not know. We go back to the city tomorrow but we still have a long voyage home. We were lucky when we came here but I am not certain that we can guarantee an incident-free voyage."

He chewed on something and then spat a piece of gristle into the fire. "Those Varangians are hard men, Baron. I have fought alongside others who would have broken when taking such losses. They would make good men at arms."

"I know but they choose to come here and serve the Emperor. They are richly rewarded for doing so."

Roger of Lincoln said, "And they earn every penny, Baron."

Dick and his archers left after dawn to search the battlefield. We ate. When they returned they had full quivers and more but their faces were grim. "The wolves and the scavengers have been at the bodies, Baron. None were buried and we saw not a single body which was whole." Dick shivered. "At least we bury our dead."

Wulfric snorted, "Normally we win, Dick and have the luxury of time. We were whipped yesterday. Had the Baron not launched that attack then Serdica might now belong to the enemy. We have become too used to victory. I for one am glad we came here for we now see the other side of war."

He was right. As the men packed our belongings onto our horses I sought out Basil. "I am to see the Emperor and then we go back to Constantinople with the wounded. I fear I shall not see you again."

He clasped my arm, Roman style. "I am pleased that I have seen you again. I have lost touch with all my other friends from childhood. I now value you as my closest friend and yet we will be divided by a continent. It is strange that you travelled around the world to see me. You have taught me much."

"And I, too, have learned. If you should ever find yourself in the land of the Franks then come and visit with me."

"I doubt that I shall survive this campaign. War is neither as easy nor as glorious as I expected."

It was like looking in a mirror of time. This had been me when I had left for Normandy and England. "You are alive and you have learned. You will be a better leader now. You have good men and they will follow you for you do not lack courage." I smiled, "Perhaps you are less naïve now."

"Perhaps." He went into his tent and returned with a torn piece of parchment and a wax candle. He dripped some of the wax on the parchment and sealed it with his ring. "Here, take this to my home. There is just my mother there now and we have many rooms. If she is not there, she sometimes spends summer in the mountains, then show this to my steward. You and your men will be more comfortable there when you are in the city." He handed me the parchment. "It is little enough that I can do. Besides my mother will enjoy speaking with you. She always liked you. She said you were the only one of my friends who was polite and she was a good friend to your mother."

We embraced and I left. That was the last I either saw or heard of my friend. I like to think that he survived and succeeded but there were dark days ahead for the Byzantine Empire.

There was more order in the city as we made our way through to the headquarters of the Emperor. His guards, other than the Varangians, were more in evidence. We learned later that more reinforcements had arrived during the night. The Emperor did not receive us in his chambers, instead, he came out to greet us. His Strategoi stood behind him along with slaves. The Varangians formed a square to keep the crowds away. As soon as he spoke I knew that this meeting served two purposes. Firstly it rewarded us but secondly it was a piece of rhetoric to inspire his people. He wanted them to see the defeat as a victory. A slave brought out a trunk and Emperor John Komnenos stood upon it.

"Baron Alfraed of Stockton, yesterday you helped to throw back the Magyar barbarians and save the life of the Emperor. For that we thank you. You have brought us a new ally, King Henry of England and Normandy. You have shown that we have many friends in the west. For that we thank you. And, finally, you have shown us that with a handful of men who fight with passion we can defeat these wild barbarians. For that we thank you."

He waved his arm and a slave came with a document in a document case. "Here is the treaty for your king." The slave handed it to me. A second-handed me a smaller document. "This is an Imperial pass. You shall travel freely in my land." He then made a larger gesture and eight slaves came towards me and my men. They carried small chests and caskets. "This is a small token of our esteem. It is little enough. It is the treasure taken from our dead enemies. It is yours." We were each handed a chest. Mine was the largest.

"I have one more duty for you and your fine warriors who espouse all the values of Caesar's legions. I would have you escort the heroes who are wounded back to our city. With you watching over them I know that they will be safe. In the Empire, we look after our heroes!"

Almost as though prompted all of the guards began banging their shields and chanting, "Emperor!" I caught the Emperor's eye and saw into his mind. He was genuinely grateful to us but was using it to his advantage.

I bowed, "Thank you, Emperor. I know that your men are great warriors and you will drive these invaders from your land."

The Emperor descended and returned to his chambers. A young officer took my arm. "If you will come with me, Baron I will take you to the men."

There were just six huge wagons drawn by oxen. Inwardly I groaned. It would be a slower journey south than it had been north. They were driven by armed servants. Beneath the canvas awning, each wagon contained ten men. Three of the wagons contained Varangians.

The young officer pointed to a smaller wagon with a team of two horses. "That is the wagon for your use. The Emperor has filled it with other rewards for your heroism. Farewell."

We wasted no time. We put our chests in the wagon along with our spare clothes, weapons and the banner. "Leofric, you sit on the wagon with the driver. You can watch our treasure. Tie your horse to the rear. Come. Let us return home. We have many leagues to travel."

I had Dick and my archers ahead of us as we headed south. Wulfric and Roger brought up the rear leaving John and me to lead our wagons back to the city. We moved steadily although not swiftly for the oxen were not capable of speed. For that reason, we travelled so long as there was light. The drivers were unhappy for they wanted us to spend the night in the mansio. A few clouts from Wulfric changed their mind. Our charges were happy at the progress.

That first night, as we ate around the campfire, we spoke with some of the Varangians. They were keen to know how Athelstan and the others had adjusted to a life of peace. As the most senior of them, Erre the Saxon told us, "Our service to the Emperor is over. We have been wounded and to serve in the Guard you have to be fully fit. Some of us will become bodyguards for fat merchants and others will become mercenaries. What your father and his oathsworn did is unique."

And so, each night, I told them of our journey home. Wulfric and the others then added their tales of the lives they lived in England. We also learned much about them. All had travelled down the rivers from the land of the Rus. Their backgrounds were all different. Some had been those fleeing a Norman world, as my father had done. There were few, now, of them. Others had come from the land of the Rus and the Norse for a better life. Despite their present predicament none regretted their choice. Over the next ten days, we got to know them well.

We examined the wagon for the other gifts mentioned by the Emperor. There were fine swords and spears, some helmets and two suits of mail armour. He showed his gratitude more generously than King Henry, that was certain.

As we neared the massive Theodosian walls Erre the Saxon waved me over. "Baron, me and some of the men would like to ask a boon of you."

"If it is in my power then I will do so."

"Some of us wish to travel to England. If we worked our passage could we beg a berth on your ship?"

"You need not work. I would be honoured to take you back but we do not travel as soon as we get to Miklagård. I have a few days of business to conduct."

"That suits us, Baron, for we have loose ends to tie up too."

I knew that many of them had liaisons in the city and some even had offspring. I suspected that the ones who wished to return to England would be the ones without children. "Then we will meet any who wish to return with us at my ship in the Langa Harbour three days from now."

The smiles and relief on their faces were as welcome as the Emperor's gold. The wagons stopped at the palace. We unloaded the wagons but kept our treasure cart. The ones who did not seek a passage insisted upon clasping our arms. We had been bonded in battle and it was a sad farewell.

We headed for the harbour. The gifts from the Emperor would be safer on board our ship and Dai could arrange them to make the ship sail more efficiently. The chests we would take to the Forum and exchange them for coins. They would be easier to transport. I noticed it was riding a little lower in the water. Dai had been busy. He had loaded the aft hold. He had a frown when he greeted us. "I am glad you have returned Baron; I have serious news. The Normans are stopping Imperial ships between Sicily and Africa. The trade from the west has almost dried up. It is said it is part of the Duke's plans to become king. Our journey back looks likely to be more dangerous than the one here."

He pointed to his ship. "I paid some of the local boys to dive beneath my ship and scrape the hull. We will travel a little faster home."

"I see that you have loaded a cargo." There were half cut logs laid above what looked like amphorae.

"Aye, I bought amphora of oil and spices as well as some cedar wood logs. They will all fetch a high price in England and Normandy. One man's misfortune can make a fortune for another. If the trade has dried up then the prices will rise."

"We have more men to take home and these chests." I pointed to the cart. First, we will exchange them for gold coins and then bring them back. I told my new men to meet us here in three days. Can you be ready to sail by then?"

"That suits. I will have my cargo shifted to the stern to allow more room for your men. The extra numbers give me comfort. Will you be staying aboard?"

"No, I have business in the city. How about you and the rest of the men, Wulfric?"

"If it is all the same to you, Baron, we would like to explore this fabled city and spend some of our gold."

"That is fine. John and Leofric do you wish to stay with Wulfric or accompany me?"

John looked at Wulfric and grinned. "I think I will stay with Wulfric, Baron, if it does not offend."

"It does not. Leofric?"

"I will stay with you."

"Good. We will go to the Forum of Theodosius with the cart. There are those there who will buy our treasure from us. Gold and silver coins will be easier to transport."

I left my leather hauberk, gambeson and shield on the ship. I would not need those. When we reached the market I think that our appearance intimidated the traders for they gave us an incredibly good price for our treasure and we all left with much gold and silver.

"I will take the cart back to the palace and then seek the house of my friend." I pointed to the forums. "If you wish to buy goods to sell at home then the markets are there but do not pay the first price. Haggle. They will expect it." They nodded, "And Wulfric…"

"Yes, Baron?"

"Look after the men."

He grinned, "I will be as their mother!"

John mumbled, "Just so long as you do not kiss me goodnight!"

After we had left the cart and horses at the palace we made our way towards the gate of Eugenius. Basil's family had a huge house that overlooked the Bosporus. Basil's father had been a successful general who had started a business importing and exporting spices. He used his military contacts and was soon the richest man in Constantinople. He had died from eating bad oysters but his business, according to his son, was still successful. His mother, Sophia, had a sound business mind herself. She was descended from one of Constantine's daughters and was as close to royalty as one could get. She was a fine lady.

I did not have the opportunity to knock on the huge and impressive door for it was opened by a butler. "I am a friend of Turmachai Basil here to visit with his mother."

He frowned both at my appearance and my smell. The baths in Serdica were a long time ago. I think he was about to turn us away as beggars when Basil's mother appeared, "Is that Alfraedus son of Ridley? It is! Come in! Cassius, go and prepare two guest rooms." She threw her arms around me and hugged me. "Basil is not here."

"I know I went with him to Serdica." Her face fell for despatch riders had brought news of the battle to the city already. "Do not worry, domina, he is safe. A few cuts and bruises but nothing worse than we suffered playing as children."

She saw Leofric, "And who is this? Your son?"

"This is Leofric, my squire. I am a Baron now and serve King Henry of England. Leofric does not speak Greek."

She smiled at him and I nodded to him. He stuttered, "I am pleased to meet you." The Greek was awful but she threw her arms around him and hugged him too.

"First you must bathe. When Basil's father returned from wars he always smelled of horses and blood." Cassius had returned, "Take our guests to the bathhouse." She beamed at me. "This is a joyful reunion Alfraedus. How long can you stay?"

"I must sail for England in three days."

"Then I have three days of pleasure ahead of me."

The slaves were experts and we were bathed, shaved and cleaned as well as I could ever remember. When we were being dried Cassius came in with expensive tunics. "Domina asked you to wear these. She will have your old clothes cleaned." His tone of voice suggested that he would have had them destroyed rather than cleaned.

Leofric's eyes lit up when he felt the fine fabric. "Baron, this is too good for me to wear."

I smiled, "You will offend the lady of the house if you do not. When you speak to her use the title domina."

He nodded, "I am sorry that my language is so poor."

"You do more than well enough. Do not be embarrassed. This is a fine lady and I know she likes you."

The meal was a delight although there were more courses than I had had since I had left this fabulous city. The food was brought in a steady stream and we were never over faced. I spent the first part telling of my adventures and my father's death. She asked about Leofric for she was fascinated by his colouring and complexion. Finally, she asked me about the campaign in the north. I was as circumspect as possible but eventually, she said, "Do not try to spare my feelings, Alfraedus. I was the wife of a soldier for many years. Tell me honestly how my son did."

"He is brave and he is a good leader but he is too reckless. I think he may have learned his lesson for many of his men died in one of his charges."

"His father was ever the same but you, I think you are like your father. You are a thinker and yet you do not lack courage do you?" I shrugged. "False modesty does not become you. Your King Henry would not have entrusted this mission of yours to a fool."

"You may be right but it takes me away from my family."

"People like us have a responsibility to others. We cannot think of ourselves. Tell me about your family."

That was easier ground and I spoke of Adela and my children. I could see, in her eyes, that she ached for grandchildren. That would depend upon the gods of war.

"It is late and I know you will be tired. What are your plans?"

"I need to buy some presents for my wife but first I have to visit my father's old house."

"Ah yes. He gave it to his freedman, Atticus did he not?"

"He did but one of my father's men told me that he had hidden something there and I feel honour bound to collect it."

"Good. Then do that in the morning and in the afternoon we shall find some fine things for your family." She stood and came and hugged me. "I thank God that you have come, Alfraedus son of Ridley, for you have made me feel young again and made a lonely old woman feel needed once more."

The next morning I rose early, for having put this task off for a long time I was keen to finish this quest. We hurried north through the city towards the fort of Petrion which was close to my father's home. Although smaller than Sophia's it was still substantial and the gift of the house to a freedman was a generous act. I felt a lump come into my throat as we approached for this was where I had grown up and was where my mother was buried. It still appeared to be well looked after and cared for. I hoped that Atticus had not sold it. If he had done so then it would make my task harder.

When the door opened I saw Atticus and he had aged. He looked ancient but his blue eyes still sparkled. "Master Alfraedus! You have returned!" To my embarrassment and consternation, he burst into tears.

I hurried us in. "It is good to see you, Atticus."

"Come, Master Alfraedus, and your servant. Come to the garden. I will get some iced lemon."

He led me to the enclosed garden and we sat on the cedar seat my father had made for him to sit on. Atticus went away to get the drinks and I stared at the lemon tree. I could not see any sign that the ground was disturbed. Perhaps Athelstan had been mistaken. He was old after all. Atticus returned. He was ever the servant but he had been a loyal steward for my father and deserved the reward of the house

As we drank the sweetened iced lemon drink I told him of our adventures and my father's death. He welled up at that point and then asked about the others. I told him all. Even as I told him I knew it sounded as though the deaths had made me leave England.

"Have you come then, Master Alfraedus, to claim your home?"

I laughed, "Of course not! My father gave you this and besides, I live many leagues in the cold north. This is a fleeting visit only." I stood and walked over to the tree. "I was told that, beneath that tree, my father's favourite, was buried an urn."

I surprised Atticus, I could see that. "He never told me."

"I think he told no one. He only confided in Athelstan when he was dying. Could we dig and see if there is an urn?"

"Of course." He went and fetched a spade.

He was about to start digging when I stopped him. "Young Leofric has a strong back and he can dig. Sit with me and we will watch."

I gave the spade to Leofric who set to with a will. He had cleared quite a space and I felt sure that there was nothing when there was a clunk as the spade struck something. I could watch no longer and I joined Leofric and we cleared the spoil from around the urn, which was soon visible, with our hands.

"That is a surprise, Master Alfraedus. I have lived here all these years and I never knew." He suddenly stood. "I will return soon." He hurried indoors.

I was too distracted with the urn to wonder where he had gone and we carefully pulled it out. It had survived remarkably intact. The top was sealed with wax and I took out my knife and ran it around the edge to break the seal. I levered off the cork stopper and a musty smell struck me. Reaching into its depths I felt around and found a piece of cloth which I pulled out. Very carefully I unwrapped it and saw, sparkling in the morning sunlight, a beautifully cut blue stone. It was as Athelstan had described it, the pommel stone from Harold Godwinson's sword. What did this mean?

I held it in my hand and felt a shiver run down my spine.

Atticus returned and he, too, held something in his hand. "My lord, after you and your father left I was cleaning out the rooms and I found this lodged and hidden beneath a chest. I would have sent it after your father but I knew not where he would be. I had forgotten it until you found the urn." He opened his hand and I saw a golden wolf with two blue eyes. It was half the size of the freedman's hand. The stones were the same as the pommel stone but were much smaller. There was a loop that showed that it could be worn around the neck. I had seen similar tokens around the necks of the Varangian Guard but they were normally Thor's hammer. He handed it to me. Once again I felt a thrill as I touched the metal. I looked up at Atticus. "What does this mean?"

"I know not, sir. I had never seen it but the place I found it was where your father kept his old clothes from the time he had first come to the city."

I now had a mystery to solve but I knew that I had been meant to come here. The punishment I had received was nothing of the kind. The Norns my father had mentioned wanted me to come to Miklagård and to claim my inheritance. They wanted me to possess these two treasures. I knew not why …yet.

"Have you a leather thong, Atticus?"

He scurried away and returned quickly with one. I threaded the token onto it and tied it around my neck. The blue stone of the eyes and the pommel, I noticed, was the same blue as the blue of the surcoat. It was almost unnatural. Leofric dropped to one knee, "Baron, this is a sign."

"I know."

"But what does it mean?"

"I have no idea at all and perhaps we will never discover the reason. It may have died with my father but these two objects will change my life. Of that I am certain."

Part 4 Odyssey
Chapter 15

Sophia was true to her word. She found me the most wonderful presents to take back. There were dresses for Adela and cunningly made toys for the children. She insisted on buying some bowls and dishes for our home which she had carefully packed in straw and sent to the ship. Through her contacts in the market, we took back sacks of spices at ridiculously low prices as well as cases of lemons and oranges. We also managed to buy two bolts of fine blue cloth that I would be able to use for my surcoats. It came from the east and its journey was in the weave of the fabric for it smelled of spices and the east. All of the goods were packed in chests that were watertight. Sophia had a good head for business and she knew the vagaries of the sea. As she said to me, "What is the point of paying a high price for goods and then allowing them to deteriorate when you transport them."

When I tried to pay for the goods she had acquired for us she chastised me, "What else have I to spend my money on? Your mother and I were friends and she was taken by the Lord far too early. My son is away and I want to indulge you." She had laughed, "I am enjoying this. Your children whom I will never see may be the grandchildren I will never have. I am a young woman once more."

All too soon it was time to go. It was sad for all of us. Leofric had grown more than fond of the generous lady and I knew that she had enjoyed the laughter and the company. The house would be emptier when we left. Her final gift to us both were two suits of lamellar armour. Leofric's had been Basil's when he was younger but mine was the armour of a strategos. It was her husband's. "Basil has one suit but you shall have this. I have heard that the seas are now dangerous. Protect yourself. If I do not see you again remember that I think of you each night, along with my son and your name is sent to God with my prayers. If I am not meant to stay in this world then I will watch over you and Basil from heaven."

I left with a heavy heart and I heard Leofric sniffing back the emotion he felt. We said not a word on the way back to the ship and Dai. We would be returning home but I was sadder now than the first time I had left.

The ten Varangians who had been wounded and were returning to England with us were already at the ship when I arrived. I got to know them on the voyage but at that moment in time, I was distracted and wanted to be alone. "Whenever you are ready, Dai, we can set sail."

All of our presents and purchases were in the hold but I had the pommel stone in a leather pouch around my neck along with the wolf token. They made me feel better; it was as though I had a link to my father. He had left the stone for a purpose. I could not divine the thinking behind it. As we headed out to sea I stood, alone, by the bow castle. Meeting Basil had also been unexpected. In my three days in the city, I had not met any of my other old friends. Had I been meant to see him? Was he what I would have been if I had not left the city? A sudden gust of wind brought the smell of the city to my nose and I knew that was it. I had not been ready to receive the pommel. I had had to prove myself. I was now ready to use it. The question remained; for what?

I turned, suddenly, and saw my men below me, peering over the side for their last look at Miklagård. All of them had a connection to the stone. The Varangians had left England for the Saxon King, Harold was dead. The Normans had driven Dick and his folk to become outlaws. Wulfric and Roger dressed as Normans but in their hearts they were Saxon, they were English. The stone bound them all for none of us were Normans. We were English.

I took out my sword and looked at it. I would have Alf set the stone in the pommel. The stone needed a home and my sword was as good as any. I would make my father and his dead comrades proud of me. My life's mission, now, would be to be true to my roots. I would do what was best for my people. I slid the blade into the scabbard and descended to the hold. I wanted to be amongst my men. I stood just to one side of them so that I could hear the banter and see the faces.

Erre the Saxon was the leader, that was obvious. He now limped although not badly. As a Varangian, he failed the test of perfection which they applied. Wulfric could teach him to ride. He would have a purpose. All ten of them wished to fight. I had knights who could make good use of their skills as men at arms. During this long voyage in late summer, I would find out more about them. I knew from both my father and Wulfstan that not all who served in the Guard were men who could be trusted. Our journey home would be an odyssey and a test of their ability and character.

To look at all of them now it was hard to see the Housecarls of Harold. The Varangians were more refined. Underneath they were the same but outwardly they were different. None looked like the rough Saxon warriors who were their heritage. All wore the flowing clothes they had purchased in Miklagård. It was cooler. They would change, no doubt, once we passed the Pillars of Hercules but for the moment they all looked almost civilised with trimmed beards and hair. They all smelled of the baths for all had partaken. It was the sailors who smelled as pungently as we would have once done.

All of my men had spent their coin wisely. I had chosen my best men. They had bought fine weapons, clothes and goods to sell in England. The hold was now full. Half contained the cargo of the captain and our precious chests whilst the other half was our home. We had yet to rig the canvas awning. Once we left Byzantine waters then we would become a ship of war once more.

Three days out of the city we rigged the awning and I had Leofric sharpen my sword. He had become closer to me since our stay at Sophia's. The experience had given him a yearning for finer things and, I think, a home. I was watching him when Erre the Saxon approached me, "Baron, I have been speaking with Wulfric." I nodded. "He tells me that there is a place for such as us in the conroi of knights. Is that true or was he making fun of us and giving us hope where there is none."

"You should know that Wulfric is never foresworn. He speaks the truth." He nodded. "Have you not had enough of fighting?"

"Most of us are younger than Wulfric. If we had not been wounded then we would be in the Guard still." He smiled. "It was a good living."

"I know. How much did you receive, thirty nomismata a month?"

He shook his head. "That was in the time of your father. We were paid thirty-five nomismata a month."

"You know you will not earn as much as that in England."

"From what Wulfric told us there is more opportunity to earn money after battles."

"That is right. If you are successful then there is plunder." I saw him hesitate before speaking. "What you should know about me, Erre the Saxon is that I like openness and honesty. Ask what you will. There is no question which will offend me."

"That is what we heard. We would serve you, Baron. It seems that this is *wyrd*, it was meant to be."

There was that word which I only ever heard from men such as this. "And I will say this; when we reach Normandy, for we call there first, if you still wish to serve with me then I will take you to my banner. I would not have you make a rash decision. The journey will be long and, I daresay, will not be free from conflict. This is a small boat. I would not have you swear and then regret that oath."

He nodded, "You are like your father, Baron and we will abide by your request although it would take a Kraken or a dragon to dissuade us."

I nodded and then smiled, "Of course you know you would have to learn to ride and fight from the back of a horse."

He laughed, "If giants like Wulfric and John can do that then it must be possible."

We headed south after we had left the islands of Greece and the Aegean. Leofric sat, in the bow castle, looking at the standard. He looked up as I approached, "Baron, your livery and your standard..."

"What of it?"

"There is something missing." He pointed to the blue. "The blue is right. It is the same blue as the stone and it is meant to be but Lord Fitzwaller had a standard which was almost the same." He pointed to the two stars. "He had stars similar to this. You need something which marks you, Baron, and tells people who you are." He suddenly looked down. "I am sorry, Baron, if I have caused offence."

"You have not and you are right. Carry on."

"I had thought...," he shyly pulled out a piece of cloth from his tunic, "I have made this from one of the surcoats of the dead Kataphractoi." He shrugged, "It was such fine material that I did not want it to go to waste. The Turmachai said I could have it." He held out a rearing wolf.

I took it from his hand. The Kataphractoi had worn red surcoats. Leofric had made this one as large as Wulfric's two hands. The edges were neatly stitched too. "This is fine work. What did you have in mind?"

He spread the banner and placed the wolf so that it was below the two stars, one yellow and one red. "It looks to me like the wolf is you and the stars are your father and Wulfstan watching down on you."

I felt a shiver down my spine as though the spirits of the dead were speaking with me. "I like it. Make it so."

He grinned and took out some thread and a bone needle. He had nimble hands and he set to. I descended, feeling happier and walked to the steering board and Dai. He had a frown that contrasted with Leofric's joy.

"What worries you Welshman?"

"We have had an easy voyage up until now but soon," he pointed west, "we have to pass to the south of Sicily. Do we sail close to that island where Normans await us or risk the coast of Africa and the pirates?"

"Where is there more danger?"

"Even with the extra men, we cannot out row the Africans. They have huge crews and are fearless. We have more chance of escaping a Sicilian vessel for it would be more like this one."

"Then you have an easy decision to make."

"Except that they will be waiting for us."

"If you sail the ship then I will direct your course and use my mind to outwit these Normans." He nodded, seemingly satisfied. I turned and called, "Wulfric, gather the men around."

Curious they soon sat around me in a circle. "The captain tells me that soon we might be attacked by Normans from Sicily. I intend to flee but it is likely that we will have to fight. From now on we wear gambeson and, those who have them, leather hauberks."

Erre said, "But, Baron, we have mail."

"As I have now but we are at sea. If you fall overboard in mail then you will die. Obey me in this and we all have a chance of survival. John and Leofric you will be with Dick and the archers in the bow castle if we are attacked. Your five war bows may be the difference between success and failure. The rest of us fight as a wedge. Erre, you organise the new warriors to fight behind Wulfric and Roger." He looked a little aggrieved, "I know my warriors and we fight as one. You understand?" He nodded. "Then let us prepare for war and pray for peace."

It was when John was checking the leather straps on my shield that I realised Leofric's idea would incur an expense for me. Every shield would need repainting and every surcoat would require a wolf stitching on to it. It would be worth it. When Leofric finished the standard he brought it to me and held it out so that I could see it. One of the Norse Varangians, Olaf Leather-Neck suddenly put his hand to his throat. He grasped something beneath his tunic and closed his eyes to invoke protection.

Erre asked, "What is the matter with you, Olaf? You look like you have seen a ghost."

In answer, he took out the token he wore around his neck. It was a crude version, made of base metal, of my wolf. "I am descended from Ulfheonar. My ancestors were wolf warriors. It is a sign."

Even Wulfric could not help touching his crucifix. Leofric said, "Show them, Baron. It is time."

Hitherto I had kept the two treasures hidden. I took the wolf on the thong and showed them. Olaf nodded and said, "*Wyrd*!" He dropped to his knees. "I know that Erre the Saxon said we were to wait until the voyage was over but this is a sign. I am your oathsworn whether you will have me or no. I have sought the wolf all of my life and it is here now before me."

I nodded and, after replacing the wolf took out the blue pommel stone, "And Wulfric, you and the others should know that this was left for me by my father. I retrieved it in Miklagård. It is the pommel stone of the sword of Earl Harold Godwinson, the last Saxon King of England."

Wulfric nodded, "Olaf Leather-Neck is right, Baron. This is a sign. It seems we have not only journeyed across an ocean, but we have also travelled in time. We have entered the realm of magic and I know not whether to be cheered or to be terrified."

Erre the Saxon said, "It was meant to be, Wulfric. We met in blood and we shall end in blood. You know you cannot fight fate."

Wulfric nodded, "Aye, that is certain."

There was a purpose to each day as we began to learn how to work together. It did not take the Varangians long to adjust to our formation. Erre took the position to the right and behind Wulfric. Olaf stood behind me. When fighting on land he would be guarding John and my banner. The rest accepted those positions as merited. The Varangians had brought a variety of weapons with them. As Imperial Guards, they had been well equipped. They each had a spear and a sword. Some of them had an axe. Wulfric had picked up four rhomphaia. He had no idea how to use them but felt certain that, as he put it, "If half-arsed barbarians could use them then we could certainly learn."

I had thought we had evaded the Normans until one of the crew shouted, "Sail to the north!"

I climbed the ladder to the logs above the amphorae. There were two ships heading towards us. "Will they catch us, Dai?"

"Aye, they have the weather gauge. Even with the oars out then they would catch us."

"Then head towards the northwest."

"But that will fetch us closer to them."

"I know but trust me. This is still King Henry's ship."

"Aye, Baron!"

"Leofric and John, light a fire in the brazier. Dick make six fire arrows. Roger and Wulfric bring me four of the small amphorae of oil I was taking home. The rest of you prepare for war!"

The ship heeled a little as Dai took us northwest. It had two effects: it slowed us down, making us a more stable platform for archery and it brought us on a converging path with the two Sicilian vessels. They were too far away to see their flags but I knew them for what they were.

Leofric and John were still getting the fire going safely and the others surrounded me. I explained what I intended. Wulfric and my original men were not surprised but I saw the Varangians were impressed with my plan. "It may not work but this way we have a fighting chance. I believe we can take the crew of one but two would overwhelm us. Dick, you and the archers get to the sterncastle. Wulfric you and John have the strongest arms. When I give the command then hurl the amphorae at the mainmast of the other ship. We will be close when I give the command so Roger you must protect Wulfric and Erre protect John." The brazier was going. "Leofric you take your shield and guard Dai with your life. If he falls then we are doomed." He scurried off. "As soon as the arrows have been launched then douse the fire. I would not set fire to our own ship." Roger took a bucket and drew a pail of seawater. He placed them next to the small brazier. "Now get to your places. The main mast is our keep!"

In the time it had taken for us to prepare the two ships had closed to within a hundred paces. They had separated so that they could approach us from each side and that suited me. I now saw the standard on the nearest ship; it was John of Palermo. I went to the steering board and, cupping my hands shouted, "Why do you attack a peaceful trader?"

I heard John of Palermo's voice across the waves. "You are wanted for crimes in Syracuse. I am here to take you back to enjoy the Duke's judgement."

I said, quietly to Dai, "Take us slightly closer to him."

"Baron!"

"Do not worry. I know what I am about." To the Sicilian, I shouted, "I do not trust treacherous Sicilians. I will refuse your offer of hospitality and the dubious judgement of your Duke."

In answer, a flurry of crossbow bolts flew across the water. It was a waste of bolts for half of them did not make it and the other half thudded harmlessly into the side of the ship. I looked to the waist of the ship and saw my two oil throwers ready to throw. Their protectors had their shields ready. John of Palermo's ship drew closer and closer. I saw two Sicilians swinging their hooks around in the air. They would grapple our ship and draw it next to theirs where they would overwhelm us. If I had given the command then Dick and Griff could have killed them. I wanted them to close with us. Now that the range was closer their bolts began to strike shields. The motion of their ship was such that there was none of the usual accuracy you expected from crossbows. One of Dai's sailors was struck in the arm but he carried on working.

When they were twenty paces from us they threw their ropes. The one aimed at the bow fell short but the other smashed across the topmost strake, bit into the wood and the Sicilians began to haul their ship closer. Half of the men were pulling on the rope which suited me too.

"Ready to throw?"

"Aye Baron, give the word!"

I felt the thud as a crossbow struck my shield. I saw John of Palermo pat the crossbowman on the back. This was personal for the Sicilian. Dick and the archers were hiding behind the mainmast close by the brazier. The Sicilian ship's stern was less than three paces from ours and the mainmast just five when I shouted, "Now!"

Wulfric's first throw was too high and it struck the top of the mainmast where the cross mast met it. It shattered and showered the men below with broken pot. John was more accurate and his two amphorae were thrown in quick succession striking the bottom of the mast. The ships were less than three paces apart. Wulfric was angry with himself and he threw the amphorae so hard that it struck John of Palermo on the side of the head, knocking him down and showering him in oil.

"Now Dick! Leofric sever the rope!"

Three flaming arrows flew straight and true. I heard the thud as Leofric's sword sliced through the rope and the Sicilian's stern began to drift away. Flames leapt up the bone dry canvas and ignited the sides of the ship. The next three arrows flew and one of them struck John of Palermo who had stood. The fire arrow did not penetrate his mail but it made him a human fireball. He ran screaming towards the stern and within a few moments, the whole ship was ablaze. I heard the hiss from behind me as the brazier was doused.

"Dick, get to the sterncastle and, well done." I looked to the other side and saw that the second Sicilian had altered course. "Dai head further north." He shook his head but obeyed. The move slowed us down and the second ship was closing. However, the doomed fire ship was being pushed behind us. I watched as it began to sink slowly in the water. The captain of the second ship had a choice, he could steer to the right of the doomed ship but that would slow him down even more or he could steer to the left and move further away from us. He chose the longer route.

"Wulfric get the oars out. We need to do some work!"

"Aye my lord."

I joined my men at the oars. There were eighteen of us and six oars. It took a few strokes to help the new men adjust but soon we were flying through the water. I did not intend to do this for long but I wanted sea room between us and our pursuer. From my rowing position, I could see Dai. He kept glancing astern. When he began to smile I knew we had outrun our enemy. He shouted, "We have lost him, Baron, he has gone about."

"Stop rowing!" They all began to cheer. "Captain, take us further south, away from Sicily. I think we have used up all of our luck now!"

We all drank deeply from the barrel of beer that we had brought from Miklagård. I saw Wulfric take a coin from Erre. I cocked my head to the side and asked, "What was that about?"

Wulfric grinned, "I bet him we would not only defeat them we would not suffer any losses. He did not believe me."

"I wondered why he gave me such generous odds!" I laughed. It was a sign that my men were bonding.

It is said that the Gods of old liked to play with men. Ulysses had suffered just so when on his own Odyssey. The lookout in the bow castle shouted, "Sail to the north-west!"

He pointed and I saw the Sicilian ship making towards us. He had come from a low bank of cloud and was less than a mile away. I hurried to the steering board. "What are our options Captain?"

He looked up at the pennant. "The wind favours him a little over us." He pointed astern. "The other ship still shadows us. Our lookout spies his masthead when the waves are right." He gestured with his head. "We could outrun him if we headed south."

"And in doing so we would put ourselves within the grasp of the men from Africa."

"You have it in one. They would swarm all over us and destroy us no matter how good your men are."

"Thank you, Captain, then I can see that we have but one choice: we race to fight this one Sicilian and then head west and north as fast as the winds will carry us."

Dai pointed to the skies. The low cloud from which the Sicilian had emerged was not the only one. A storm was brewing. "Soon we will be fighting Mother Nature as well as the Sicilians."

"Do the best you can."

"I am sorry about your oil, Baron. Those four amphorae would have cost a pretty penny."

"What price a man's life? How is your sailor?"

"He will live and he can help me with the steering board. If we have a storm then he will be needed here."

"Get your weapons. Dick, have the archers in the bow castle. John and Leofric take your bows to the sterncastle. You two must aim for the steersman. Wulfric, we will gather around the mainmast again,"

As I approached them I heard them all laughing. We were about to go into battle and they were laughing. "What is funny Wulfric?"

"I just asked Erre here if he wished to take another bet and he said he would rather bet with the devil. At least he would stand a chance with him."

The Sicilian was making directly for us. I saw that he would meet us with his bow. This was a canny captain. It minimised the damage we could inflict on his crew. If we turned south then we would fly into danger. We had to maintain our course no matter how perilous. I drew my sword and hung my shield from my shoulder. I would not hold it unless I had to. I could use two hands with my sword. I saw that Wulfric had his shield similarly placed but in his left hand, he held a rhomphaia. He saw my look and shrugged, "I thought I would give it a try. I doubt the men on that ship will have seen one. Perhaps I can confuse them."

There was an air of optimism amongst all of the warriors who fought with me that day. I remembered that John of Palermo had worn mail before he had been sent to a fiery death. If these wore mail too then they might have an advantage. I would have to use my quick hands and feet if I was to win. The deck was not pitching too badly. If this were in the deep sea then we would struggle to keep our feet let alone fight. Perhaps that was why pirates used this sea for their trade.

Unless they rammed us, the Sicilian ship would have to turn. I could not see him ramming us for he would risk too much damage to his own vessel. When he turned, we would have one chance to slay his steersman. "John and Leofric a gold piece for whichever of you slays the steersman. When they turn it will be a good opportunity."

They waved their acknowledgement and I saw them selecting their best arrows.

As we closed, I was acutely aware that I only had a gambeson and a damaged hauberk for defence. It was not enough against a knight in mail. I could see that there were at least ten men in mail on the other ship and many more who looked as though they knew how to fight. Luckily there appeared to be fewer crossbows or perhaps this knight was wiser and was saving them for when they would do the most damage.

When they were less than fifty paces from us they began their turn, it was so slow that I thought they were going to ram us. Their captain was a skilful sailor and our bows drew inexorably together. None of us had fought on top of the cedar logs which protected the amphorae. I had judged it too unstable a platform. Standing where we were made us level with the top of the side of the boat. Our enemies would descend from a height to fight us. It was not the way I would have arranged it but Fate....

My archers needed no commands. Dick and his two archers slew the crossbowmen while John and Leofric rained arrows at the steering board. Their captain was protected but the warrior protecting him fell to an arrow and was flung astern. A sailor stepped in front of an arrow that was destined for his neck. This captain bore a charmed life. I switched my gaze to the ship which loomed next to us. They had taken down their sail to make the ship steadier and they launched themselves over the side. A number of things happened all at once: the captain was flung overboard as two arrows struck him in the chest and the mailed men leapt aboard. One misjudged the gap and fell screaming to be pulverised and crushed between the two hulls.

Some had chosen to land on what they thought was a firm deck. The Cedar logs moved alarmingly as the mailed men leapt onto them. They had no chance of a good footing and Dick and his archers made short work of them as they flailed around like the tortoises of Korfu when they are placed on their back. The rest, however, landed successfully and the hold was filled with a mass of writhing fighting bodies. There was little space to swing a sword. I saw more men leap aboard and we were in danger of being swamped, quite literally. Out of the corner of my eye, I saw the wounded sailor leap forward with a rhomphaia and hack through one of the ropes which bound us. The stern of the Sicilian began to move away from us and we were just held by the bow rope. Our sail was still unfurled and we began to tug the ship around.

A knight lunged at me with his sword. I flicked the tip away and punched with my shield. The moving ship was not impeding our balance but the weight of the knight's armour was causing him more problems than my leather hauberk. As he lurched back he held his arm up to regain his balance. I swung my sword two handed into his ribs. His mail and gambeson stopped my sword penetrating but it must have cracked his ribs for he reeled. He smacked his sword into my side as he fell. I raised my sword above my head and as he struggled to find his feet and brought my weapon down hard upon his neck. His ventail held my sword briefly but I used a sawing action which tore through the links. I saw terror in his eyes as I forced him down. The ventail fell away and I saw that he was no more than twenty summers old. It was too late to halt my sword and it ripped through his throat and neck. He fell in a bloody heap at my feet. Around me were writhing pairs of men engaged in a deadly dance of death.

I twisted my sword out and spun around to find another foe; there was no shortage. I saw an enemy man at arms leap from the side towards Wulfric. I swung my sword sideways at the head of the man. He had no coif and my sword sliced through to his brain. I used his body as another stepping stone and, reaching the side of the ship, sliced through the last rope which held us. Free from the dead weight of the ship we leapt forward so violently that many of the pairs of men fell to the floor. I saw a knight quickly rise and raise his sword to finish off Erre. I used two hands to bring my sword down on the back of his head. I did not cut the helmet but I drove it down hard and he stumbled to his knees. Erre ripped his sword up between the knight's legs and into his guts.

The knights were dead and the last of the men at arms were soon slaughtered now that there were no more reinforcements. I stood panting. It had been hard work. My warriors went around ending the pain of our enemies and tending to our wounded. Leofric raced to my side, "Baron! You are wounded!"

I looked down at him in surprise. He put his hand to my side and it came away bloody. The leather hauberk had finally given way. "Take it off, Leofric and find some honey."

Wulfric had received a cut across his forehead. I could see the bone beneath but he grinned at me. Waving his hand at the bodies he said, "A right good haul, Baron; mail, swords and, when we search the bodies mayhap some coins too."

It was ever thus with Wulfric. Death was an occupational hazard. There were four warriors who would not swear allegiance to me for they lay dead. I looked at the other six. They were not sad for their comrades had died a good death. While I had my body sluiced down with seawater Leofric found some honey. It would have been better if it had been heated but we dared not risk a second fire. The wound was bleeding but it was not a deep one. Wulfric and my men stripped the bodies, friend and foe before throwing them over the side. The Sicilians were dumped unceremoniously overboard but words were said as each Varangian returned to the sea. Erre suddenly pounced on an arm that had been chopped off a Sicilian during the battle. I wondered what he wanted it for.

Leofric wiped most of the blood from my side and then began to smear the sticky honey on the wound. Miraculously the blood flow slowed and then stopped. He wrapped a bandage tightly around it. "Pull it as hard as you can, Leofric. It helps the healing process." Since arriving in England, I had learned much about medicine.

He poured me a horn of ale which I quaffed. "Have we lost the enemy?"

Leofric nodded. "They both gave up. I think our teeth were a little too big for them."

"We were lucky, Leofric. You fought well and you did not panic."

He smiled, "I am learning to be a thinking squire, Baron."

"And you think right well."

Wulfric approached, "What do we do with the treasure, Baron?"

"See if any of the mail fits the squires; if not we take it home. If any want the swords then they can have them. As for the rest then you divide it."

"There is much here, Baron!"

"Good. The men deserve it. And I hope that our journey is more peaceful from now on."

The loss of blood and the effort had tired me and I lay down amongst the bedding in the bottom of the hold. I was suddenly woken by a roar from the rear of the ship. Thinking we had been attacked I grabbed my sword and clambered, stiffly, up the ladder. My men were all at the stern. I wondered what it was. They parted and I saw Erre hauling on a rope. "We eat well tonight Baron!" He suddenly gave an almighty heave and a shark, as long as a man, was hauled on board. Wulfric's axe ended its threshing.

I looked at it in amazement. "How?"

John laughed, "He used the arm and one of the hooks the Sicilians used. He towed it behind the ship and the shark took the bait!"

I was learning much about my men as we headed across that normally placid sea. I watched as Dai had his crew secure the cedar logs which had moved about during the battle. They had helped us, that was for sure.

Chapter 16

The mail from one of the two knights fitted Leofric well and it was finely made. The wearers had all been young. They had seen this as a chance for glory and had paid the price. It had been a harsh lesson for them learning how to fight on a pitching boat against men such as Wulfric and the Varangians. Dick and the archers took three of the swords. They had short ones but had seen the wisdom of carrying longer ones. They would wear their scabbards on their saddles rather than on their waists; if we ever managed to reach the safety of home.

We barely had time to enjoy our moment of glory after the division of spoils for a mighty storm blew up. I had seen these before. This was not like the storms we saw from our home on the Tees. Those storms sometimes raged for days. This was a hotter and quicker storm. It erupted like a volcano from nowhere but it spewed torrential rain and hailstones. The clouds appeared and turned night into day. The air became heavy, like armour, and then the winds began. The deck pitched and tossed like a skittish horse and the normally small waves rose like cliffs. The rain did not fall it crashed onto the ship and was so heavy it appeared to be a sea that was falling. It was so dark that I saw some of the new men clasp their crosses and drop to their knees as they cowered down in the hold.

We had little time for the luxury of prayer for the hold began to fill with water which spilt in from the wild sea. There was no protection from the sea save our canvas awning and the few cedar logs. We formed two chains of men to pull pail after pail of seawater from the bottom of the ship. Wulfric and I worked at two ends of the hold and it was backbreaking work. I bent, dragged, lifted and then took another pail to bend, drag and pull once more. It was relentless. I felt the warm flow of blood from my wound which had opened as I stretched and lifted each bucket full. We seemed to be losing the battle. The water rose above my ankles and soon reached my knees. My muscles burned so much I thought that I would have to stop. I kept going for to cease would mean that the hold would fill with water and we would sink. I renewed my efforts for I had to get home to my family. The King's mission faded into insignificance. This was about saving a tiny ship in the middle of an ocean. All else was irrelevant. As I passed a bucket to Dick I touched the blue stone around my neck. It seemed to give me the energy to carry on.

We kept going for what seemed like hours. Time almost stopped for the sky remained so dark and we could not see the passage of the sun. And then the water stopped rising. We were winning. I found more energy from somewhere. When the level dropped blow my knees then I spied hope and by the time it fell to my ankles and the motion of the ship was less violent then I knew that we had been spared. The water which remained was too shallow to be gathered by the pails and so I laid the pail down and almost collapsed on a sodden sack of lemons.

The wounded sailor looked over. "I will come down and clear the last of the water, Baron. You have done enough." He clambered down next to me and took a piece of sponge such as they find in the Aegean and began, one handed, to soak up the water and squeeze it into a pail.

Leofric and Wulfric hauled me to my feet, "Come, Baron, we must get you on deck for your wound is bleeding. We need light to attend to it."

They pulled me up to the fresh air and a clearing sky. I rolled on my back atop the cedar logs. There was no doubt that they had saved us for they had kept some of the water from us. The ship had been damaged. The sail, or the remains of it, hung in tatters and I saw that the bow castle had been swept away. The bow of the ship looked naked. My men stripped my sodden clothes from me. Leofric brought out the honey and smeared it on the wound. We needed no seawater to wash it this time. The storm had washed me clean and soaked me already. Wulfric tied the bandage this time and he pulled it so tightly that I winced. "I am sorry, Baron, I shall have to kill you with kindness."

As the storm abated the wind died and the motion became much easier until we stopped. Dai made his way down to us. "That was a close-run thing, Baron. I lost two men over the side." He pointed to the sail. "We will have to rig the spare sail."

"You have one?"

He nodded, "Aye but it is close to the stern behind the amphorae."

My heart sank. "You mean we have to move the amphorae?"

"Not all of them. If your men clear a passage to the side then I can send two small men to pull it out." He shrugged. "I am sorry, Baron. It is normally in the part of the hold where you are sleeping. I did not think when I loaded my cargo."

This was disappointing. His incompetence would cost us dear. My men were exhausted already. I began to rise. "Very well. Get me my clothes Leofric."

Wulfric shook his head. "Leofric get the Baron his clothes but keep him here. We will do the work. Right boys let us show these sailors how real men work."

They all took off their sodden clothes and descended to the Stygian depths beneath the cedar logs. They were so wet it was more comfortable to work naked. The calm sea meant that the amphorae could be stacked on the logs without danger of falling. Even so, it took many hours to clear a passage large enough to accommodate the two slight sailors. It seemed to take an inordinately long length of time to drag the reluctant sail from its nest. I could see why when the two exhausted figures flopped the snake-like canvas at the feet of Wulfric and the others. It was heavy and unyielding. Although my men were exhausted, they helped to drag the canvas up to the mainmast.

"Wulfric, we will have to replace all the amphorae before we can hoist the sail."

I saw a look of exasperation on the face of my Sergeant at Arms but he rose, wearily to his feet. "Right boys one last effort and then we sleep the sleep of the dead eh!"

It was almost dark by the time they had finished and the last amphorae had been tied in place. I then watched as the three sailors and Dai hauled the new sail into place. My men pulled on the sheets to haul it up but even so it took a long time. Had a pirate or a Sicilian chanced upon us then our odyssey would have ended there and then for we were in no condition either to move or to fight. The wounded sailor steered although there was so little wind that the ship barely moved. It was pitch black by the time they had finished and my men collapsed into the hold, still damp from the storm and fell asleep. I had had the least work to do and I dragged myself to the steering board.

I pointed with my thumb, "Captain, get some sleep."

"But Baron you are a lord!"

"And I have done the least work in the last few hours. I am rested. I will watch with your sailor here and I will rest on the morrow."

"Thank you."

He nodded and curled up like a cat at our feet. His snores soon told us that he was asleep. "I will take the steering board if you tell me the direction."

"Are you sure, Baron?"

"You have a wounded arm. My wound will not stop me from steering." He moved to one side and I sat on the chest Dai used as a seat and leaned against the wooden steering board.

"A little more to your right, Baron." I made the adjustment. "That is it. Keep her steady."

The rudder did not come directly from the stern but was offset to the right. It took skill to steer. Over the next few hours, I learned how to steer. It was not easy. The sailor, Gwynfor, was a patient man and pleasant to talk with. It seemed this was just his second voyage and he had gone to sea to get the money together to become a farmer. He came from Wales and the little rock they call Anglesey. That was beyond the reach of King Henry and there the land was freely available to men like Gwynfor. So long as he had the money to buy sheep then he could farm his own land without having to ask the lord of the manor.

He pointed to the wound on his arm. "This is a small price to pay. We all have a small share in the oil, wood and spices. When we sell it I will be able to travel to Myfanwy, buy my sheep and build my home. This will be my last voyage."

"And have children."

"Aye, lord, and have children."

"You will have tales to tell them."

"Baron, I will be able to tell them tales until they are grown. I watched in awe as you and your warriors fought many times your number. I felt certain that my life would end as a slave in Sicily."

"I do not think that I am fated to die here." I unconsciously fingered the blue wolf. "I still have a destiny and I still have something to do with my life."

"Here Baron, I am rested and I will take over." We swapped places and I found that my arm ached. It had been more tiring than I had thought. "I am curious, what do you yet have to do? You are a mighty lord and a great warrior. What else is there?"

"I know not but when I returned to Constantinople, I discovered something from my father's past and until I know its purpose then I will keep searching."

"You have a family, Baron?"

"I do."

"What of them? If I had a family then I would keep them close and keep them safe."

"I have people who watch out for them."

"But they are not you. I know that I would give my life for my family." He laughed, "And I do not even have a family yet. I just have a girl who will be my wife when I return."

We watched in silence for the remainder of the night. He had given me much to think about. Was I being a bad husband and father by doing what I did? Of course, I could not help this absence but I knew, in my heart, that if the Empress was in danger then I would leave my family in an instant to serve her. It did not mean I did not love my family but I was tied, through blood and honour with Empress Matilda. All the plotting and machinations of the great, the good, and the bad were embroiling me in events that had little to do with me. I do not think that my father envisaged such a future when he left his favourite lemon tree in his little garden in the east.

Dai woke before dawn. "Thank you, Baron. That rest has done me good. You have shown me a different side to knights on this voyage. I expected an idle lord who would order us all around but you have been as one of us. And yet you need not have stirred to help."

I laughed as I began to head towards the hold. "If I had not stirred then I fear this ship would now lie at the bottom of the sea. Those who sit and watch are the ones who die. A man must do all that he can to survive. That is life."

When I awoke the men were all seated on the cedar logs. Erre was squeezing lemon juice on the butchered flesh of the shark. Leofric pointed to it and said, "Erre here thinks that the lemon juice can cook the flesh of the fish. How can that be, lord? Is it magic?"

"I know not. Where do you learn this Erre?"

"I had a woman in Miklagård, Baron. She had been taken as a slave from the east and she showed me how to do it. I have only ever done it with smaller fish but we have cut this up as small as we can. I will try it first."

I nodded, "Where is she now?"

He shook his head, "She died. She was carrying my child and something... well, she died." He shrugged, "*Wyrd*."

There was little else to say. Life hung by a thread and a man, or a woman made the most of the short time they had on this earth.

He finished and said, "We leave it for a short time and it should be ready."

Surprisingly enough it was cooked, or at least it did not taste raw and it was not tough. I would not have liked to live from it but we were all so hungry that the whole of the beast was devoured. As events turned out that might have been the difference between survival and destruction. "Sail to the east. It is a Dhow! Barbary pirates."

Although the wind had risen the pirates would use oar power. Dai shouted, "Baron, we are not far from the Pillars of Hercules. If we can make them we stand a chance. They like not the dark waters of the deep ocean."

"Right boys. Let's get the oars out!" Wulfric had taken the decision without me. I sat next to John and Leofric. "Baron, your wound."

"You bound it Wulfric and it will not bleed. Come let us row!"

As we rowed Olaf Leather-Neck began to sing and it helped our rhythm. There were not many verses and soon we all joined in.

Bend the back and pull the oars
Take this ship to foreign shores
Find the girls and take the gold

Baron of the North

Live today we'll never get old

Swear the oath and take the blood
We fight for the jarl as oathsworn should
If we die we'll meet once more
On Valhalla's distant shore

Bend the back and pull the oars
Take this ship to foreign shores
Find the girls and take the gold
Live today we'll never get old

I heard later that he had learned the song when sailing down the rivers of the Rus. It was a Viking song. It seemed appropriate somehow. Disappointingly Dai shouted, "The Arabs are still gaining on us. You will have to keep rowing."

If I thought that would have made my men downhearted it had the opposite effect. Olaf Leather-Keck shouted, "I am not going to be beaten by a bunch of half-naked hairy arsed Arabs who would sell their mother if the price was right. Put your backs into it!"

Bend the back and pull the oars
Take this ship to foreign shores
Find the girls and take the gold
Live today we'll never get old

Swear the oath and take the blood
Fight for the Baron as oathsworn should
If we die we'll meet once more
On Valhalla's distant shore

Bend the back and pull the oars
Take this ship to foreign shores
Find the girls and take the gold
Live today we'll never get old

We're sailing home to England fair
We sail to fight for the Baron there

After two renditions I realised that Olaf had changed it slightly. It had changed from Jarl to Baron.

"They are not gaining but they are still within sight of us."

Although I barely had the breath I shouted, "How far to the Pillars of Hercules?"

"Not before nightfall, I am afraid. It will be a long afternoon."

I could see that the men were tiring. "One man in each oar take a break."

Erre said, "But they will catch us."

"They will gain I know but if we all row until we are exhausted then they will catch us. This way they will catch us but we will still have some fight left in us."

Wulfric chuckled, "Want to take a bet Erre?"

In answer, Erre shook his head and he and Sven the Rus stood and joined me and Ralph of Wales. "Get water and a lemon for each of us. It will sustain us. We can wait for food."

Sven the Rus said, "Aye, Baron, it is not good to row on a full stomach."

They went to the hold and I took the opportunity of going to the stern to view the Arab dhow myself. I saw that it was half a mile away. I could see the gleaming, sweating, black bodies as the dhow slid through the water. The ship bulged with the pirates. Their ship rode lower in the water than we did and that gave me an idea.

"They are gaining again, Baron. We should have men on each oar."

"I know but the men were tiring. Dai, do you have ballast aboard?"

"Ballast?"

"Aye stones, that sort of thing."

"We have some and the two sea anchors are made of stone."

"Where are they?"

"Gwynfor, show the Baron where the ballast lies."

As we passed him Ralph of Wales handed me a lemon which he had cut in two. I squeezed the sour juice into my mouth and then washed it down with the water from the skin. Immediately I felt refreshed both inside and out. "Ralph and Sven come with me. Erre, give a lemon and a drink of water to each of the rowers."

We went to the most forward part of the hold. Here it was narrow. There were twenty or so large stones. "We will carry four of them to the cedar logs."

When we had manhandled them up to the cedar logs I was happier. Erre gave me a curious look and Ralph laughed, "Do not try to read the Baron's mind, Erre; just wait and be amazed. It is better that way."

I saw that the enemy was still gaining and we switched rowers. The extra power held the lead for a while longer. After the third change, they were less than four hundred paces from our stern. "How far to the Pillars?"

Dai pointed ahead to a low smudge on the horizon. It was too far for us to reach. I took the fateful decision. "Wulfric stop rowing. Store the oars and arm yourselves. Dick, take the archers and the squires to the sterncastle."

When Wulfric and my men had gathered they looked astern. "There are many of them, Baron."

"I know Wulfric and we cannot fight them."

"You will not surrender surely! They are savages and will sell us to the slavers!"

"No Dai. They will come alongside and we will drop these four heavy stones and stove in the bottom of their dhow. "

Ralph slapped Erre on the back, "I told you!"

"Dick, I want you and the archers to make life difficult for these pirates. Go for the leaders and those at the tiller. With luck, you might discourage them enough to give up the chase."

Dai shook his head, "I would not gamble on that Baron. These are desperate men. Look how overloaded the boat is."

Erre pointed to the waters behind us. "And I would not give much for the chances of any man in the sea now." Since we had thrown the bodies overboard and Erre had used the arm as bait we had been constantly followed by a squabbling shoal of sharks. Their dorsal fins appeared every now and then from the sea.

Dick waited until the dhow was a hundred paces from us. That was well within their range but they did not loose their precious arrows blindly. Each chose a target. There was a large overweight, half-naked man whose gleaming black body made a huge target at the bow. He was beating a drum for the rowers. Two arrows struck him in the back but the layers of fat and muscle stopped them from striking a vital area. Three other arrows hit two rowers on our side of the boat.

I heard Dick curse and watched as he carefully chose the perfect arrow. The others watched as it soared high and struck the drummer in the neck. At eighty paces we saw the blood fountain high in the air and he fell. The other four then released their arrows and this time three men died. One fell overboard and there was a sudden bubbling of the sea as the sharks pounced to tear the corpse to shreds.

I hoped that would have been enough but I saw the rowers rearrange themselves and warriors appeared with shields to protect them. They still closed with us, albeit slower and Dick and the archers only scored minor hits on the crew.

"It looks like we will need the stones. The ones who do not have stones use the javelins to stop them from climbing aboard. Dick and the archers will be able to thin them out too."

It seemed that Nature conspired with the Arabs for the wind began to drop and the oar-powered dhow began to gain rapidly on us. I brought my shield around as the Arabs hurled spears at us. Most clattered harmlessly on the cedar logs but one stuck in Roger of Lincoln's shield. He pulled it contemptuously from the shield and hurled it back to sink into the chest of a giant covered in gold and jewels. As his body fell into the sea I reflected that the sharks would have a rich meal.

My archers were causing such devastation that the captain panicked and brought his dhow in before the oars had been retracted. Some of them sheered and splintered. Many of the rowers were speared by splinters and there was much confusion. I saw that there had to be fifty or more warriors still alive in the dhow.

The dhow nudged next to us. It was much lower than we were and they would have to climb the sides of the cog to board us. "Now!"

The four stones were lifted and then dropped. They fell quickly and such was the effect that two of them went straight through the planks of the hull. The other two crushed men and must have cracked the dhow for, with an alarming creak and groan, it split in two and the crew were thrown into the water. The blue waters became a maelstrom of churning, bubbling bloody terror as the sharks gorged themselves on the thrashing pirates who desperately tried to flee from the monsters of the deep. It was in vain. As we headed west we saw in the darkening sea of red that all of them perished. No one would return to Africa and their families would ever wonder the fate of their men. As we passed the Pillars of Hercules just after dark, I wondered if, like Ulysses, we were doomed to sail the seas for year upon year. Already the journey seemed to have taken longer than our outward voyage. I clasped my wolf token and prayed that we would reach home soon.

Chapter 17

The weather worsened as we passed through the Pillars of Hercules. That was not surprising. It was now close to the beginning of autumn. On the first morning after we had left the calmer waters of the Mediterranean Dai asked to speak with me.

"Baron, I fear the weather. I would put into a port sooner rather than later to offload and sell some of our goods. With the Sicilian blockade, we will make as much here as we would in England."

"But where is safe?"

He pointed to the east, "This is the land of the Muslim. They value spices but it is, perhaps, not worth the risk. We should make for Aquitaine and Bordeaux. It is the first Christian country we can safely reach."

"Very well then, Bordeaux it is."

It took many days to beat up the coast. We were all on watch, perpetually. Although this was not the Mediterranean filled with the threat of pirates there were minor warlords who could put out to sea in fast oared ships to take advantage of helpless Frankish merchants. The banks of storm clouds out to the west kept us within sight of the coast and danger. The captain, of course, was correct. This did make sense. Bordeaux was famous for its wines and we could make double profits by selling some of our cargo in Aquitaine in return for wine and then the rest in Normandy and England. Captain Dai could make enough money to buy a second ship although I doubted that he would do so. He seemed to be a solitary man. I could see him ending his days on the high seas. What would he do with all of his profits? At least my men and I had a purpose. My family, my castle and my people would all be better off for my endeavours.

We were now travelling into colder, damper weather and we had all changed from our fine eastern clothes back into the heavier garments from home. Many of the clothes we had brought and bought were the worse for the wet. The chests Sophia had given me for the gifts for my family were the exception. Inside all was dry and the clothes and presents were in perfect condition.

The Gironde is a long and wide river and we found shelter from the tempestuous weather we had endured. I knew little of the region saved that it was ruled by a Duke called William and that it was fiercely independent. I wondered at our reception and I made sure that, as we sailed up the river to the fortress city of Bordeaux, my men were all well presented. We had not had time to change the surcoats but that would have to wait for England and my wife.

The port was well maintained and they were used to dealing with foreign ships of all types. I saw huge warehouses next to the river filled with barrels of wine. We were, of course, viewed with suspicion when we docked. Dai had never been there and, with the bow castle gone, we looked more than a little odd. The people spoke Poitevin but they understood Norman. Armed guards accompanied the port official who came to greet us or perhaps to warn us off. My Varangians looked more like pirates and brigands than warriors of an English lord.

"We are here to trade."

He looked down his nose at Dai who had spoken. "And what can a Norman have that is worth trading?"

I smiled for Dai had expected such a response. "Cedarwood," the official nodded, "lemons," he became more interested, "olive oil," his eyes widened, "and of course many spices such as pepper, saffron, cumin and coriander." His mouth actually dropped open.

"You have been to Constantinopolis?" He used the old name for the city. Dai nodded. "But we have heard that the Normans in Sicily have blocked the route. They are trying to strangle the Empire. There have been no ships for weeks."

"Nonetheless we managed to evade them. The Baron of Stockton here and his men are doughty warriors."

It was interesting the change which came over the official. He became fawning, "I am certain his grace the Duke would appreciate meeting someone who has bested the men of Sicily."

I nodded, "I will leave you to discuss the trade, Captain. Is there someone who could direct us to the Duke?"

"Of course. Gilles, take the Baron to the castle."

Gilles was curious about our appearance. The Varangians, in particular, looked both exotic and barbaric. I explained how we had fought against real barbarians and these were now my warriors. "You live close to the Scots then Baron?"

"I do."

"Are they not barbarians too?"

I smiled. I think many of the knights there would have taken offence at being called a barbarian. "They are fierce and wild fighters it is true but their knights dress like you and me."

Duke William was roughly my age and I liked him immediately. He too had a young family. Once Gilles had explained who we were and how we had reached his land we were treated well. My men were taken to the main square where they could enjoy the taverns and my squires and myself were taken to the main hall. His wife was a frail-looking creature, Aenor de Châtellerault, who sadly died the following year. He had three children. His only son, William, was a pleasant little boy but he too only survived his mother by a year. It was the Duke's eldest daughter who made the greatest impression not only on me but all that she met. Eleanor was just seven years old but she was both bright and confident. She acted much older than her years. I came to know her well but that was a long time in the future. She took a close interest in all that we had to say. She was a good listener.

The Duke was fascinated by my account of the defeat of the ships which had assailed us. "Then you must have had experience as a seaman before, Baron."

"No, your Grace. I could not sail a ship to save my life but I applied the rules of the battlefield to the sea and they seemed to work."

He nodded, "You are a quick learner then. Your King Henry is very ambitious is he not?"

I wondered if this was an attempt to make me disloyal. If so, it failed. "King Henry is careful to protect his lands. His father conquered England and Normandy is his by right."

He held up his hand, "I do not wish to offend. I too am ambitious but here we do not have the army which your King has at his disposal. I was merely thinking that with men such as you a leader could do almost anything. If you should ever tire of service to King Henry then there will be a place for you here in Aquitaine. I need men who have battle experience."

I nodded, "I am grateful and flattered by your offer but I swore an oath to the King and, in my family, such oaths are sacred."

Eleanor suddenly interrupted, "As it should be!"

Her father silenced her with a glare. "I am sorry, Baron, my daughter is a little forward."

I smiled, "There is nothing wrong with that. In my land, they have a phrase which is *'shy bairns get nowt'* which translated means that children who ask for nothing get nothing. Your daughter is right to express her opinion."

"But she is a girl!"

"King Henry's daughter is a woman and she was Empress of the Empire and is now heir to England and Normandy. Women can wield power too."

I could see that I had made a friend for life of Eleanor; not that I had said what I had for that reason. The Duke also reflected upon my words. "Will you stay with us, Baron? For a while at least."

"I am sorry your Grace. Normally I would be happy to do so but seeing your charming family has made me realise how much I miss my own. I am anxious to be home. The blockade means that both my King and my family might fear for my safety."

He smiled and ruffled Eleanor's hair, "I understand. My family travels everywhere with me."

"Would that mine could but I am a warrior who is often called upon to go to war. I make the most of my precious moments with my family."

They accompanied us to the wharf. Eleanor raced forward and reaching up said, "I would like you to visit with us again, Baron Alfraed."

"And I promise that I will do so. Who knows I may bring my own family here to see your beautiful land."

As we sailed back up the Gironde I was pleased that Dai had made us call in at the port. King Henry was all about making alliances. I felt that I had made one too. It would remain my secret. Who knew when I could use it to bargain my way out of a corner. Who knew when I might need somewhere I could find sanctuary? Dai was more than pleased. He had traded half of our cargo for wine. My men at arms had also made a profit but I feared that the Varangians would consume their profits before we ever saw England.

The Orne and the coast of Normandy was a welcome sight. I would not be home in time for the harvest. The voyage had taken longer than we could possibly have imagined. I was just grateful that we had survived intact. My mission was almost over.

As Dai nudged his ship towards the wharf he said, "Baron I will sell some of my cargo here and the rest in London."

I cocked my head to one side, "What you are really asking is permission to delay returning me and my men to our home."

He smiled and nodded, nervously, "Aye lord. I am anxious to sell my cargo when it is in prime condition. And I would like to hire sailors to replace those we lost. I do not like to sail shorthanded; especially with winter so close"

"Just so long as we land, unload and leave then that is satisfactory. I have delayed my homecoming long enough."

The wharf was not a large one and was some way from the castle. I went with my precious parchments to the castle taking only Leofric and John. When I reached the castle I was told that the King was in Rouen and I cursed my misfortune. Rouen was a day's ride away.

"I need three horses."

The Castellan looked ready to object to my request. To forestall him I held up the documents I had brought. "I have travelled halfway around the world on the King's behalf and he will be less than amused if he discovers that you prevented me from fulfilling my duty."

He saw the wisdom in acceding to my demands and he gave us three poor palfreys. We rode back to the ship. "Wulfric take charge here. I will be in Rouen for a couple of days. You may be able to sell your trade goods here but keep the men, all of them, well behaved. I do not want a delay when I return."

Wulfric nodded and heeded the warning. "Do not worry, Baron, the men are all as anxious as you are to return home to England."

We headed north through an autumn rainstorm along muddy roads. Our clothes became filthy and we had no spares with us. The King would think he had three vagabonds returning to him.

Rouen was now the royal court. It was better positioned for the King to react to danger from either Flanders or France and since Matilda's marriage, the border with Anjou was more secure. As we rode through the streets I could see the liveries of many lords. It looked like a conclave of knights. I left John with the horses for I wished a speedy return to Caen and the ship. Robert of Gloucester greeted me as I waited in the ante-chamber. I had not seen him for some time and there was an uneasy air between us still.

I took the parchments from Leofric. "I have the treaty from the Emperor."

His eyes widened, "You have succeeded? I thought your early return meant you had failed."

"Early return? I thought we had been away longer than expected."

"It is known that Emperor John is like all such men; he does nothing hastily and considers the ramifications of everything."

I shrugged, "He did not seem that way to me." I pointed to the closed door of the Great Hall. "There seem to be many knights in the city this day."

"My father is rewarding those who served him well in the recent wars." He smiled at me, "I believe you are one such. Had he known you were about to arrive he might have delayed the ceremony. Still, he can reward you in private. That way King David will not be offended."

I smiled. It was as though the ice between us was thawing, "I am never worried about offending the Scots."

He laughed, "And I feel the same about the Welsh. Although they are quiet at the moment. They are like an itch I cannot scratch."

"I shall be telling the King but, in case he does not know already, the Normans on Sicily are blockading the Empire. I have heard that their Duke is about to become a king."

Robert frowned, "Aye we had heard such things. It is a good job there are many leagues twixt their Duke and my father for I think the two of them would clash. You escaped without incident though?"

I shook my head and told him of my clashes both on the outward and homeward voyages. He smiled, "Fortune favours you although it is said that fortune always favours the brave or is it the reckless? You do take chances, Baron."

"We have but one life, my lord, and one chance to achieve. I take my chance. I have seen too many brave men die with dreams unfulfilled. That will not be me. When I die I hope that men say of me that I never gave up."

"Gave up what?"

"Living!"

The door opened and a flurry of finely dressed and noisy knights erupted. They looked at me as though I was a beggar. I ignored them all for I saw, in their midst, Stephen of Blois. Our eyes fixed. There was mutual hatred between us. It had existed ever since he had tried to abduct Empress Matilda. No matter how much he deceived the King and the Earl he would never fool me. I knew him for what he was, an enemy of the Empress and of me.

When they had emptied the room the Earl shepherded us in. The King's face lit up. "Baron! You have exceeded my expectations. I had thought you would have been away another six months at least."

I smiled, "We were fortunate." I took the sealed leather containers with the precious parchments and documents. "Here is the treaty and letters from the Emperor."

"He acceded to my request?"

I nodded, "If I am to be frank, my liege, he could not see what you had to gain from an alliance which could never be more than symbolic."

The King smiled, "Let us just say that it suits me. Now sit and drink some wine whilst I read."

I sat with the Earl and a servant poured us wine. I nodded to my squire, "And some for my squire too."

The servant looked to the Earl who nodded. He then turned to me and said, quietly, "You do treat your inferiors well, Baron."

I resented the tone but I smiled, "Those inferiors watch my back in battle. Of course, I treat them well. Only a fool would do other." I sipped the wine. It was not as good as that which I had shared with Duke William but I nodded appreciatively as I drank. I had offended the Earl and the King before. The lesson had been learned; do not express opinions.

The King read. Every now and then he would look up and stare at me then he would resume his reading. Finally, he laid down the documents. He waved to the servant, "Leave us. And if your squire would wait outside too."

Leofric was not offended and, after bowing, he left.

The King tapped the documents. "This is better than I had hoped. The Emperor thinks highly of you." He looked at his son. "The Emperor offered him a position in Constantinople; did he tell you that?"

The Earl looked at me, "No he did not. And you refused?"

"I have a home on the Tees and a family besides my father took the decision to return home and I think of Stockton as my home now."

"Our young knight here saved the life of the Emperor, without mail!"

The Earl laughed, "Now that does not surprise me in the least."

"I sent the prying ears from the room for you deserve to know why I have made this alliance. The Pope is being wooed by Louis of France. The new Emperor of the German Empire is an implacable foe. I may have secured my southern borders but we are still vulnerable. That is why I had to appease the Scots. King David has his spies here and when I announce, tomorrow, that you have returned from Jerusalem and are forgiven then he will believe that I have punished you. The Emperor in Constantinople is beyond the power of the Pope. I can stay within the Church and yet not bow the knee to the Pope if I have an alliance there. Now, do you see?"

I nodded, "But you should know, your majesty, that the Emperor is pressed on all sides by enemies."

He smiled, "Aye but Count Fulk and others are now carving out kingdoms in Outremer. Soon they will be a wall to protect the eastern side of the Empire." The King tapped the document, "I believe that will allow the Emperor to reconquer some of the lands to the west; who knows, perhaps even Italy."

"You have heard of the blockade?"

"I have."

The Earl said, "And the young Baron here has sunk a Sicilian ship and fought off two others with just one small cog."

"Indeed. Then you have done well." He stood, "Now I wish you to go hunting with me tomorrow. The other knights who are here will participate too."

"I had hoped to return home, my liege. And my family is still in London. They will be anxious to see me."

He waved his hand airily, "Another day or two will not hurt and, besides, I insist." He smiled, "Your family is safe; believe me."

"I came with just these clothes, sire."

"I think we can furnish you and your squires with some clothes. You shall stay here with me."

I nodded. I knew when I was beaten. The King had plans for me. I could not see why he wished me to stay but I could not afford to antagonise him. "Then I will be happy to do so."

With the horses stabled and my squires jammed into a tiny room next to mine, we were supplied with clean clothes. I used the fact that we were in the King's castle to have hot water and a bath fetched so that we could, at least, appear clean. Leofric had become quite adept at shaving and grooming me so that by the time we were ready for the feast I looked presentable.

Before we left for the meal I said, "You two will be expected to wait upon me this night and then eat with the other squires. Keep your ears and eyes open and your mouths shut. Not all those who are present are allies. Some are enemies. You can drink to your heart's content when we return to Stockton. I will be drinking little. And tomorrow we hunt boar and you know how dangerous they are."

They both nodded, seriously, "We will my lord."

Having bathed I was one of the last to arrive. The King and Earl had still to make an appearance. The ones who had arrived early were busy drinking and I saw, across the Great Hall, Stephen of Blois. He was surrounded by his usual coterie of knights. Then, to my delight, I saw a friendly face. It was Rolf, another of the knights of the Empress. I saw that he had saved a seat next to him and all thoughts of Stephen of Blois were driven from my mind as I headed for him.

He grabbed me in a bear-like embrace, "The Earl told me you were here! It is good to see a friendly face in this sea of courtiers!"

"And it is good to see you."

"Sit and tell me about your adventures! The Earl said you had been to the east?" He handed me a goblet of wine.

I lowered my voice. I could trust Rolf. "The tale you must spread is that I went to Jerusalem when, in fact, I visited the Emperor."

He grinned, "I knew the rumour of begging forgiveness could not be true. Tell me all."

Before I could begin my saga we all stood as the King and the Earl entered. They marched to the head of the table and we were waved to our seats. The King spoke, "You are all here for you have all done me some service in the recent wars. This is to celebrate and now Baron Stockton has returned from a pilgrimage to Jerusalem so that all his sins have been forgiven. Tonight we feast and tomorrow we hunt!"

I felt the eyes of Stephen of Blois boring in on me. I ignored the attention.

"So, my young friend, there is intrigue." Rolf's voice was low.

"There is indeed. It is almost Byzantine!" I told him of my journey, John of Palermo, the battle with the Magyar, the rhomphaia, the voyage home and the sea battles. Finally, I confided in him about Aquitaine.

He nodded sagely. "You do right not to tell the King of Aquitaine. It is as well to have some secrets. The high and the mighty keep enough from us. You have done well. Will he reward you?"

"He said he would but who knows. Besides, it would only be a title. I have as much power now as I can handle. In terms of riches…" I took out my two treasures and showed them to him beneath the table.

"They are fine indeed. And yet you know not their origin?"

"No. Perhaps Osric may know. He is the last of my father's oathsworn. I will ask him when I return home." I surreptitiously returned the treasures and said, "And that is enough of me. What brings you here and how fares the Empress?"

"Ah, that is not such happy news. I will be returning in the morning to Anjou. I brought a letter from the Empress to her father. Things are not good between the Count and the Empress. He is a boy. He is petulant and he is arrogant. I would have fetched him a clout many a time had the Empress not held my hand. She is desperately unhappy. They sleep in separate rooms and he spends all his time fornicating and drinking. It is not a marriage, it is an alliance."

"I feared as much. And with Count Fulk in Outremer young Geoffrey has free rein."

"He does. I came here because our mistress wishes to leave her husband and return to England."

"And what did the King say?"

"He forbade it. He commanded his daughter to be a good wife and stay there."

"He is my liege lord but there is little to like about King Henry. He uses people as though they were toys."

"He is like his father." He smiled, "And now tell me of your home and my friends, Edward and the others."

The mood was lightened as I told him all. It made me feel better too for the news from home was all good. Wulfstan's death had been in the past and the hurt was now gone. Rolf, like me, knew that Wulfstan died a warrior's death. His family was another matter but Wulfstan had died the way he wanted to, surrounded by his dead enemies. As we parted Rolf clasped my arm, "I will be gone before dawn but I will write to you with any developments. I will use a code for you are a clever man. The Empress will be my sister in the letters."

I nodded, "And tell her that Edward and I are ready to come to her aid should she ever need it."

"She knows and," he hesitated, "she thinks fondly of you."

I slept happy that night with that thought in my head.

Chapter 18

Rolf had, indeed, left by the time we rose. Most of the knights had been well in their cups the night before and were the worse for wear. After watered beer, bread, cheese and ham we gathered in the armoury to collect our weapons for the hunt. John and Leofric would be on foot and they chose hunting bows. Most of the other squires and attendants chose crossbows. They would be on foot. I took a boar spear to go with my sword.

I saw that Stephen of Blois was there too and he had four surly looking men with him. They looked like men at arms rather than squires. The Earl and the King arrived and they were also attended by two men. In addition, there were the King's foresters with a pack of hounds. They would bring the prey to us. In my own land, I preferred hunting by stalking. I believed it made you a better warrior. The King, obviously, preferred quicker results.

"Come, my friends, let us see who can claim first blood this day!" We all knew it would be him. He was at the front and his foresters would drive the beasts towards the man who paid them.

John and Leofric jogged easily behind me as we followed the King and the Earl. They were at the fore, as was their right, and the odds were that they would make the first kill. It took us some time to get into the heart of the forest. It was coming on to winter and the wild boar would not be foraging far and wide. It was a good time to hunt as the young pigs would have left the sow and would still be succulent. The honour went to the one who killed a large, older boar but the younger ones had the better meat.

We heard the horn and the hounds barking. We all knew that means they had the scent of the boar in their nostrils. Without being told my two squires strung their bows and held two arrows next to them. We had learned it meant they could release faster and with a wild boar hurtling towards you then speed was of the essence. The horse I rode was still the palfrey we had been loaned in Caen. He was not a good horse. He was neither swift nor responsive. I suspect he was getting towards the end of his life.

The sound of the hounds grew closer and I readied my spear in the overhand position. I would not be the first to strike for the King and the Earl were forty paces ahead of me. I saw the King stand in his stirrups and shout something. I could not make out the words. Then he and the Earl hurtled forward. I spurred my weary beast after them. I arrived in time to see them both plunge their spears into an old sow. They leapt from their horses, which their retainers grabbed and went, with their swords, to finish off the dying beast.

Now that my horse was up to speed he was hard to slow down. Suddenly the mate of the sow charged towards the King and the Earl from the undergrowth close by. As luck or fate would have it my path took me closest to the beast. As the King and the Earl turned to face the fierce tusks of the angry boar I stood in my saddle and threw my boar spear at the neck of the animal. It was a reaction throw and it was not well aimed. It was not a killing strike and it just buried itself deep in the animal's shoulder. A wild animal always reacts to the nearest threat and that was me and my horse. He whipped his wicked head around and ripped his tusks into the belly of my horse. My palfrey reared and screamed in pain as he was eviscerated. I had the presence of mind to kick my feet free from the stirrups so that I rolled away.

As I lay winded I saw the tusker turn, having torn his head free from my horse's guts, to charge towards me. Two arrows from my squires hit his flank and that allowed me to regain my feet and draw my sword. As two more arrows struck the animal I prepared myself. I would have one strike and one strike only. I waited until the last minute and then stepped aside, swinging my sword at the back of the boar's neck. He was wounded but he was wily and he turned too. I felt the edge of my blade sinking into his neck. I had used two hands and the blow was mortal but the boar, even in its death throes still tried to turn and gore me. Its tusk caught my leg and the weight of its falling body made me fall. It saved my life. Even as I fell first one and then a second crossbow bolt zipped over my head to thud into a tree behind me.

Leofric and John whipped their heads around to see the assassin. There were many to choose from. At least eight retainers had their crossbows in their hands. As I rose, slowly, to my feet I saw that two of Stephen of Blois' men were hurriedly reloading. I knew who the assassins were. It would be hard to prove but I knew.

The King and the Earl ran over. "Baron! We owe you our lives."

"Are you hurt?" The Earl pointed to my leg which had been scored by the tusk of the boar.

"It is nothing. My horse saved me from worse." I went to my horse which was dying. I took my sword and slit his throat. He did not deserve more pain.

The King came and embraced me. "We have even more reason to honour you, Baron." He turned to his retainers. "We have enough now. Take these beasts back to the castle and find a horse for the Baron."

"It is fine your majesty. It is not far to walk."

"Are you certain?"

"I am. I will have my squires for company and the walk will stop the wound from stiffening. This is not my first wound."

The animals were quickly trussed and taken leaving us alone in the woods. I went to the tree and took the bolts from the trunk. It took some effort to withdraw them. I put them in my tunic. "Did you see who loosed the bolts?"

Leofric said, "I thought it was the men of Stephen of Blois but I could not be certain."

"You are right and they will now try to finish their work." They both looked around. "They will lay an ambush for me which is why I spurned the offer of a horse. I would rather end this threat today. Stephen of Blois will not have time to hire more assassins before we leave for home. I do not want an ambush on the road to Caen. Your skills as falconers are now needed. I want you to the left and right of me; about forty paces before me. Move silently and I will pretend I know not how to move through the forest. I will make enough noise to flush them out."

"That is a risk, my lord."

"It would be Leofric if I had any but you two. When you see them then strike true! I need no prisoners!"

I let them hurry on and then I blundered and limped through the forest. I had been trained by Wulfstan to be silent and it took an effort to make noise. I limped although I was not in pain. The cut had stopped bleeding and caused me no discomfort. I wanted the killers to think I was wounded worse than I actually was.

I now knew how the animals we hunted felt. I was the prey and I knew that I was being stalked. I was relying on two young squires and my life was in their hands. I could have taken up the King on his offer of a horse but I had known that would have allowed Stephen to ambush us on the road to Caen. This way I would decide where the ambush would be; here in the forest.

I became aware that the birds ahead had stopped singing. Suddenly two huge wood pigeons took flight. I dropped to one knee and a crossbow bolt thudded into the tree next to me. I drew my sword and ran towards the crossbowman. I could not see him but I had seen the flight of the bolt. He would be rapidly reloading his weapon. To my right, I heard a scream. I put it from my mind. I also ignored the noises I could hear from my left. My squires were there and this enemy I faced was ahead of me.

I saw him. He was dressed in green which made him harder to see and he dropped his crossbow as he saw my approach. He began to draw his sword. I held mine in two hands and just behind my body. As I ran up to him I began to swing. His sword was slow to release from its scabbard and he barely made it. My blade clanged into his so hard that sparks flew and his one hand was not as strong as my two. The edge of my sword scored his leg. I did not give him the chance to escape. I whirled around and brought my sword into his right side, beneath his sword. Such was the force that my blade, striking his side, was only stopped by his spine. His lifeless body crumpled at my feet. I went back to the tree and took out the bolt. It had the same markings as the other two.

Leofric and John materialized at my side. "I am sorry Baron. I saw one warrior and went after him."

"As did I. We were overconfident lord and took too long to kill them. You nearly died."

"But I did not Leofric and all is well. Go and search the bodies and I will search this one."

I found the man's purse. In it were four large silver coins and a golden one. It bore the mark of Blois. Around his neck, he had his good luck charm. It was a crudely made hawk. It had not done him much good and I took it. I had a purpose for that. His weapons were poor and I left them.

My two squires returned and showed me the coins they had collected. They too bore the mark of Blois. I gave them my coins. "Here, a reward from the dead. Now let us get back before we are missed."

It took longer to get back than I had anticipated. My wound began to ache and I could not move as fast as I would have liked. As we approached the castle I saw a party heading out to meet us. It was Robert of Gloucester with some of the foresters.

He reined in, "We were worried when you did not return."

"My leg slowed me a little."

"Did you see any others while you were returning? My Lord Blois is missing two men."

"We did not see *two* men, my lord." I hated lying and I did not have to. For some reason, Stephen of Blois had told the Earl his own lie.

Something in my voice must have alerted the Earl for he said to the foresters. "You may return to the castle. I will walk with the Baron." When they had gone he asked, "Where are they?"

"The three of them lie dead in the forest. They tried to ambush us."

"Are you certain?" I nodded, "There were three of them?"

I took out the bolts I had collected. Two of these were aimed at me when I killed the boar. The other when we returned. Had my squires not been such good archers then my body would lie there instead of the assassins."

"Did you know them?"

"My lord, you and I both know that it was Stephen of Blois who put them up to this. He has tried before."

He nodded, "Yet my father will hear nothing of this. He needs the brothers to be a buffer against France and he trusts them. You can not mention this to him. It will cause trouble."

"He may trust them but I know that Stephen of Blois wishes to be king and to do so he has to stop the Empress from attaining the throne. I am her protector. We both know that. So long as I live the Empress is safe."

"Then I pray you live longer. Will you say anything?"

"No, but I will let your cousin know that he has failed. I would return tomorrow to Caen and thence home. Will you help me persuade your father to allow me to travel?"

"Of course. It is the least I can do."

I made a visit to the priests and healers. My leg was bound and they took the opportunity of examining my side. The honey had worked but they cleaned it up for me. I gave them a coin for the poor for their trouble. I visited the King before the feast. The Earl of Gloucester was there already. The King greeted me warmly. "Here he is the mighty slayer of boars! You have another skill. Is there no end to your talents?"

"I was in the right place at the right time, my liege."

"You are too modest. I look forward to hearing your tales from the east."

"Sire, I would return tomorrow to Caen and thence to home."

"My son told me you would make such a request. Is our company so abhorrent that you wish to flee?"

"No, my liege but I have been away from my home more than I have been there lately. My men on the Tees are good warriors but you appointed me Baron of the North for a purpose did you not?"

"You are right. I am being selfish. I enjoy your company." He held his hand out and the Earl handed him a ring. "I had this made for you while you were away. It is a seal to go with your new title. You are now the Earl of Cleveland."

I bowed and stuttered my thanks, "I am honoured, my liege." Then, as I opened my hand I saw that the seal was a rampant wolf. How could this be?

The King saw my look and smiled, "I know that it is not your sign but you have all the attributes of a wolf. We are the lions but you are the wolf. You keep the other wolves from our doors." He handed me a document. "Here is the letter for the Castellan at the Tower. Your family have enjoyed my hospitality long enough."

"Thank you."

As I left the Earl came with me. "I knew of this before but I dared not mention it for my father enjoys his surprises. However, I can give you a warning. Cleveland is the land south of the river. That is subject to the see of York however your lands, Stockton, are subject to the Palatinate of Durham."

"As I know."

"However what you may not know is that, as a result of your treaty, my father can ignore the Pope. It was the Pope who appointed Bishop Ranulf. The next Bishop will be appointed by my father."

"I understand." The King was being generous but I now had three masters: the King, an Archbishop and a Bishop. My life would become more interesting.

My new title was confirmed at the feast and, generally, I was applauded for my title. The last one to congratulate me was Stephen of Blois. The smile was not in his eyes and his hand, as I took it, was like a cold and lifeless fish.

"You have been lucky so far, Earl. I pray your luck continues."

"And I know you have had bad luck lately so I will give you a gift which might bring you better fortune. It is a good luck charm. It is crudely made but…"

I dropped his dead assassin's charm in his hand. His eyes narrowed and he smiled. "Thank you but I need no charms. Still, I am sure I can find someone who will find a use for it."

I said quietly, "Then he had better be more skilled than the owner of this one."

We left before dawn. We reached Caen by noon for the horse I now rode was a much better mount. The ship rode a little higher in the river for Dai had obviously done some good trading. As we approached I said to my squires, "Say nothing about the attack. I will tell Wulfric and the others when it is right."

"Aye Baron."

Dai's smile told me how successful his trading had been whilst Wulfric and my men also looked happy. "Are we ready to sail, Captain?"

"We are, my lord. And soon we shall have you home."

I was reflective as we sailed north to London. I had asked my squires to remain silent about the attacks but not about my new title. They could not wait to tell Wulfric and the others. To my surprise, they were all delighted. It was just a title but, to my men, it made me the equal of Robert of Gloucester. I did not point out to them that Robert of

Gloucester was illegitimate nor that I now served three masters. I allowed them to bask in the reflected glory of serving an Earl.

The Thames was as busy as the Golden Horn. England was now a hub of commerce and ships travelled from all parts of the mainland. Perhaps the blockade of the Empire had affected the English trade. Whatever the reason we struggled to find a berth. "Dai you can sell some of my wine and spices with your own."

He nodded, "How much my lord?"

"Just half. When can we sail?"

"It will take time to trade and then we shall have to wait for the tide. It will be the morrow."

That was a longer stay than I wished but I had no choice. Old King Canute had tried to defy the tides and had failed. I was a mere knight. I turned to the Varangians. "I have fulfilled my part of the bargain. We are now in England. If you wish to become my oathsworn then I will take you all as my warriors but if you wish to become your own men then I bid you farewell."

Erre looked at the others and stepped forward. "I will speak for us all, Earl Alfraed. We will be your oathsworn. Our minds have not changed since Miklagård. In fact, if anything, our resolve has hardened. You are like Earl Harold would have been. You are a warrior and we will follow you unto death."

They knelt before me. I took out my sword and holding it by the blade offered them the hilt. "Do you swear to follow me and protect me and my family?"

They chorused, "We do!"

"Then I will be as a father to you and protect you unto death!"

And so I gained six fine men at arms. It proved to be one of the best decisions I ever made for none of them ever broke their oath.

My first task was to go to the Tower for my family. King Henry had told me they had been happy. The proof would be in my wife's eyes. The Castellan read the document and smiled, "The guards will miss your family, Earl. They have enjoyed their stay here and been popular with everyone." He gestured and they came forth.

I was amazed at how much William had grown. He ran up to me and threw himself in my arms. I was nearly knocked over. Then my daughter hurled herself quickly towards me and kissed me too. I was sad that I had missed her first faltering steps. She had gone from a toddler to a younger version of William and I had missed it all. Scotland and Constantinople had occupied my time when she should have.

Then I took my wife in my arms and, without worrying about what people thought, kissed her hard. She pulled back and, with eyes wide, said, "I need not ask if you missed me! The women of the east were not attractive then, my husband?"

"Compared with you even the fabled Helen would have been a dullard!"

I took the time Dai needed for the trades to buy some material for the wolf emblem on my surcoat. The King's choice of signet had been almost supernatural. Wulfstan would have said, '*Wyrd.*' I would not ignore such a sign. My two stars would now be replaced by a wolf and I could not wait to give Alf my sword for him to fit the blue stone in the pommel. It was not a Christian thought but I knew that the stone would bring me good fortune and make me a better warrior.

My men carried their belongings and we returned to the ship. I spent the afternoon, night and next morning telling them of my adventures and of my new title. Had I known I could have taken longer to tell for we did not leave when Dai had predicted.

As events turned out we were in London for three days. A mixture of trades, inclement weather and tides meant we did not leave for home when I expected to. It was now the middle of autumn and the weather we had to endure as we travelled north was some of the worst I had ever experienced. It seemed we were being tested. The poor ship had endured much already. Dai was already worrying about the condition of his ship as we passed along the eastern coast of England.

"Have you somewhere I could repair my ship on the Tees, my lord?"

"We have."

"Then, with your permission, I will spend time there. I would not risk the winter storms with my ship in the condition it is."

"And you are welcome for you have served me well, Dai the Welshman."

We pulled into the Tees on a cold damp morning when there was a hint of frost in the air. Our light clothes from Constantinople would not see the light of day until the next year. But my castle was all the more welcome for the fact that it was home. After the east, Bordeaux, Caen and Rouen, it seemed an insignificant little pile of stones but it was my pile of stones. Now that I drew close I felt a sense of relief. It could have been that my people would just have received the news of my death. Instead, I returned with riches, fine presents and a new title.

Harold was there to greet me. He too had grown. He clasped my arm, "I am glad to see you back, Baron."

Adela said, "He is now Earl, Harold."

"Earl! And not before time!"

My men and Dai's sailors began to offload the cargo and we stood to one side. I asked the question which had been on my mind for the last few days, "Is all well, Harold?"

"It is, my lord. There has been peace. The harvest has been the best for years and we have been lucky with the animals. Few died. More settlers have come so that Elton is now thriving once more."

I knew what that meant to my former squire, "I am pleased. And the other manors?"

His face darkened a little, "They are all well but, I am sorry to say, my lord, that Osric has joined your father and the oathsworn. He died last month and is buried with the others."

Although it was to be expected, for he was old, it still came as a terrible shock. I had not been there when the last of my father's men had died. Equally important was that there was now no one left alive who could tell me about the wolf token and the blue stone. The mystery had died with Osric. I would never discover what they meant. My new life was as an Earl but I now knew less about my past than I thought I had.

Epilogue

It was a joyous Christmas. My wife was delighted with her new pots and clothes. Sophia had bought quality and my wife recognized it. Perhaps I would take her east to meet Basil's mother. The spices had proved a hit and we had the best Yule I could ever remember. The weather was not as cold as it was normally and so my wife invited all of my knights to tell them of my new title. It was a wonderful celebration. I was flattered by the apparent genuine expressions of pleasure from my knights. When all had left I was able to enjoy my castle and my family. I got to know my children and they me.

As the winter grew colder we had a rider who came from the south. He had messages from the King and, more importantly, a letter from Rolf, my brother in arms. The King's letters were terse and business-like. They were instructions for the spring. The other letter was the most important. I went to my western tower to read it alone. It had been written, as he had said he would in code, but I knew its meaning without the need to decipher it. I took a deep breath as I broke the seal on the letter. I carefully unfolded it and began to read.

Earl Alfraed,

Congratulations on your new title. Your brothers here in Rouen are pleased that you have been so justly rewarded. I have some interesting news to impart. My sister and her husband have parted. It was not meant to be. At the moment she stays with me here in Rouen but she is keen to visit London. Perhaps if she does then you could visit her there?

My best wishes to your wife and your family,

Rolf,

Knight of the Empress.

I was both surprised and yet not surprised. Rolf had told me that all was not well in Anjou. The Empress had left her husband and was coming to England. What did the King think of that and did she expect me to do something? I had more questions than answers but a sudden thought filled my heart with dread; if she was in London then she was away from the protection of both her husband and her father. The brothers from Blois had a manor in London. Could the Empress be in danger? My happy, settled life in the north in the bosom of my family was now thrown into disarray by this news. I had a duty to my family, my people and my knights, not to mention the King, but the Empress might need me. What would I do?

The End

Glossary

Allaghia- a subdivision of a Bandon-about 400 hundred men
Akolouthos - The commander of the Varangian Guard
al-Andalus- Spain
Angevin- the people of Anjou, mainly the ruling family
Bandon- Byzantine regiment of cavalry -normally 1500 men
Battle- a formation in war (a modern battalion)
Cadge- the frame upon which hunting birds are carried (by a codger- hence the phrase old codger being the old man who carries the frame)
Conroi- A group of knights fighting together
Demesne- estate
Destrier- war horse
Fess- a horizontal line in heraldry
Gambeson- a padded tunic worn underneath mail. When worn by an archer they came to the waist. It was more of a quilted jacket but I have used the term freely
Gonfanon- A standard used in Medieval times (Also known as a Gonfalon in Italy)
Hartness- the manor which became Hartlepool
Hautwesel- Haltwhistle
Kataphractos (pl. oi)- Armoured Byzantine horseman
Kometes/Komes- General (Count)
Kentarchos- Second in command of an Allaghia
Kontos (pl. oi) - Lance
Lusitania- Portugal
Mansio- staging houses along Roman Roads
Maredudd ap Bleddyn- King of Powys
Mêlée- a medieval fight between knights
Musselmen- Muslims
Nomismata- a gold coin equivalent to an aureus
Outremer- the kingdoms of the Holy Land
Palfrey- a riding horse
Poitevin- the language of Aquitaine
Pyx- a box containing a holy relic (Shakespeare's Pax from Henry V)
Serdica- Sofia
Surcoat- a tunic worn over mail or armour
Sumpter- packhorse
Tagmata- Byzantine cavalry
Turmachai -Commander of a Bandon of cavalry
Ventail – a piece of mail that covered the neck and the lower face.
Wulfestun- Wolviston (Durham)

Stockton Castle

Historical note

The book is set during one of the most turbulent and complicated times in British history. Henry I of England and Normandy's eldest son William died. The king named his daughter, Empress Matilda as his heir. However, her husband, the Emperor of the Holy Roman Empire died and she remarried. Her new husband was Geoffrey of Anjou and she had children by him. (The future Henry II of England and Normandy- The Lion in Winter!)

Hartburn is a small village just outside Stockton. My American readers may be interested to know that the Washington family of your first President lived there and were lords of the manor from the thirteenth century onwards. It was called Herrteburne in those days. In the sixteenth century, the family had it taken from them and it was replaced by the manor of Wessington, which became Washington. Had they not moved then your president might live in Hartburn DC!

Books used in the research:
- The Varangian Guard- 988-1453 Raffael D'Amato
- Saxon Viking and Norman- Terence Wise
- The Walls of Constantinople AD 324-1453-Stephen Turnbull
- Byzantine Armies- 886-1118- Ian Heath
- The Age of Charlemagne-David Nicolle
- The Normans- David Nicolle
- Norman Knight AD 950-1204- Christopher Gravett
- The Norman Conquest of the North- William A Kappelle
- The Knight in History- Francis Gies
- The Norman Achievement- Richard F Cassady
- Knights- Constance Brittain Bouchard

Griff Hosker July 2015

Other books by Griff Hosker

If you enjoyed reading this book, then why not read another one by the author?

Ancient History

The Sword of Cartimandua Series
(Germania and Britannia 50 A.D. – 128 A.D.)
Ulpius Felix- Roman Warrior (prequel)
The Sword of Cartimandua
The Horse Warriors
Invasion Caledonia
Roman Retreat
Revolt of the Red Witch
Druid's Gold
Trajan's Hunters
The Last Frontier
Hero of Rome
Roman Hawk
Roman Treachery
Roman Wall
Roman Courage

The Wolf Warrior series
(Britain in the late 6th Century)
Saxon Dawn
Saxon Revenge
Saxon England
Saxon Blood
Saxon Slayer
Saxon Slaughter
Saxon Bane
Saxon Fall: Rise of the Warlord
Saxon Throne
Saxon Sword

Medieval History

The Dragon Heart Series
Viking Slave
Viking Warrior
Viking Jarl
Viking Kingdom
Viking Wolf
Viking War
Viking Sword
Viking Wrath
Viking Raid
Viking Legend
Viking Vengeance
Viking Dragon
Viking Treasure
Viking Enemy
Viking Witch
Viking Blood
Viking Weregeld
Viking Storm
Viking Warband
Viking Shadow
Viking Legacy
Viking Clan
Viking Bravery

The Norman Genesis Series
Hrolf the Viking
Horseman
The Battle for a Home
Revenge of the Franks
The Land of the Northmen
Ragnvald Hrolfsson
Brothers in Blood
Lord of Rouen
Drekar in the Seine
Duke of Normandy

Baron of the North

The Duke and the King

Danelaw
(England and Denmark in the 11th Century)
Dragon Sword
Oathsword
Bloodsword
Danish Sword

New World Series
Blood on the Blade
Across the Seas
The Savage Wilderness
The Bear and the Wolf
Erik The Navigator
Erik's Clan
The Last Viking

The Vengeance Trail

The Conquest Series
(Normandy and England 1050-1100)
Hastings

The Aelfraed Series
(Britain and Byzantium 1050 A.D. - 1085 A.D.)
Housecarl
Outlaw
Varangian

The Reconquista Chronicles
Castilian Knight
El Campeador
The Lord of Valencia

The Anarchy Series England 1120-1180
English Knight
Knight of the Empress

Baron of the North

Northern Knight
Baron of the North
Earl
King Henry's Champion
The King is Dead
Warlord of the North
Enemy at the Gate
The Fallen Crown
Warlord's War
Kingmaker
Henry II
Crusader
The Welsh Marches
Irish War
Poisonous Plots
The Princes' Revolt
Earl Marshal
The Perfect Knight

Border Knight
1182-1300
Sword for Hire
Return of the Knight
Baron's War
Magna Carta
Welsh Wars
Henry III
The Bloody Border
Baron's Crusade
Sentinel of the North
War in the West
Debt of Honour
The Blood of the Warlord
The Fettered King
de Montfort's Crown

Sir John Hawkwood Series
France and Italy 1339- 1387
Crécy: The Age of the Archer

Baron of the North

Man At Arms
The White Company
Leader of Men
Tuscan Warlord
Condottiere

Lord Edward's Archer
Lord Edward's Archer
King in Waiting
An Archer's Crusade
Targets of Treachery
The Great Cause
Wallace's War

Struggle for a Crown 1360- 1485
Blood on the Crown
To Murder a King
The Throne
King Henry IV
The Road to Agincourt
St Crispin's Day
The Battle for France
The Last Knight
Queen's Knight

Tales from the Sword I
(Short stories from the Medieval period)

Tudor Warrior series
England and Scotland in the late 14th and early 15th century
Tudor Warrior
Tudor Spy
Flodden

Conquistador
England and America in the 16th Century
Conquistador

Baron of the North

The English Adventurer

Modern History

The Napoleonic Horseman Series
Chasseur à Cheval
Napoleon's Guard
British Light Dragoon
Soldier Spy
1808: The Road to Coruña
Talavera
The Lines of Torres Vedras
Bloody Badajoz
The Road to France
Waterloo

The Lucky Jack American Civil War series
Rebel Raiders
Confederate Rangers
The Road to Gettysburg

Soldier of the Queen series
Soldier of the Queen
Redcoat's Rifle

The British Ace Series
1914
1915 Fokker Scourge
1916 Angels over the Somme
1917 Eagles Fall
1918 We will remember them
From Arctic Snow to Desert Sand
Wings over Persia

Combined Operations series 1940-1945
Commando
Raider

Baron of the North

Behind Enemy Lines
Dieppe
Toehold in Europe
Sword Beach
Breakout
The Battle for Antwerp
King Tiger
Beyond the Rhine
Korea
Korean Winter

Tales from the Sword II
(Short stories from the Modern period)

Other Books
Great Granny's Ghost (Aimed at 9-14-year-old young people)

For more information on all of the books then please visit the author's website at www.griffhosker.com where there is a link to contact him or visit his Facebook page: GriffHosker at Sword Books or follow him on Twitter: @HoskerGriff
or visit his Facebook page: GriffHosker at Sword Books

Printed in Great Britain
by Amazon